# PENWOMAN
### Elin Wägner

ELIN WÄGNER (1882-49) was active in many fields. She was a radical feminist and pacifist; and an environmental campaigner ahead of her time, notably in *Väckarklocka*. (Alarm Clock, 1941). She made her name as a journalist and suffragist in Stockholm, where she wrote her early novels including the bestselling *Pennskaftet* (*Penwoman*). From the house and writer's retreat she later built in the province of Småland where she was raised, she travelled widely in interwar Europe to lecture and gather material, and developed an international network of contacts. She was closely involved with the Women Citizen's School at Fogelstad, which ran pioneering courses in women's civic and political rights and responsibilities, and from 1923 a tireless contributor to *Tidevarvet* (The Epoch) a weekly journal with similar goals.

Her many novels include *Åsa-Hanna* (1918), *Dialogen fortsätter* (The Dialogue Continues, 1932) and *Vinden vände bladen* (The Wind Turned the Leaves, 1947). She was elected to the Swedish Academy in 1944. Her bold and innovative narrative technique, overlooked by critics who conventionally pigeonholed her as a provincial or purely autobiographical novelist, has been the subject of recent research.

SARAH DEATH has translated works by many Swedish writers including Alexander Ahndoril, Victoria Benedictsson, Fredrika Bremer, Astrid Lindgren and Sven Lindqvist. She has twice won the George Bernard Shaw Prize for translation from Swedish, for Kerstin Ekman's *The Angel House* and Ellen Mattson's *Snow*. In 2008 she was awarded the Swedish Academy's Translation Prize. She is Editor of the journal *Swedish Book Review* and an Honorary Research Fellow at University College London.

Some other books from Norvik Press

Kjell Askildsen: *A Sudden Liberating Thought* (translated by Sverre Lyngstad)

Victoria Benedictsson: *Money* (translated by Sarah Death)

Hjalmar Bergman: *Memoirs of a Dead Man* (translated by Neil Smith)

Jens Bjørneboe: *Moment of Freedom* (translated by Esther Greenleaf Mürer)

Jens Bjørneboe: *Powderhouse* (translated by Esther Greenleaf Mürer)

Jens Bjørneboe: *The Silence* (translated by Esther Greenleaf Mürer)

Johan Borgen: *The Scapegoat* (translated by Elizabeth Rokkan)

Fredrika Bremer: *The Colonel's Family* (translated by Sarah Death)

Suzanne Brøgger: *A Fighting Pig's Too Tough to Eat* (translated by Marina Allemano)

Camilla Collett: *The District Governor's Daughters* (translated by Kirsten Seaver)

Kerstin Ekman: *Witches' Rings* (translated by Linda Schenck)

Kerstin Ekman: *The Spring* (translated by Linda Schenck)

Kerstin Ekman: *The Angel House* (translated by Sarah Death)

Kerstin Ekman: *City of Light* (translated by Linda Schenck)

Arne Garborg: *The Making of Daniel Braut* (translated by Marie Wells)

Jørgen-Frantz Jacobsen: *Barbara* (translated by George Johnston)

P. C. Jersild: *A Living Soul* (translated by Rika Lesser)

Viivi Luik: *The Beauty of History* (translated by Hildi Hawkins)

Runar Schildt: *The Meat-Grinder and Other Stories* (translated by Anna-Liisa & Martin Murrell)

Amalie Skram: *Lucie* (translated by Katherine Hanson & Judith Messick)

August Strindberg: *The Red Room* (translated by Peter Graves)

August Strindberg: *Tschandala* (translated by Peter Graves)

Hjalmar Söderberg: *Aberrations* (translated by Neil Smith)

Hjalmar Söderberg: *Martin Birck's Youth* (translated by Tom Ellett)

Hjalmar Söderberg: *Selected Stories* (translated by Carl Lofmark)

Hanne Marie Svendsen: *Under the Sun* (translated by Marina Allemano)

Anton Tammsaare: *The Misadventures of the New Satan*

Helene Uri: *Honey Tongues* (translated by Kari Dickson)

# PENWOMAN

by

Elin Wägner

Translated from the Swedish and
with an Afterword by

Sarah Death

Originally published in Swedish as *Pennskaftet* (1910) by Ljus förlag.

Norvik Press Series B: English Translations of Scandinavian Literature, No. 45.

*A catalogue record for this book is available from the British Library.*
ISBN 978-1-870041-74-4
First published in 2009 by Norvik Press, Department of Scandinavian Studies, University College London, Gower Street, London WC1E 6BT.

Norvik Press gratefully acknowledges the financial assistance given by the Swedish Academy towards the publication of this book.

Norvik Press was established in 1984 with financial support from the University of East Anglia, the Danish Ministry for Cultural Affairs, the Norwegian Cultural Department and the Swedish Institute.

e-mail address: norvik.press@ucl.ac.uk
website: www.norvikpress.com

Managing editors: Janet Garton, Neil Smith, C. Claire Thomson.

Cover illustration: Elin Wägner standing beside the 1913 petition for women's suffrage. Photograph reproduced courtesy of the Women's History Collections at the University of Gothenburg library, website: www.ub.gu.se/kvinn/

Cover design: Richard Johnson

*Printed in the UK by Page Bros. (Norwich) Ltd, Norwich, UK*

# Contents

\* \* \*

\* \* \*

# Translator's Acknowledgments

I am grateful to Helena Forsås-Scott, London, for her unstinting assistance and enthusiasm, and for commenting on draft versions of the text. The definitive Swedish Academy edition of *Pennskaftet* (Svenska klassiker series, 2003), which she edited and annotated, has been an invaluable source of information, although any errors that remain are my own. I also wish to thank Solveig Hammarbäck, Växjö, for generous help with language queries.

Sarah Death, February 2009

# CHAPTER 1

For a person who was once in love with a stationmaster, there are most certainly more pleasurable ways of spending the day than being carried across Sweden at a leisurely pace on a stopping train.

In those days, when he was head station clerk and the only man in the world, all those stations through which a person now finds herself passing – Nässjö, Mjölby, Katrineholm – were as many imagined homes, where one knew the price of wood and meat and how to find a little cultured company. Since then, it is true, they have reverted to being sooty little halts of no significance, but a person still does not pass through them with indifference, for she has never loved anyone else. And all the while, as kilometre is added to kilometre, she is chaperoned by the certainty that, as inevitably as growing older, she is being drawn closer to that junction to which he was promoted, where there will be a twenty minute stop for dinner, or whatever one chooses to call it. A person had at any rate decided a whole week ago not to leave the carriage this time, but did not think it would help much, for she had long since abandoned any expectations of herself. She might turn her back to the carriage window and take out her sandwiches, but one is destined to eat one's own past sliced and cold, and when the train has stood there for twenty minutes she rises hurriedly to her feet, as if she has forgotten something vital, and hurries out onto the platform to wander up and down and with thumping heart steal a glance or two through the dirty panes of the booking office, until finally the man she would do anything to avoid emerges from a door marked 'Entry Prohibited'. He bears the Red Flag under his arm, but it no longer has the same marvellous, symbolic meaning as before, when he conquered a person in Its spirit. His back is broader, his neck thicker, his deportment self-satisfied, and he pretends not to recognise a person, but does once bellow: 'Keep away from the track!' One might wonder if he ever thinks back to an unpleasant winter's night at about three o'clock on an empty station, where a solitary signal light glittered on mournful wet tracks that ran south and north to lose themselves in a bottomless, dripping darkness; wonder if he ever remembers a long, heart-rending conversation that ended in a life and death tussle on the tracks as the train from the continent stormed into the station; one wonders if it is just a dream, that it was this same purplish face which back then, white as a corpse in the flickering lantern light, leant over someone as she was slung, half-dead, up onto the train, which surged out of the station again, carrying someone where she did not want to go. But no, it is not a dream, for if a single thing is true in this world, it is that someone loved him beyond measure, and would so gladly have dedicated her life to the modest task of keeping the curtains white at the windows of Sweden's sootiest station.

'Finnsta, ten minutes!' announced the conductor, and Cecilia's thoughts immediately supplied: imagine if it had been 'Finnsta, ten years'. She allowed her tired gaze to scan the red, smoke-grimed station house, wondering what it would have been like to spend her days up there in the middle front flat, and lie listening to the trains pounding past in the night. At that moment it struck her that she had now installed herself in all the major stations between there and Eslöv, and wondered what name the medical experts would give to such a condition.

Here, however, something was afoot. She leant out of the window, deeply grateful to the lady with so many flowers and friends who had chosen to depart from Finnsta on that very day and on that most desperate of trains. She was still standing on the platform with her back to the carriage, while her friends gathered round her in a semicircle and Cecilia, who could see only a long travelling coat and the veil of a hat, tried to imagine her face by scrutinising her friends, without reaching anything close to a conclusion. They seemed to comprise the leading female society of the place: the county law officer's wife, the manageress of the stationer's shop, the postmistress, and here came the stationmaster's wife with a sprig of geranium that had until a few moments before been adorning the upstairs window. Their demeanours expressed the self-importance so typical of a newly appointed committee, yet simultaneously a sort of maternal pride, and a profound wish to express their thanks in a way that the departing lady would not forget. The formalities of leave-taking progressed round the group and then a male voice, presumably the law officer's, proposed 'Long live woman, in the person of Ester Henning'; there were enthusiastic cheers and then it was time to climb aboard, for the stationmaster was blowing his whistle with an apologetic gesture to the town's guest, saying he 'was sorry but had no choice'. The mystery was now solved: Dr Ester Henning took classes in hygienics at the school where Cecilia was a language teacher, and they had occasionally encountered each other in the corridor and at staff meetings. Nothing was therefore more natural than for Cecilia to help her open the compartment door and gather up the flowers, half of which she had dropped in the corridor. This despite the fact that Cecilia, in all the years they had worked together, had never made any overtures to the Doctor, whom she viewed rather as a cripple regards someone with the full use of all limbs. Her very vitality, her clear voice and clear laugh, her healthy complexion and brown eyes – as Cecilia saw it – utterly unclouded by cares, got on her nerves. The Doctor for her part had always been in too much of a rush, had too much on her mind to notice the quietest and least approachable of all the teachers in the school, but at this unexpected meeting, and with the prospect of several hours' journey ahead of her, she nodded and beamed amicably across the floral tributes from Finnsta, and said, 'How nice to run into a colleague; we shall be able to keep each other company back to Stockholm I assume?'

Cecilia courteously expressed her pleasure at the meeting, adding with a gesture towards the flowers, still lying in a heap on the seat: 'You seem to enjoy a singular popularity in Finnsta, Dr Henning.'

'Oh, it's not me,' said Dr Henning modestly, but inside she was delighted that the other woman had given her such a natural opening to talk about her favourite subject. For although she had just reached the end of a lecture tour, repeating the same words for ten days until her vocal chords were almost worn away by votes for women, she was instantly willing to start again. Admittedly she was used to converting on a larger scale, but she was profoundly aware of the importance of every soul won for the cause, and would gladly sacrifice her travelling time to Cecilia. If it proved successful, she would not be the first person the Doctor had converted on the Swedish state railway system. Since Cecilia said nothing, she therefore continued:

'No, as I say, it's not me, but women's suffrage.'

'Oh, really?' said Cecilia politely.

'Yes, you see,' Dr Henning went on, 'it's all because I was in Finnsta to set up a new branch, and now these flowers will serve the cause even further, since the WSA, the Women's Suffrage Association,* is launching its autumn campaign at a meeting tomorrow, and the General* will be surrounded by stocks and asters. She will be so pleased about that, for although she has a glasshouse and a large garden of her own, these are from her youngest branch, and we always love our youngest best, as you know.'

'Well no, not really,' replied Cecilia, seeming to draw back a little.

A pause ensued; the Doctor sat looking at Cecilia and trying to recall what she knew about her, to underpin her own observations. She seemed to remember hearing that her father had been a manager of traffic, and of aristocratic descent; that the daughter had lived at home until the death of her parents a few years before; that she was very gifted at languages; and that she had had some kind of affair. In actual fact, you could tell all that just by looking at her. Her fine-boned face and pleasant manner, so quiet and yet so self-assured, spoke of her patrician background, as did her ability to keep her face politely empty as she uttered some courteous phrase in her reticent voice, while her thoughts were presumably engaged elsewhere. And as for her 'affair', one did not need to be a doctor to see that she had some old, mishandled sorrow to drag around with her.

If only I could get her involved in our activities, mused Ester Henning, it would be a boon to her, and we would have an extra soul and an extra arm and perhaps a new channel for reaching the upper classes.

She began to speak, of how well she had been received in Finnsta and how interested everyone had been. Cecilia remained politely indifferent, but when she did occasionally put in a question, she betrayed such profound ignorance that the Doctor, utterly shocked, finally burst out:

'But Miss Bech, you can't have the first idea about our work for women's suffrage!'

'No, I have not,' she replied, unaware that it was blasphemy to utter such words.

The Doctor let her hands sink into her lap.

'Are you really trying to tell me that you, a self-supporting, modern woman, can live in Stockholm entirely outside something so splendid (she put particular emphasis on the word), something so important, as women's fight for the vote?'

However often Dr Henning's experience showed her that this was possible, she was equally surprised and nonplussed every time, and would never find a satisfactory solution to the mystery or become resigned to it.

'I live outside everything,' said Cecilia, modestly but without shame. 'It was only very recently I chanced to hear that we had lost Norway.'*

The Doctor remained silent for a moment, but she was busy thinking.

'Perhaps you think it inexcusably tactless of me to engage you on this subject?' she asked.

'By no means,' said Cecilia, 'because I know how fervently interested you are in it yourself, Dr Henning.'

13

'Well yes, you see, it really is indefensible – and I say this for your own good – to be so utterly absorbed in simply earning a living. You are a teacher; you may be sure that you will never enjoy a reasonable salary, that we will never convince the authorities of the justice of equal pay for equal work, until we win the vote. Once we have that, it will be easy to open the eyes of the blind and the hidebound.'

'I am not absorbed in my work either, really,' replied Cecilia, 'and I have as much money as I need. I am entirely alone.'

'And is that true of all your colleagues? Are there not those obliged to wear themselves out giving private tuition because they cannot support their mothers or pay their study debts on their salaries alone? Are there no widows who have been obliged to step into the role of family breadwinner?' The Doctor looked sharply at Cecilia and noted with satisfaction that she blushed.

'Well ye-es, of course, and votes for women is a fine notion,' she said, continuing in a mildly complimentary tone: 'and I suppose we should all be grateful to you, Dr Henning, grateful to those who have the energy to do all that work, but I could not – '

'But if you are absorbed in neither your work nor your family, you must have something else to live for?'

'Must have – no, surely it would be pretentious to think one could not live one's life even without that?' said Cecilia with imperturbable calm. Another station. How many rooms might there be in the stationmaster's apartment here? Was this not the one that came with a lovely, large garden? Oh dear, it will be better when I get to Stockholm.

From far away she heard the voice of the indefatigable Doctor: 'Do you think there is any point my trying to get you involved in our work?'

'I do not know; I have so many years of blindness behind me,' Cecilia said softly.

No need to tell me that, thought Dr Henning, but she said, 'At least come along to the meeting tomorrow; that can do you no harm. We can accomplish a lot between our tears...'

Cecilia smiled.

'This is no miracle cure I am offering you,' the Doctor went on, 'but a very simple, harmless one, tried by many sick people – I am treating you as a patient, you see. For you, I prescribe work and comradeship.'

'But deeds without faith, what use are they to you?'

'Faith will come, make no mistake,' said Dr Henning hopefully, 'and in the meantime, you can still be of use. A horse or a porter probably hasn't much faith, but can still be absolutely indispensable. If you, for example, undertook to work in the campaign office for a few hours a week, stuffing envelopes and writing addresses, a great deal would be achieved.'

'I understand,' said Cecilia. 'And it comes as a huge relief to me that you are not speaking in terms of "The Great Cause" and "Our Goal". But have you not more than enough horses and porters fighting over those tasks already?'

'Well, yes, but our movement is short of money, and unpopular with the sorts of people who make donations. What do rich women care about the suffrage, and what do they care for their thousands of poor sisters, to whom the vote could bring both justice and bread? We need a workforce which demands neither food, nor payment by the hour, and that is heart-breakingly hard to find. If not before, you will believe me when you see how enraptured they are, the girls, when I bring you along in triumph to number six, Lästmakaregatan. That's where we have our campaign headquarters,' she added by way of explanation.

'Can I work myself into the ground?' asked Cecilia, who had had an idea.

'Most certainly,' said Ester Henning gaily, 'there are unrivalled opportunities for that in our movement. I could show you several people who have achieved it in a surprisingly short space of time.'

'My word, I believe you understand me,' said Cecilia in amazement. 'Perhaps I should give it a try, on condition that you do not expect me to show the least amount of interest, and that I can just get on with menial tasks without anyone explaining to me what they are for. For if anyone does that, I shall walk away. I was once engaged to give language lessons at the YWCA...'

She sighed.

'We shall ask no more of you than clear handwriting,' Ester Henning assured her, 'But don't blame me if your interest is aroused of its own accord, because it will happen.'

'Are you so sure of that?' Cecilia asked, regarding Ester Henning with a sardonic smile that did not perturb the latter in the slightest.

'Let me give you a little example of how precious the cause can become to one, after one has been serving it for a while,' she said. 'I have come from Normandy, where I went in a state of excessive exhaustion to lie in silence by the Atlantic Ocean, I who spend eleven months out of twelve holding forth...'

'One should suffer one's torments beside the great oceans,' put in Cecilia expertly.

'Yes, and then go to the great cities and find new ones,' said the Doctor, throwing out her hand. 'Have you been to Normandy?'

'Yes, but it was a long time ago.'

'Well then, you know just how healing and invigorating it is to be far away from everything, to lie there on the edge of the precipice, where France plunges straight down into the waves, and feel like a piece of the green, salt-washed French turf, while the tide ebbs and flows and the sea advances on the land, thundering like the tramp of heavy hooves...' The Doctor had inadvertently launched into one of the phrases from her latest lecture, and a longing expression came into Cecilia's eye, the look of the cowed schoolmistress on her way back to the classroom and the autumn term.

'But,' Dr Henning went on, 'in spite of all that, when I received a telegram one day from the E.C. – the Executive Committee – ' she corrected herself with a sympathetic smile, 'asking me to fit in a lecture tour on my way home, I immediately woke up and felt touched, as you are when you set eyes on some dear old face after a long separation. I felt I would rather be a humble suffrage campaigner in Stockholm than a carefree stretch of turf by the Atlantic, and rather see my homely, grateful Swedish audiences than the sun sinking over the coast of France.'

'Rather inhale the air of the Good Templar Hall in Finnsta than the cool, salty winds bearing tidings straight from the continent of America?'

'Yes,' said the Doctor with conviction.

'That sounds suspiciously like religion,' said Cecilia.

'Yes, I know we first workers for the cause did feel rather like the early Christians, as we held our much-derided meetings in the strangest places and laid plans for crossing the sea of opposition and indifference in which we found ourselves. I do believe our enthusiasm was rather like that of the first Christians, too. And now what are you smiling at so sceptically?'

'At the fact that you think I will reach that point. I? Religion requires life, after all, and someone like me...'

'Yes, yes,' said the Doctor, 'we must content ourselves for now with letting the Executive Committee be your nurses and Lästmakaregatan your convalescent home. Oh ye of little faith.'

'Little faith! Try telling a horse who has collapsed in front of his load that he is to address envelopes for votes for women!'

Cecilia had said it so calmly, and yet you could see her as the fallen horse lying helpless in front of its load, no longer even trying to struggle to its feet. Ester Henning felt both deeply sympathetic and a little embarrassed at having got so carried away. Here she was, rich and happy with everything life had to offer in the way of love and work, and in an hour she would be reunited with her husband and little boy, who were to join the train at Flen, and they would travel back together to their beautiful, happy home; was it any wonder the horse eyed one so reproachfully when one happened to cheer too loudly?

'I quite forgot: I was supposed to be trying to sell some pamphlets,' she said, and vanished with a bundle of literature under her arm.

When she returned after a lightning tour that had yielded excellent results – because once all the passengers knew their

*Forget-me-Not* magazines\* off by heart, they were grateful even for suffrage pamphlets – she found a new passenger in the compartment and Cecilia leaning back in her corner, her face sealed and her hands resting on her lap with an immobility that was as deliberate as it was forced. Ester Henning wondered for a moment if she expected to convince anyone that a person can sleep with such bitter consciousness etched all over her face. She would be left in peace for a while, at any rate, if that were her wish.

But it was Cecilia herself who raised the subject once more.

'How do you find time for everything? After all, you have the suffrage campaign and your practice and home and husband and children.'

'My practice is not so large,' said the Doctor with a good-natured smile, 'but it is certainly true that I neglect it somewhat for the suffrage. For many of us, the greatest sacrifice we can make for the campaign is to give it so much of the strength that we should really have invested in our own life's work. But what is one to do: no sooner does one start to work for some special interest, and see and think a little about the current state of society, than one inevitably ends up back at women's suffrage. It has been a meeting point for all of us, coming from so many different directions and all with some matter dear to our heart waiting for us.' At this the Doctor momentarily looked a little subdued, but she soon brightened up again.

'We must do the best we can, but do you know what I feel sometimes on evenings when I have to get up and break the family circle – which by the way does not happen as often as the pillars of society imagine, because I always try to wait until the children are in bed – and my little boy says in his resigned way, "There, I just knew we were too cosy here together," do you know what I feel?'

Their mute fellow traveller looked up with curiosity from a penny novelette.

'Pangs of conscience?' suggested Cecilia.

'Pangs of conscience for occasionally sacrificing family contentment to the Cause? No, how can you think that? Neither pangs of conscience nor anxiety, because it is only in reactionary novels that children lie down and die if their mother has the audacity to go to a meeting. Oh no, what I feel is a wild urge to get at all the rest of you, who keep your distance, to shake you into sharing the burden with us; those of you without commitments, whose time is your own, yet spent sleeping and grieving!' Her brown eyes glittered, and she looked straight at Cecilia, clearly referring to her. Their travelling companion plunged back into her book with an amused smile, to avoid any risk of getting caught up and dragged along to a suffrage meeting. So that's what they were like, those suffragists.* Which of the lady doctors could she be, and married too?

Cecilia sat in silence, her lips pursed.

'Those of you on your own,' went on Ester Henning, 'without anyone tugging at your skirts and begging you to be back soon, what is to stop you giving all your spare time to our work? You simply have no experience of conflicting interests, unlike those of us who are the central figure in a little circle, where everyone depends on us. You have no excuses for staying away, but by your indolence you force those of us who have hitched ourselves to the load to pull with more strength than we possess. I am convinced there must be a meaning in some women being on their own, without a home and a family.'

Cecilia stared at the Doctor.

'Meaning? Oh no,' she said from the bottom of her heart.

But Doctor Henning did not permit herself to be diverted from her train of thought.

'Oh yes,' she said a little severely, 'as long as there is still so infinitely much that women can do for women, so many mountains of ignorance to be blasted away, so much campaigning to rouse those who are slumbering, in a word, so many more days' work than workers to do them. The meaning, of course, is that they are to give all the care and affection they have not expended to the women's cause.'

'In other words, the strain of spiritual starvation will drive them to work?'

Cecilia regarded her with something akin to distaste.

'That wasn't exactly what I meant, but it is true enough.'

'Well, I happen to think one should have loftier motives for dedicating one's life to something,' declared Cecilia. 'How can one do any good, if one's starting point is no more than an egoistic desire to find something with which to fill one's life? Why, then it is mere chance whether that turns out to be women's suffrage or bridge.'

Dr Henning sat in silence for a time, perhaps feeling she had hit the wrong note; all that could be heard was the pages of their fellow passenger's book being turned, and at such a rate that she must have reached the exciting part.

'You mustn't think that is what motivates our people in their labour,' Dr Henning said, 'even if that is the way some of them began. But the strength to persevere, that comes when they start to feel solidarity with their sex, so its pain becomes their pain, its degradation their own degradation. And anyway,' the Doctor smiled thoughtfully, 'the cause is great, even if we are small; it is in fact greater than most of us, as we go about our daily work for it, ever realise, or see in a wider context. As long as we are doing honest work, what does it matter how we were driven to it in the first place? No, I come back to what I said just now: I believe it is those of you on your own, who are called above all others.'

'Those are hard words,' Cecilia said softly. 'What would you say, if a woman from among those you call the chosen ones came to you with her lonely heart and asked: why me?'

She stood up quickly and pressed her face to the carriage window. Beyond it, the dark forests and autumn-gold slopes of Sweden were slipping by in the gentle afternoon light. She stared blindly ahead, seeing nothing but the outlines of her own face in the glass, contorted with pain, always her own face.

Not a single word more was spoken until they reached Flen. As soon as the station was announced, the Doctor hurried out onto the platform to greet her husband and child, and the joy of their reunion echoed right into the compartment. Cecilia was just thinking with relief that the family would have to find seats elsewhere, when a happy, beaming Ester Henning stuck her head round the door and asked if she might introduce the real Dr Henning and his son.

'We have been having a long and fascinating discussion lasting halfway across Sweden,' she added by way of explanation to her husband.

'No need to tell me what you ladies were talking about,' said Dr Henning, eying his wife. '"Working for women's suffrage is the best medicine ever invented", am I right? Soon we won't need any other doctors, since it's a cure for everything.'

Ester Henning laughed and surreptitiously stroked her husband's coat sleeve, thinking herself unobserved. 'You always say I never prescribe anything else, but what if those who are already working for votes for women fall sick?'

'Then you write out a prescription for yet more campaigning, my little doctor, I know you.'

'My husband is even more convinced than I am, if that is possible, of the necessity of women having the vote,' declared Ester Henning, turning to Cecilia, who said with a smile that she realised as much.

'Yes,' said the other Dr Henning, 'and my greatest wish is that they get it, while there is still a little left of my wife. Just imagine: a third of my precious month's holiday gone on converting the provinces! Leaving me and my son to our own devices! But I have taken my revenge, and made him into a Conservative!'

On entering the compartment, the boy had at once sat down beside his mother and become engrossed in a cowboy and Indian book, keeping a tight and loyal grip on her hand as he read. But now things had gone too far, and he was obliged to intervene.

'Oh Father, how have you the heart to call me Conservative?' he asked in a tone of injured innocence that made the whole company burst out laughing, which once again caused the young man to seek safe refuge with his mother for himself and his political convictions. But it did not take long for her to console him with repeated assurances that she had never doubted his Liberalism. And with the same radiant pride with which all mothers boast of their children's remarkable qualities, she confided to Cecilia that Erik had promised never to cast his vote 'before Mother has got hers'.

The train finally reached Stockholm central station and as they were preparing to take cabs in opposite directions, Cecilia made her farewell by extending to Ester Henning a hand that ached with sorrow.

'Well?' said the Doctor quizzically.

'Yes, I shall try, to come to the meeting tomorrow.'

# CHAPTER 2

The lodgers came in from their respective rooms and cast hungry looks at the dinner table; the non-residents who took meals gradually assembled. It was the first of September, so there were quite a few newcomers; people introduced themselves, stumbled over names and said nothing of note. They sat down at the table in silence, a silence eventually broken by one of the regulars asking: 'But where's Penwoman?'

The feared, thin-lipped smile gathered itself about the landlady's mouth, but before a reply could work its painful way out, the jovial chief cashier seated on her left intervened, for as the senior member of the company he enjoyed an undisputedly special position, and could get away with it.

'She'll be busy as usual, I expect,' he said, and the landlady shrugged her shoulders with a malicious smile, but was obliged to hold her tongue.

'Yes, that taxing job of hers at the daily paper,' came a voice, emphatic, self-satisfied and with a distinct Scanian accent, from the other end of the table, where a young aesthete with rounded cheeks was sitting. 'I passed her ten minutes ago; she was standing in a crowd of other street urchins who had gathered round a fight, craning her neck to see what was going on. Just as I went by, I heard her screeching, "Yes, he went that way, I saw it with me own eyes, officer!"'

They laughed at the Scanian's imitation of the Stockholm vernacular, and those who knew Penwoman said to the newcomers, 'That's so like her.'

At that very moment, a small, delicately built girl was

standing in the doorway, regarding the large, motley gathering round the table with thoughtful impudence. Her pale blonde hair was shiny and wavy, framing a thin, angular, irregular but rather attractive face; at the back of her eyes, grey and deep-set, glittered the memory of something freshly experienced.

'We are already seated,' said the landlady.

The corner of the girl's mouth twitched silently at this sensational piece of information as she cut across to the door of her room, scrutinising *en passant* the soup tureen, in which a few impassioned strips of red carrot swam among numerous globules of grease, and said casually: 'No soup for me, thank you.'

After a while she returned, made a brief apology and sat down at the vacant place. On the first of the month there was always a risk of being obliged to break bread with someone whose table manners were repulsive, so she ran her eye over the company round the table, dwelling a second longer on the new arrivals. On one new young man, who looked extremely embarrassed at being caught staring at her, she bestowed a smile of secret complicity, as if to say: 'Do you think I don't know they've been talking about me?' and she paid a moment's thoughtful attention to Cecilia's pale, shuttered face. The Scanian whispered something across the table that sounded like, 'What happened then, did the police catch him?' causing her to ask him in a penetrating tone to speak up and get whatever it was off his chest. Apart from that she sat quietly, listening to the conversation of the older diners: the landlady; her more prosperous sister Mrs Bodin, married to a deputy judge, who had come to settle her daughter in Stockholm; Mr Tillberg the accountant; Mr Jessen, who called himself an editor and did proofreading for the newspapers; and a plump, elderly spinster, who had been introduced as 'the authoress, Miss Anderson-Jublin'.

'Well now,' said the landlady, looking sharply at all her guests, 'beer and milk have both gone up again.'

Anyone in the company who did not drink beer invariably

drank milk, so they should all have felt this was aimed at them, but they were too used to such pronouncements to take much notice. The old woman had put up her prices at the start of the quarter, so there was no danger of her being able to do it again for a while.

'Yes,' said Mrs Bodin, as no one else spoke, 'It's remarkable that you can provide such excellent fare at that price.'

To take the edge off this strategic remark, the chief cashier furrowed his pale brow in concern and sighed, 'Yes, these are expensive times we live in.'

'If that were all,' moaned Mrs Bodin, 'but things are much worse, it seems. Arrogance has infected those in charge, children learn nothing but nonsense at school, the workers imagine themselves as good as people from better families, and nobody dares to contradict them; they get things all their own way.'

'As good as? They are far superior,' said Jessen, 'If we were all as well off as the workers, we could be content.'

'Why don't you work then, Mr Jessen?' asked Penwoman.

They pretended not to hear her. The Scanian applauded ironically.

'No, our national and local governments care nothing for saving public money, so we shall all soon be ruined by taxes,' said the landlady, who if boarding house gossip were to be believed, falsified her tax returns. The rumour had started because Mr Jessen, who compiled them for her in his capacity as a man of letters, was always allowed a card party on the first day of March, the day after the returns were due in.

'My husband says it's all these hundreds of committees that are ruining the country,' said Mrs Bodin.

'Yes, them and the teetotallers,' added Mr Jessen.

'Indeed, and it will probably only get worse when women get the vote, because then they will ban alcohol altogether,' said the authoress, smiling at him. 'But let us hope that will not be very soon.'

Editor Jessen hated women's suffrage campaigners even

more than teetotallers, if that were possible.

'They ought to know better,' he said. 'They should stay at home and concentrate on duties fitting for them, and not interfere in what they don't understand. Has there been too much manliness in Parliament until now, I ask you?'

'I do agree,' said Mrs Bodin, 'that a woman should be a woman first and foremost. It's so much nicer that way. What business is it of ours, how the men run the country?'

'Come up to the press gallery with me one day and listen to what they are discussing, Mrs Bodin, 'and you'll see that it's very much our business,' put in Penwoman from her corner.

'No thank you,' said Mrs Bodin.

'Art must surely be superior to politics?' interjected her Arts and Crafts daughter, who thought she was going to be a textile designer, and was dressed accordingly.

'Ah yes, art,' said the plump authoress, feeling impelled to contribute to the discussion, this being her subject area.

'Not all women can compose decorative damper cords,' said Penwoman, who always resorted to crudeness sooner or later, once the authoress and the textiles girl got started.

'No,' said the authoress, who hated Penwoman with a passion, yet had to share a room with her, 'but all women who have a little – I wouldn't like to say beauty – '

'Oh no, don't do that – '

'...but charm, can get whatever they like from a man anyway, and the vote will never help them achieve that. Think what a great thing it is to be a woman,' – Penwoman contemplated her roommate's figure and nodded in agreement – 'and feel the power of femininity over men. I think men would despise me, if I started agitating for the vote.'

'I think so, too,' said Penwoman.

'But why are they making such a fuss about votes for women?' – the conversation at the bottom end of the table had opened up to all – 'They can vote for a man as Member of Parliament, after all, can't they Mother?' said the textiles girl.*

'I don't know,' said her mother. 'We have fortunately been

too happily married in our community to feel the need to form any suffrage associations. Why do women need the vote, anyway? We have our position in society through our husbands, thank God; we have influence indirectly, through our sons, if we want; and to manage our affairs we have our kind bank managers. What is more, there are so many excellent men in the Upper Chamber, to whom God has given the gift of ruling the country, and to them I continue to give my silent vote, as I have done up to now.'

So saying, she rose from the table and sailed into the parlour, where they were all now trying to make themselves at home among the garish, uncomfortable items of furniture claiming to be in the rustic, peasant style.

On Penwoman, however, the room had exercised a mysterious charm ever since she had realised that its interior, cold, pretentious and empty as it was, with the slovenly, dishonest touch added by the cheap, ugly knick-knacks, had unconsciously become an image of the boarding house owner herself: the limitations of her soul made manifest in furniture, its miserable nature betrayed in flower vases. Cecilia, on the other hand, from whom this cruel, secret pleasure remained hidden, had hated the parlour from the first moment, and intended to withdraw swiftly to her own room, but stopped as she heard Penwoman, who had clearly not yet had anything like enough of an argument, throw out an inflammatory: 'You should have been at the suffrage meeting yesterday evening!'

The journey suddenly came back to her, her promise to Ester Henning, how hopelessly slack and forgetful she was.

'Oh, I forgot I was supposed to go!' she burst out involuntarily.

Penwoman gave her the same thoughtful, attentive look as before.

'Are you a suffragist?'

'Oh no,' said Cecilia, 'But I had promised to try to do them a service, and now, just imagine, I have broken my promise.'

'They're cowardly and unreliable, too,' noted Mr Jessen in

a loud whisper, intended for the authoress, but heard by the whole room. 'They deny their faith for fear of the Jews.'*

For the first time, Cecilia was on the verge of a smile – as Penwoman observed with pride – at the thought of denying anything whatsoever for fear of Mr Jessen. And so as not to seem to be running away, she revised her plans and sat down with a cup of coffee.

The chief cashier tried for a second time to steer the conversation onto more neutral ground: 'Well, my dear Penwoman,' he said, 'Have you had a busy day? What poor victim have you been interviewing?'

'My dear Chief Cashier,' said Penwoman in the same tone of voice, 'It's pitiful enough, without my needing to talk about it. You can read all about it when you go to the barber's tomorrow.'

'Are we to get an account of the fight on Tegnérgatan, too?' asked the Scanian sarcastically.

'I presume you've all had one already,' retorted Penwoman, who had been well aware of the Scanian's presence, though he had not realised it. 'But yes, you would get one, the like of which you'd never dreamt of, if I were allowed to write as I shall be able to, one day.' A small, clenched fist thumped down on the table.

'Tell us anyway, Penwoman,' said the chief cashier, and since he was her only supporter at the boarding house, she obliged.

'As I was passing on the tram, I saw a girl, all bloody, come hurtling out of a doorway on Badstugugatan and run off down Tegnérgatan. I got off, of course' – half the company giggled at her 'of course' – 'and saw her man coming after her with a broken beer bottle in his hand. He stood there, looking round, then he saw her trail of blood and charged off after her, cursing, but when I got back with a policeman, he'd disappeared. You might have thought the girl would have been beside herself, all slashed as she was, but she still had the presence of mind to send the policemen the wrong way, and she was hissing and spitting and cursing me when I put him straight. One evening when she's feeling better and I'm coming home late from the paper, she'll batter me to death, but how was I to know she loved him that much?'

'That simply can't be possible,' said the textiles girl, who had been getting frantic signals from her mother to leave the room, but had not complied.

'Possible,' said Cecilia in a calm tone that seemed to decide the matter, 'oh yes, that was presumably why he hit her.'

Penwoman regarded her in amazement. The new arrival was so much older than herself, and looked like a woman of sense and experience, but she clearly had no notion of the reality that lay behind a scene such as the one just described.

'Maybe "girls like that" should get the vote, too?' said Mr Jessen, turning to Penwoman with a withering smile.

'I can't think of any who need it more,' she said, holding his gaze unflinchingly. 'But you can rest assured, Mr Jessen. Their papers definitely aren't in order. The most they can hope for is to go to Communion, and not even that without special absolution.'

Then Mrs Bodin got to her feet without a word and beckoned her daughter, who dragged herself reluctantly away to go with her mother to the evening service at the Oscar Church.

'You always find the singing and organ music so inspiring, my dear. On the fifth Sunday after Trinity you composed a tea cosy.'

Penwoman watched them go triumphantly, though she knew she had done something that would cost her dear. She was so used to being the one from whom every mother tried to protect her young sons and daughters.

For the third time, the chief cashier tried to rescue the situation.

'What would you rather have, Penwoman,' he asked, 'the vote or a new hat?'

'I would rather *have* neither,' she said, 'because I want to earn both the vote and the price of the hat myself.'

'Yes yes, you're a modern woman and all that, dash it all,' said the Scanian, 'but the fact of the matter is, you are going to have to content yourselves with being given the vote as a gift. I shan't deny it you, and though I think it damned unaesthetic and unbecoming to vote, I have high hopes of women simply not noticing they have the right. The only risk might be if the clergy pointed it out to them, to enlist their votes on the reactionary side. Well then, let them all compromise themselves, that would serve them right!'

'No, on the contrary,' said Editor Jessen, 'It will be social democracy that gains. Think what a boost there will be to the numbers of ignorant voters walking into their trap! Wives will follow their husbands, because they don't know any better. What do they care if the country collapses? No, give us women like Kristina Gyllenstierna!* They can have the vote by all means, the minute they step up and ask for it. But we have no need whatsoever of English suffragettes, French *pétroleuses* and Russian anarchists!'

'Hearing you talk,' said Penwoman, contemplating his purple face, 'reminds me so very well what they mean about silence being golden.'

Mr Jessen, who was not a popular member of the company, counted the smiles around him with fury, got up and walked out.

'Well Penwoman, you'll soon have driven them all away,' said the Scanian, smugly admiring his pretty reflection in the landlady's largest pier-glass from his vantage point in the most comfortable chair.

Penwoman, catching her breath after the heat of the battle, looked up: 'Oh no, do you think so? I don't mean to. But it's impossible for me to stay calm when anybody attacks women's suffrage.'

'No, it can't be easy for someone with such a pugnacious spirit to be a woman,' he teased. 'Tell me, Miss Penwoman,' he said, squinting up at her, as she stood by the door, 'Wouldn't you love to be a man?' Penwoman screwed up her left eye and pondered for a moment.

'No, but wouldn't you?' she asked in turn.

When the Scanian went out to the hall to put on his coat shortly afterwards, he was accompanied by one of the newcomers, a young man, who had not said a word throughout.

'I don't know if we were introduced. Mr Block, trainee architect.'

'Mr Tufve, clerk. Well, what did you make of that menagerie?'

'I thought that little Penwoman seemed a splendid sort of girl,' said the architect, who had introduced himself in order to find out more about her.

'Well, it's all a matter of taste,' said the other man with a malicious smile. 'For my part, I am not at ease with young girls who don't, er, may I offer you a cigarette?'

'Thank you, but what do you mean, sir?'

'Nothing. I speak no ill of a lady, it's just that I wouldn't want her socialising with my sisters. And if I had a fiancée – ' he shuddered.

'I can't imagine she would want to socialise with my sisters,' said the architect, thinking of those little farmer's daughters in Östergötland, 'but apart from that – '

'Well, it depends on the sisters,' said Tufve, who was an only child, 'but mine have a reputation to think of.'

'So why hasn't *she*, then?'

'You ought to be able to see that, even on your first day here. Not even her enthusiasm for the vote has been able to lend her a cloak of respectability, just so you know.'

'I set great store by girls without too much of a reputation; they are usually the most pleasant, so that's fine by me,' said the architect.

'Well, get to know her as well as I have,' said Tufve, 'and it will be pleasanter still.'

The architect whistled. 'Indeed?' he said.

'Oh yes,' replied the Scanian, bent over his galoshes. 'And you won't be treading on my toes,' he added. 'I've finished with her.'

Mr Block looked strangely pleased, and set off with long, happy strides for the architects' firm where he slaved away his afternoons.

# CHAPTER 3

'Sorry,' said Penwoman, sticking her head into Cecilia's room, 'I took a lot of trouble to invent a reason for disturbing you, but it went out of my head the minute I knocked. I expect it'll come to me in due course. Anyway, the real reason was to ask you if I could stay in here for a while; nobody saw me come in, and nobody will think of looking for me here. I've got my outdoor clothes with me, so they'll think I've gone out, but I haven't the energy; this is my evening off, and I'd planned to lie on a sofa and just rest,' she said with a pitiable little smile.

'Sit down,' said Cecilia kindly, 'or in fact, if you are tired, come and lie on my sofa, no of course you can, it is a sofa meant for idleness. And tell me, if you want, what the matter is.'

'It's really hard,' said Penwoman with a sigh of pleasure. 'Oh no, not the sofa, but the problem of my roommate. It's my only free evening all week, and she has to be authoring. Nothing makes me so livid.'

'But you are an author yourself,' said Cecilia, taken aback.

'By my soul I'm not! I write to live, and I live to gain a bit of sense and maybe one day be able to become an author. But even if I were one, it wouldn't help matters. I got back from my holidays to find my previous, nice, illiterate room-mate replaced by this authoress! The landlady thought it would be ideal to have "two lady authors in the same room". What exquisite psychology! But I shall teach her that it won't do. You must have noticed her, all eighty, soulful kilos of her.'

'Oh yes,' said Cecilia, shaking her head at Penwoman's description of Miss Anderson, 'she was telling me over breakfast that she has been commissioned to write an article.'

'At breakfast, was it?' Penwoman exclaimed triumphantly, scrambling to her feet and sending cushions flying in all directions. 'So she was having me on after all, because when I got home at dinnertime and jeered at her because she was still at it, she told me she had just got the job and been given two hours to complete it by the editor. Now she's sitting with her feet in cold water to draw the blood from her head, groaning over her conclusion, and I shall tell you why I ran away: it was so as not to be obliged to take that woman and her article in hand, once she gave up. Because they would both have been equally useless, I know that from experience. I'm fed up with being her midwife. She's happy enough to despise me in between times, oh yes, because I'm a professional journalist and have to write about everything, even "things that don't interest me," and "without being in the mood".'

'So she has no permanent situation herself, then?' asked Cecilia, who would always politely discuss whatever seemed uppermost in her guests' minds at any given moment.

'No, how could you think so? She comes from a good family, and her brother-in-law is a Judge Referee to the Supreme Court. Do you think he would let her, even if she wanted to and was capable of it, sit in a press seat in the main auditorium at Central Hall with the other hacks and then dash down to the editorial office to write reports in the middle of the night, or set off for Söder at two minutes' notice to interview a tailor who's won the lottery, or a worker's wife, whose husband fell off a roof an hour before, or an old woman accused of being a baby-farmer?'

'So what does she write about?' probed Cecilia.

'Good question! She's really a governess, you see, at least that's what she was most recently employed as, after trying everything under the sun. She's one of those old spinsters longing for a purpose in life. You know them, don't you? They're the ones who keep all those thousands of spurious courses going, from Shakespeare to decorative ways of serving butter; oh, I've seen it all right, because I've written about every one of them. These women didn't get a chance to study anything properly

when they were young, of course; they always had to make way
for their brothers, or it wasn't convenient and somehow never
happened. They're well aware of their ignorance, so as soon as
there's any new course on offer, they sign up. They sit there at
their desks getting wrinkles, growing old and bent from all that
jumble of superficial knowledge, but they can't cope with a man,
or earn their daily bread, oh no. So she decided to give up her
profession and become an authoress; it would give her such a fine
purpose in life, and she had always found it so easy to write. She
thought she would be able to live freely and independently with
the help of some nice, fat fees and that people would recognise
her and say, "Look, it's her, she writes so well."'

'And what actually happened?'

'What happened? She had a terrible job placing her
manuscripts to start with, and got behind with her rent and
couldn't work out who it was that had stirred up all the
newspaper editors in Stockholm against her, she said. But then
she had an idea: she started writing anti-women's rights articles
and they were hugely sought after, you see. Now she's learned
the best way of doing it: she goes to all our meetings and reads
all our literature to get material, and then she watches out for an
occasion when there's a lot at stake for us, and it would make an
impact for a woman to be speaking out against us. She ferrets out
things we avoid talking about for the sake of solidarity and good
comradeship, and scatters as much doubt and dissent as she can,
and people say: see, women themselves don't want any
improvement in their position; they don't think they are mature
enough, so why should we give it to them?'

'You paint a dreadfully black picture,' said Cecilia, 'of so
much malice in one person.'

'Oh, it does no harm if I speak a little ill of her, because
there'll still be so many people praising her; she's all puffed up
with conceit, the old jackal. Give me an honest housefire report
for nine öre a line any day!' said Penwoman complacently.

'Presumably you don't write for the same newspapers?' asked
Cecilia, to establish whether an element of professional envy

might explain her hard judgment of the authoress.

'I should think not,' replied Penwoman with a laugh. 'I'm not *entirely* without religion. Naturally I only work for those parts of the press that have suffrage on their political programme. And anyway, they wouldn't want me anywhere else,' she went on after a moment's reflection.

'Well this is undeniably tiresome,' said Cecilia. 'If you absolutely have to share a room with somebody, could it not be an ordinary, I mean a proper, journalist?'

'That would work, all right,' conceded Penwoman, 'and there is one here at the boarding house, in fact. But the awful, unbelievable thing about him is that he doesn't want to share with me. He sees me as the embodiment of two sworn enemies: Woman and the *Liberal Morning News*.\* We don't keep the same hours, either; he always gets home later and drunker than me.'

'Come in here, when her writing gets too much, until you can find another colleague,' interrupted Cecilia, not really liking this line of talk. The next moment, she regretted her offer. For what would happen if the young girl came and took her at her word at one of those times when solitude was her only means of concealing her grief?

'Well thank you, that's fine, then,' said Penwoman, as if she had been expecting the invitation all along. 'How mild and soft and pleasant it is in here; how have you managed to make the room so like yourself in just a week? There's no need to answer,' she went on, as Cecilia thanked her for the compliment with a smile, 'I can see for myself that it comes of your being such a pronounced person in every respect. Even your gloves, that were out on the woodbox this morning, size six and a quarter, lying serenely one on top of the other, had that mild, worn-out, indifferent – they were your gloves, weren't they?'

'No, but you can pretend they were, and write a column about them regardless,' said Cecilia and smiled, 'But by the way, do tell me your name. I have only ever heard your – *nom de plume*.'

'Ah yes,' said Penwoman, 'I'm grateful my nickname is no worse; in a boarding house one has to be prepared for anything.

My other name is Barbro, a terrible, handicrafts sort of name, and then Magnus. Perhaps you'd actually like to call me by my name? There's not a soul in the whole of Stockholm who does.'

Cecilia thanked her with some astonishment. After just a few days, the girl was treating her like an old friend when she, through all those lonely years, had not made a single one. Grief was all too jealous a comrade.

'I don't really think you fit in here at Mrs Bengtsson's,' Penwoman chatted on from her pile of cushions. 'You have to be prepared to use coarse language here – as you've no doubt already noticed I do – and know how to make yourself as feared by your fellow cattle as by the landlady and her staff. But you, you're far too refined; you won't know how to give them a good bellowing when they serve you cracked eggs for breakfast – and she will, you know, as soon as the initial politeness wears off. Good God, you should have a home of your own; I mean, everything about you is crying out for it.'

She noticed Cecilia had suddenly gone rigid, but went on: 'It's glorious, isn't it, to have got so far that we aren't dependent on men in that respect at least, unless we choose to be, of course. A person can have her work, a two-roomed apartment with a kitchen, and a slave to look after them and her.'

'Can she?' said Cecilia. 'I do not know anyone who has all that, so it can hardly be usual. After all, you have not managed it yourself, Barbro.'

'No,' said Penwoman, unconcerned, 'because I'm not mature enough to set up home yet, and anyway, I can't afford it.'

'But someone like you, who *can* afford it,' she went on, 'and I assume you can, because I know exactly what you pay for this room with the shower, the best one on this floor. I assure you it would cost no more to rent a place of your own and have someone to keep house. Wait a minute.' Before Cecilia could blink, she was alone, but before she had time to gather her thoughts, the girl was back. She said she had just written an article about the desirability of self-supporting women being paid enough to afford a home of their own, and here – she held out a notebook full of jottings – were her calculations. She never for a moment considered that Cecilia could be anything other than vastly interested, and consider her every word a revelation.

'They say we lack resilience, and that is no doubt true, but why?' she went on, sermonising in the words of her article. 'Well, because we lack that elixir of life which a woman finds in her own home, her own peace and quiet, her own food and a maid. I for my part can't promise to survive even fifteen years more, if I'm to live in a boarding house. But just wait until the self-supporting women start setting up home, filling the whole of Stockholm; each home will be like a little powerhouse, and the world will be amazed by what we will achieve.' Cecilia sat staring straight ahead; she was not paying attention but thinking about the housing advantages accorded to Sweden's stationmasters.

'Wouldn't it be splendid,' Penwoman persisted, 'to get home from work and be able to close your own front door and be received by a slave, with whom there was no need to exchange a single word, other than to say, "Bring me some hot water and put the dinner on the table, Stina."'

'Such a thing really never occurred to me,' said Cecilia, who was now starting to get vaguely interested. 'You see I shared my parents' home in Stockholm for so long.'

'All the more reason for finding one of your own,' said Penwoman decisively. 'But you thought, of course, that it was the single woman's duty to make things as hideous for herself as possible.'

'What I thought was that it was of no importance, since nothing could change the fact that – '

'Yes, there we have it; my mother's just the same. Whereas in fact, the very opposite applies. You see, dear, someone who's happy doesn't need to be served her favourite dishes, doesn't need peace and consideration and coffee in bed! But as I always tell my mother, someone whose life has become "the years left to get through" can take the most mysterious pleasure in life's more modest comforts, if only she puts her mind to it. Above all, she needs a secluded place to throw up in.'

Cecilia looked up, dazzled by so much wisdom from such young lips.

'There are very different notions of what a single woman's duty should be,' she said. 'Some would say it is the suffrage.'

'Why yes, that too,' said Penwoman, glad to have aroused a little interest after all. 'But I don't count the suffrage as one of life's more modest comforts. I talk about that in an entirely different way.'

Oh, thought Cecilia, here we go again. What she said was: 'You may be right; it could be worth considering.'

'But not for too long. You know, when I was preparing for my article, just for the fun of it I went to enquire what those little apartments for girls cost. That's to say, in Stockholm they don't officially exist, so you have to ask around among the ones currently occupied by senior railway linemen, chauffeurs and widows. There's one on Blasieholmen I particularly recall, a bit old fashioned and perhaps not the height of comfort, but it had the most glorious view from the best room over the harbour and the boats, with the venerable silhouette of the Nordic Museum in the background. It was made for you,' she went on, leaping up from the sofa. 'Just imagine if it were free, what damned good luck that would be, eh?'

She was gone before Cecilia had time to reply, but without quite realising it she, too, was seized by a sudden, fervent wish that the apartment might be vacant.

'You know, I think it just might be,' continued Penwoman, coming in with the telephone directory. 'The landlord seemed terribly particular. I don't think he would have rented it out to anyone unless they were from an institution for distressed, single gentlewomen.'

Cecilia began to chuckle. 'Well then, I should suit him perfectly.'

'It's positively made for you!' exclaimed Penwoman, light-headed with delight. 'Make sure you learn the Athanasian Creed* before you go, and he might even put the rent down.'

'But my dear Barbro, your words are running away with me. It cannot all be settled in such a hurry. Whatever will Mrs Bengtsson say?'

'Leave her to me; I can easily find her another boarder to take your place,' said Penwoman blithely. 'There are so many menfolk in this town queuing up to live here, so it won't be a problem. Furniture might be, but unless I'm very much mistaken, you've got quite lot in storage in some aristocratic attic.'

'No, at Frey's Express,' said Cecilia, 'but how did you know?'

'Pah, don't you think people can tell by looking that you inherited an elegant old home? And I can see from your mournful eyes that you've got monogrammed sheets. What fun this is going to be. I shall go and ring the landlord right away.'

And so she did, before Cecilia could think of preventing her.

'It's vacant,' she said on her return, beaming with unselfish delight. 'I took the opportunity of making an appointment for you to see the landlord and view the flat. Half past eleven, does that suit you? I expect that's during your lunch break. Now the only thing left is to find you a maid,' she added, sinking back down among the cushions with a sigh of satisfaction. 'But we've plenty of time; it's a whole month until the first of October.'

'I might conceivably be able to organise the maid for myself,' said Cecilia with a smile.

CHAPTER 4

'Do you want to do a piece on the arrival of the Duke and Duchess?' asked the deputy editor, turning to Penwoman, who was standing bolt upright in the office they called the Slaves' Galley, awaiting orders.

'All right,' she said, 'how long?'

'Oh, there's no need to be economical with your words,' he said. 'We've nothing held over for today. And don't forget to give all the details of what the princesses and ladies-in-waiting are wearing, but keep some kind of democratic angle.'

'Princess X in a suit of thundercloud blue looked as if she was thinking about little Prince Y and wondering if he was teething,' suggested Penwoman in businesslike tone, but inside she was thinking how furious the fashion editor would be!

'Yes, that sort of thing; steer a course between our democratic male readers and our royalist female ones; keep them both happy. Have you got a police pass?'

'Yes, I flirted one out of the Commissioner, remember, that time he wanted to recruit me as a detective.'

The deputy editor was too used to Penwoman's irreverent references to the city's figures of authority to react to this.

'They'll be here at three,' he said. 'So if you were thinking of smartening yourself up, you'd better get off home at once.'

'A female journalist's ablutions always leave her prepared for a low-cut neckline,' declared Penwoman recklessly, quite forgetting the holes in her gloves. 'I'll never rival the Swedish Telegraph Bureau, anyway, but if you want me to hold my own against the *Stockholm Daily News,** you'll have to pay me better.'

'How are you getting on with those letters to the Editor on

41

"Women and Dress Reform"?'* the deputy editor hastened to ask.

'Oh, the one in favour of rational dress is done, but the one attacking it isn't due in until tomorrow. It does take me a little while to reverse my opinions on the subject.'

'Well, just long as they're provocative enough,' urged the deputy editor.

'Isn't what I write usually, then?'

'Oh yes,' he laughed, 'it certainly is. How's that Sunday article "Women and the Comet" going?'

'I haven't had time to think about it yet. You, of all people, know how much I've had to do.' But he was engrossed once more in his long list of the day's assignments, and did not hear her.

A couple of hours later she was standing by the platform at the central station, waiting for the Duke and Duchess with a knot of newspapermen of all political complexions.

The zeal of the good journalist was upon her; she always threw herself body and soul into even the most trivial assignments, and on this occasion there was the extra frisson of annoying the fashion editor.

At the door of the royal waiting room stood the young Princess Charlotte, thin as a greyhound. She had recently married an archduke and was now on a visit to the Duke and Duchess of Halland in order, the gossips said, to try to overcome her spleen. Stockholm was presumably not her choice, but they would not let her travel to England, her homeland, for now she had changed country and religion and was supposed to forget England.

Penwoman observed her thoughtfully; in the course of her work she had encountered women in workshops, palaces, schools, hospitals, homes and on the committee of the Fredrika Bremer Society* and felt she had been afforded some fairly revealing glimpses of their fluctuating emotional life, but this young creature, more like a jewel – though so melancholy – than a human being, could hardly have a single thought in common with any of them. So what was she thinking about, then; where did her first thoughts fly in the morning? To an estate and a horse, a lord, a tea tray in her homeland? But only in a somewhat weary, indifferent way, simply because she had no work or ambition, and because the wages of work and the accomplishment of ambition were already hers.

Penwoman's heart was suffused with a strange mixture of envy and pity, which changed to pure pity when she saw the expression of loathing and scorn with which the Princess was looking across to the railway track, to the spot where her archdukely aunt, who could well be at Liljeholm by now, would doubtless descend from the train, kiss her on both cheeks and tell her that a princess had to display a greater capacity for controlling herself than other people.

The Princess sent Penwoman a sudden little look of cool surprise, and the latter told herself that the Princess, singular phenomenon though she might be, presumably found it as uncomfortable as any commoner to be the object of someone else's protracted scrutiny.

'Right, I must start minding my manners, although I'm a journalist,' she thought, going over to her colleagues and launching instantly into an animated but good-humoured dispute with the right wing. A quick look told her that the Princess had started pacing up and down the red carpet rolled out between the waiting room and the platform edge. With her next glance – because Heaven knows, she was only human and sometimes scarcely that – she intercepted to her amazement a swift, appraising look from the Princess, alive with a curiosity and interest one might not have thought her capable of.

'Fair enough, it must be her turn to stare now,' thought Penwoman, tactfully averting her gaze and continuing with much laughter and many asides to dictate the names of the royal retinue and any other notables to a delighted provincial correspondent.

The Princess continued walking to and fro, disregarding the fact that all the members of the royal party had come out and were now standing in a row by the track, and every time she passed Penwoman, she gave her a swift glance and listened to her clear, merry voice. She surreptitiously brought out a little notebook with a silver cover, wrote a few words with the pencil that dangled from it on a cord, tore out the page, screwed it up and then, without hesitating, as the train pulled into the platform and everyone, even her lady-in-waiting, was looking expectantly that way – everyone except Penwoman, that is – threw the little ball so it landed, apparently by accident, right at the girl's feet.

Penwoman had been watching the Princess with mounting astonishment, and now gave her a direct stare, as if to ask if she had understood correctly, before picking up this unexpected message from a higher world.

'I wish I were a reporter.' Written in English. Ah, so that was what she was thinking!

The Princess was still standing there, even though the official welcomes had already begun; it was as if she were waiting desperately for an answer.

'She is like a rare, royal flower, condemned to wither young,' – the phrase ran for a moment through Penwoman's trained columnist's brain – 'her eyes looking out on the world, wide and uncertain, shifting between grey and violet like the blue fox fur round her neck...'

But she realised very well that the Princess needed comforting swiftly and unambiguously, before her archdukely aunt got hold of her, and with a quick, sad gesture containing the eloquence of a whole world, she reached out both her hands in their threadbare gloves, with a hole in every fingertip. The Princess gave a delightful, fleeting smile that left Penwoman completely unsure whether she had understood or not, and hurried off to greet her princely relations. As she went, she dropped her notebook, and when she noticed this, she half turned and gave Penwoman a nod. The girl understood, slipped under the cordon that divided the crowd from its royal family, and retrieved the book with pleasure.

But why did a young princess want to be a newspaper man?

It was after five by the time she had written her article, which was full of detail, though none of it concerning the episode with the notebook. She dashed from the newspaper office, along the dusky alleyways round Klara church and on to Tegelbacken to catch a red tram directly to the dinner table. Events had unfortunately conspired to make her late for dinner several days in a row, and she therefore gave a sigh of relief when under the willow tree she found the trainee architect, waiting for the same tram.

'It's always easier if one has a fellow sinner,' was how she explained her friendly greeting, for at that moment she remembered she had had reason to put him in that category of young men, who from pure, childish arrogance interpreted the slightest pleasantry as a victory for their male charm. His undisguisedly hopeful manner towards her, which would have been impertinent in any man but this decent, artless boy, had been amusing her for a week or two, but now she felt the time had come to teach him better manners, and when he immediately suggested they go out for dinner together, with the excuse, 'If we're going to sin, we might as well do it properly', she agreed after a brief hesitation.

'How funny you are,' she said. 'Is that what you call sinning? And do you enjoy it more that way? Well, that's fine by me, provided I can choose where we go and what I eat.'

'Anything within half my budget,' he said, beaming. Penwoman was pretty, and the fact that she was also fun to be with exactly matched his experience of the less moral among girls from good homes. You can have a pretty good time with them for a relatively modest outlay in material terms; they are often cheerful and good-natured; and there's no risk of the fuss and tiresome consequences that can ensue when you consort with well-behaved, refined girls, and he should know. He had kissed both categories in dark boarding house halls.

They took their seats at a table by the window in the Rosenbad* restaurant, and in line with the rudimentary knowledge of women he had gleaned at the boarding houses of Stockholm, and the preconception he had of Penwoman as a girl of loose morals, he began casting bold, glad looks in her direction. She did not notice them immediately, however, being ravenously hungry, so then he tried to cajole her into agreeing how strange and significant, not to say slightly daring, it was for the two of them, on such short acquaintance... and alone... see those knowing looks we're getting from the head waiter...!

45

Penwoman began to laugh again.

'You really are funny,' she said. 'Just imagine you thinking that this head waiter, who's seen me here with every single colleague from the newspaper, singly or in flocks, and with various others besides, would be surprised by such a thing! You're most definitely the only one who sees anything novel in the situation.'

'And do you come here with Mr Jessen, as well?' he asked, to show he could be disagreeable too. 'It seems to me that the two of you have been exchanging plenty of confidences these last few days.'

'Oh, has it showed?' asked Penwoman, and laughed at the thought of the effect her deliberate revelation of Cecilia's four thousand a year had had on the women's suffrage-hating editor. Those were the sorts of argument he understood. No, young Mr Block would not get anywhere that way.

'Couldn't you, being so depraved, initiate me into the basics of depravity,' he proceeded to ask, leaning forward – a little too far, she thought, and drew back at once.

'Oh, tavern habits are best acquired by personal study,' she said, a little dismissively.

'Now you're misunderstanding me.'

'Yes, I thought it the most tactful thing to do,' she said calmly.

'Most tactful?'

'Precisely. I thought you would understand, if someone gave you a little hint, the need for a change of tone.'

'But you surely weren't offended, were you?'

'If you had the slightest idea how offensive that is, said in that tone, I'd summon the waiter, pay the bill and leave. But I can see that you haven't, and I'm sure it isn't your fault. You simply haven't ever been taught how to behave to a girl in a situation like this.' He stared at her in such astonishment, that for the first time that evening she felt herself losing her temper.

'Now just you listen,' she said a little fiercely. 'You are totally nonplussed that I, Penwoman as they call me, with my reputation for being a bit eccentric, having allowed myself to be invited to dinner on the spur of the moment – which incidentally I don't intend to repeat after this – am bothering to pretend to be offended. I'm right, aren't I?'

'If I were to deny it, I don't suppose you'd believe me,' he said glumly.

'No, I wouldn't. It's rational not to believe just anybody, any time. And a young woman' – she tossed her head – 'must be rational. Otherwise she'll go under, but I don't intend doing anything of the kind. I've got to draw the line. More than enough have gone under before my time.'

He said nothing, for he had no idea what he was allowed to say. Here was a case where his experience and natural quick-wittedness were no help at all.

'What a lot of things you know about,' he said finally.

'Oh, there's more,' she said, and he dared not give even a hint of a smile. 'And we need to go through it all, before we can be friends or even get on tolerably well together. I'd like to teach you something that lies quite beyond your horizon, something very pleasant called camaraderie.'

'Is that what you're in the habit of teaching young men at Rosenbad?' he asked.

'Yes,' she said.

Now he felt he was starting to discover this girl's private way of being immoral, and he thought: this is going to turn out all right, but I must watch my step. It was pretty clear, anyway, that there must be something not quite correct about a girl who needed to justify herself to a casual dinner companion. Elsa and Greta, his sisters, would never have done such a thing. For the first time in his life, he caught himself feeling proud of their infinite innocence.

'Why must you take everything so damn seriously?' he said. 'Stop beating about the bush, take off that lecturing busybody look and be yourself. They do say,' – Penwoman gave a rather sad smile – 'that you're usually merry and lively. Perhaps you think I'm some kind of saint, but I'm not, even though I come from the country.'

'In that case we aren't at all suited to each other, but it doesn't

47

matter, because this dinner won't cost much,' said Penwoman. 'It's just as well, isn't it, that we found out before we went off to the seaside at Nynäs together, say, or to the theatre? Because I like saints, as long as they're happy ones.'

'And a bit hypocritical,' he ventured, thinking he was giving a brilliant display of sharp wit, after all the scolding he had had for his stupidity.

'So you think me hypocritical?' she asked.

'Well, perhaps a little,' he said, 'but it's very becoming.'

Penwoman sighed.

'So that's what happens when I politely and loyally try to point out to you, that people can't take out a season ticket for me as if I were the opera house or the hot baths. And I've every reason for telling *you* this, as you well know.'

He replied that he most certainly did not know that; it was the last thing he had thought, and anyway he much preferred both the opera and the hot baths. But far from being embarrassed, she laughed at him, and in the end he had to admit she had been right.

'Well how was I to know?' he said morosely. 'Why must you sail under such a false flag? Let people talk about you as they do?'

'Oh, it's just a simple pleasure I allow myself. And, incidentally, an excellent way of finding out what men are like.'

He had a sudden sense of having failed an examination.

'And why do you write so indecently?' he asked.

'That's the way I feel things. What was it about my writing that our Mr Tufve – because it must be him – found indecent, then?'

'Well, you betray knowledge of things that a young girl ought not to know,' he said, delighted by his ingenious reformulation of the Scanian's more crudely expressed verdict.

'Why ought she not?' asked Penwoman, with an ominous glint in her eye.

'She ought not,' Dick Block said simply, 'because we want a woman to be delicate and pure and good and innocent, of course. That's how we visualise her, and we have to, because we can't be that way ourselves, can we now?'

'But your preference is for her to be delicate and pure at a distance, I'm sure, while for company you choose the likes of me, and those further down the scale?'

'Yes, but once we're earning four or five thousand a year and are bored with bachelor life, then we marry her.'

'If you had a fiancée, would you want her to be a "delicate and innocent girl"? Even if she were ignorant and childish?'

'Yes, how else could she be innocent?' he asked.

'Doesn't it grieve you to think that some women will have to live through what a delicate lady is too delicate to know?' she asked slowly, contemplating him as if seeking enlightenment about the customs and habits of strange tribes.

'No, but that's different, you know,' he said.

'I see. Have you never considered, you men with the gift and the power, reorganising matters so there isn't anything on this earth so improper that your sisters and fiancées mustn't know of it?'

'But just think, my dear young lady, how impossible that would be.'

'And has it never occurred to you men that it would be better if you released them into the world and let them help? If you didn't instantly condemn them, as you have me, for their knowledge?'

'I can't exactly say why, but it goes against the grain for me to think of anything like that,' he said. 'When a man is fond of a woman, he wants to protect her, I suppose.'

'It doesn't go against the grain, though, for you to think of the sort of city Stockholm becomes at night, a jungle of stone, where alleyways are the hunting ground and quarter is neither given nor accepted?'

'People can always stay indoors.'

'I can't. How often do you think I have to walk home from the newspaper offices in my skirt and jacket and be taken for fair game? But then, of course, I'm not a proper lady any more,' she added, a touch bitterly.

'Oh yes you are,' he said quickly, but broke off and blushed deeply.

They both laughed, and Penwoman raised her glass in exaggerated gratitude.

'Don't even try,' she said. 'You need to change your whole way of looking at life, before you can say that with a clear conscience. As you can imagine, I've lost all my naiveté in my profession, but I've learnt about the suffrage and a lot more...'

'Like what?'

'How to get through temptation and misfortune, better than your sisters could, for example.'

'If you fell into temptation, you'd get through the misfortune, you mean?' he asked delightedly, seeing this as his first opportunity to talk of matters personal and sexual.

'I shall never fall,' declared Penwoman very definitely. 'I shall stop, before things go that far. And you needn't sit there thinking "Well I like that, coming from her," or "She's a fine one to talk", because I'd rather die. And anyway, that question won't arise for years. For now, I can presumably be much loved, if I choose to.'

He looked utterly perplexed by her strange logic.

'But surely it's precisely when a woman's in love, that she falls?' he said.

'Oh, is that how you see the problem?' she asked with interest. 'Do all men think like you?'

'I don't know. I'm sure you know better than I, but how else could they think? Well, not if she's married, of course.'

Penwoman sat thoughtfully for a moment.

'Come on, let's go,' she finally said, rather abruptly. 'No, let me pay my share. After all, I've had a meal and learnt a lot about men for my money.'

'Couldn't we walk a little way, so I get a chance to learn about the new women?' he asked.

'You certainly need to,' she answered, laughing, and looked at her watch. 'Well, I don't have to be at the Victoria Hall* until half past seven, and some poor girl might always benefit from your having had a lesson. So' – and she raised a lecturing index finger in a newly-mended glove – 'as I see it, there's no risk of my falling, when I'm young, and can preferably still afford to wait and appraise with clear eyes, until I find the one I shall love very much, and to whom I shall give myself, without caring what it costs, because I am loved with a love that must be royally rewarded.'

They were strolling along Blasieholmen quay, and she was staring reflectively straight ahead, over the water into the Skeppsholm twilight.

'It isn't very easy for us to understand each other, of course, since I'm a woman,' she said, 'and actually it's easier for *me* to know, myself, than to tell you. But it seems to me that we women, if we want to respect ourselves, need to think, as we give ourselves to a man: this is the only man for me, and I'm the only woman for him. And not look back or forward. But it's not like that for you. There's such an enormous difference. Mr Tufve said once, when I asked him, that he'd have to find a girl really distasteful, not to want to "get together" with her, whereas we, in that situation, are investing our whole soul. So really it's no wonder, is it, that we're out of step?'

'This new woman you were talking about will just have to give a little less of herself,' he said. 'That would be more rational.'

'Yes, perhaps,' said Penwoman a little sadly, 'but it simply can't be done. No, I *shall* give my soul gladly, but if the gift isn't appreciated, I shall be braver than my mother was, or my grandmother. I shan't do as they did: leave my soul floundering and run away or let anyone who cares to trample it and spit on it. I shall take it back and cherish it and respect it just as highly as if it had never been rejected, or worse. Naturally I could go down with my love, like a captain with his ship, but if I don't, then I've no intention of letting anybody declare me unworthy of commanding other vessels, just because the one I had sank. If I knew any of your architectural terms, I'd use them, and then perhaps you'd understand me better.'

'Oh, I think perhaps I understand,' he said, ' but I do wonder how things will turn out for you, if you start living by your version of morality. And there is one thing I don't understand. In your language, what do you mean by "falling"?'

'Oh,' she said, now eager and agitated, 'that's easily explained. Falling is what I would be doing if I tried to worm my way into love at a cheaper price, if I valued myself so little that I gave

51

myself without wanting to give every last part of me and without demanding the same back. They say there's a temptation for women nobody desires to humiliate themselves and beg, or accept charity, pretending not to notice it's given with contempt. But the day I find myself standing there with my double chin and a longing inside me that doesn't match my outward appearance, feeling that if I lived, the temptation would become too much for me, I shall shoot myself. Is there anything else you want to know?' She took a few steps towards the quayside, where the dark waters of evening swirled by on their way to the sea.

He took her by the arm in feigned alarm.

'Oh, don't be alarmed,' she said cheerfully. 'Do I look as if I couldn't be...' She broke off, for perhaps it would not be appropriate to say 'loved'.

'No, of course not,' he said, with genuine conviction.

'I'm sure you must have found me very – ,' he was unsure how to put it. 'Ignorant,' she supplied with a little smile. 'But that's not so remarkable, you know.'

'Well I'm glad, anyway, that you found out how I was thinking, because otherwise I don't suppose you would have talked to me the way you just have, would you?'

'I don't know,' she said, 'I've found out so many, but I've never said this to any of them before. I don't think I've really spelled it out to myself before, just gone along knowing it in my heart.'

'You've talked to me much more than I had a right to expect,' he said, once they had turned back into the city and walked in silence for several minutes. 'But if I ask you one more thing, you mustn't be angry. It's not just impertinence. Tell me, have you – have you – yourself – ?'

'No, never,' she replied.


The trams had stopped running, and the torrential rain had emptied the streets and made the going heavy by the time Penwoman was on her way home from the newspaper that evening. She was trudging along as fast as she could, her thoughts preoccupied with the physical discomfort of the rain and wind, when at a corner of the otherwise empty road, just ahead of her, she saw a girl in some kind of shimmering, silky raincoat, beneath which rustled and glinted a sequined dress, while a red petticoat slapped around her legs with every step she took.

If that's the girl from Badstugugatan, thought Penwoman without knowing why, then she'll sense I'm right behind her and turn round.

And sure enough, she did. She had a dirty bandage round her neck.

'Oh, it's you, you bitch,' she said.

'Yes,' said Penwoman. 'How are you?' But she glanced round to check they were alone.

'They arrested him,' the girl answered her look, 'Otherwise you'd best have made yourself scarce.'

'I thought as much,' said Penwoman. 'Otherwise I'd have taken a different route. But where are you off to?'

'Why d'you ask?'

'We might be going the same way.'

The girl began to laugh. 'I reckon we are. Just as well we haven't got the same landlady, and all.'

She was walking through all the deepest puddles, and suddenly slipped in the mud and fell over. Penwoman helped her up, not without a shudder of distaste.

'Come into this doorway so you can wring yourself out,' she said.

'A girl needs to be drunk,' said the young woman.

Penwoman sighed.

'Come on now, you look a sight. Can't you try to wipe yourself down? I've got to get home. Where do you live?'

'Get lost,' said the girl.

'I'm not trying to do you good or ill.'

'Nobody can,' said the girl. 'Not any more.'

'But can I ask you...?'

'How I ended up like this? You ask away. I might tell you lies. Anyway,' she said, her dignity suddenly asserting itself, 'it's none of your business.'

But she embarked on her story, even so, and once she got started, she was not short of words. 'There was this count, see...'

'Yes,' said Penwoman sceptically.

The girl gave her a look, and then a different story gradually emerged, not as romantic as the one she had intended serving up, but infinitely more wretched. She had been sent out on the street by her foster-parents and had earned her first coppers at the age of twelve.

'It was all I knew,' she said, 'but then I was saved! I behaved myself for three years and got a place and worked like other people, though I often found it very hard, when I could've been doing nothing instead, and earning good money for it. But then I got engaged, and he said he didn't care about the past, he said, and he'd been no better himself.'

'Was he the fellow who...?' began Penwoman.

'Hah,' said the girl. 'He was neither the first nor the last, but this boy I'm talking about, the one I got to know, was a good-looker, I'd never seen anyone so fine, but then he wanted me to go back to earning money the old way, *so I did it*. Then it was if I'd never been saved, of course, and it wasn't long before the police got me again, but that's the way it had to be.'

'The way it had to be!' said Penwoman, and stamped her foot with a splash. 'Can't anything be done? Can't someone teach girls to be on their guard, tell them what happens, can't someone write...?' Confused ideas for a flyer to be handed out in streets and schools came into her mind.

'There's no point,' said the girl. 'Because when the one comes along that you believe in, it's as if you hadn't heard a word.'

Penwoman felt all her theories sinking like a bubble in water in the face of this flash of immutable truth.

# Chapter 5

A broken promise was perhaps not such an unusual experience, but Ester Henning could not shake off a certain bitter surprise at having so thoroughly misjudged Cecilia. Until the very last moment she had hoped to see her at the campaign launch and when, to the disappointment of many, she did not stay for the subsequent gathering, at which summer experiences would be compared and collated, and all of Sweden would be marked on its suffrage performance by those who had been on summer lecture tours, it was because Cecilia had not appeared. She had felt so sure of her, that she had already been anticipating her comrades' approval and delight at this new, unspent force – and then Cecilia did not even come to the meeting as promised.

Who are we working for, she wondered bitterly, as she walked home alone. They do not notice us working, nor will they notice the results. She turned the words over and over in her mind, feeling no inclination to shrug off her depression; in fact she stubbornly focused her thoughts on everything that might intensify it, and naturally there was no shortage of material. Old episodes came back into her mind; she remembered her sister-in-law not renewing her subscription to the Association when the annual cost was raised to one krona; she remembered the caretaker's grimace when she had been turned away from an election meeting several years before. There was scarcely a single little stab of pain among all those she had received in her years of work for women's suffrage that did not smart in the course of those twenty minutes walking the rainy streets.

And before she even crossed the threshold to her husband's consulting room, he could see from her face that something had put her out of spirits, and he was not surprised when her first words after asking how the children proved to be, 'Do you think all our toiling for women will lead anywhere? I'll sacrifice my life gladly, but I do want to...'

'Get something in return,' he said, putting aside his magazine with a smile. 'Well *you* might not, but our little girl will.'

'Oh, that's not what I meant.' She sat down in the patient's chair, moving it rather closer to the doctor's own. 'You see, as I walked home I was thinking: perhaps we are taking all this trouble for nothing. Perhaps women feel their lives are fine as they are. I would much rather concentrate on my profession and my home, and sometimes I think I must be mad to put so much effort into something that doesn't concern me.'

He was silent for a moment.

'You say women think their lives are fine as they are,' he said slowly, because he knew exactly how to treat her. 'I wish you had been at the clinic today.' And he began telling her of all the misery that had washed through his clinic at the big hospital, of neglected children and abandoned women, malnourishment and death.

They eagerly discussed his various cases and the social conditions that gave rise to them, and her dejection was soon forgotten.

'Thank you for reminding me,' she said at last. 'You always know. However could I forget: our own may not need us, but the working-class women do. We shall labour for them.'

'Yes, you certainly should,' said the doctor, adding under his breath, 'as long as you don't let them see you are doing it,' but his wife did not hear the last part.

'Oh, I forgot to tell you,' he added, 'it says in this evening's paper, that your friend Tilly Berg has been declared incompetent to apply for a hospital doctor's post in Karlköping. So the poor women of the upper classes do need their share of campaigning as well.'

He knew this was a piece of news that would restore all Ester's thirst for action and battle, and he was not mistaken.

'Incompetent, I like that! The very idea of Tilly being incompetent!'

The last traces of her dejection evaporated; her eyes glinted with indignation, and she could not stay in her seat but had to get up and pace the floor to give vent to her flood of emotion.

'Just you wait, you gentlemen law-makers,' she said.

As she made one of her turns she suddenly looked at her husband. He was watching her with a smile, pleased with his successful treatment.

'You know how to handle me,' she said, going over and putting her arm round his neck. 'If I hadn't got you – '

'Another thing I forgot,' he said without looking at her, but in a light, and cheerful tone, 'here's something to help prevent any relapses for a while. The provinces are calling for you again.' He handed her two letters. 'I recognise the handwriting.'

She could see at a single glance that he was right. More of those touching requests for lectures. In one place they were on the verge of setting up a new local association, in another, a weak association was going to keel over and die if it did not receive an injection of new life from the capital.

Ester Henning recalled very well how happy her husband had been at dinner that very day that they were all gathered at home in peace and quiet again, and utterly understood what he must have felt, when he retrieved the two missives from the letterbox.

Tears came into her eyes.

'Oh my dearest, there is no one like you,' she whispered, pressing her damp eyelids to his cheek.


If Cecilia was left in peace in the days that followed to repent her omission, it was thus as a consequence of those two letters and the three-day trip they necessitated. But one evening, when Ester Henning was sitting alone in her hotel room after having successfully set up a new branch, she took it upon herself to write to the breaker of promises:

'Dear Miss Bech,

It was a pity you were prevented from attending our meeting as agreed. You would have found it most edifying. Simply seeing the joy everyone present took in coming together again after their summer separation would have helped you visualise a time when you yourself will be a link in this chain of comradeship. Our General was more inspired than ever, and if you knew how much work we have planned for the coming winter, you would realise that you really cannot justify delaying a single day before coming to harness yourself to the load.

I sit here alone in my hotel room, which is an ugly, bare little place, but I feel neither lonely nor sad. A mere quarter of an hour has passed, you see, since the elect were sitting here on the edge of my bed, receiving their instructions for the future, and not an hour ago I spoke on the telephone to my husband and children, and the youngest informed me it had embroidered a serviette case with the inscription: Votes for Mama! What a child! But that is not my reason for writing to you. It is not as comfortable here as in Finnsta, remember; I am not anyone's guest here, but on the other hand I am more deeply gripped by the gravity of the moment, and I have had the pleasure of answering intelligent questions and receiving promises, small in number but very firm. I can now fall asleep in the conviction that henceforth there will be another little beacon shining within its own limited sphere.

Might you be able to come up to Lästmakargatan on Thursday at 6 p.m.? I shall be there, and could introduce you to the Hard-Labour Gang and set you to work. I look forward to seeing you.

Yours most sincerely,
Ester Henning.'

Cecilia was above all a well-mannered person, and since Dr Henning had been kind enough to renew her request, despite Cecilia having failed to appear, politeness demanded that she present herself at the appointed time. Thus she was in Lästmakargatan at a quarter to six, and was just looking for the right entrance when she ran into a whole gaggle of women, coming out of number six. As she stepped aside to let them pass, she at once caught a phrase to tell her, had she not known already, that the women coming towards her were suffragists: 'What will the

Director say, if I go in tomorrow and ask permission to go and lecture on votes for women in Norrköping?'

Cecilia scrutinised them with a certain curiosity as they went by – a handful of women of different ages and standing, their faces generally a little worn and sharp-featured, their dress free of vanity, but as far as she could see from this brief inspection, not sharing any other characteristics to indicate why they, among thousands, had made active work for women's suffrage their task.

Did any of them, she wondered, come to the job as impoverished and listless as she?

At the end of the row, walking a few steps apart from the rest was a thin, elderly woman, white-haired and imposing, flanked by two shorter friends resembling nothing so much as a pair of anonymous letters. She looked sharply at Cecilia, who blushed and bade her a good evening; to have failed instantly to recognise Miss Adrian, the well-known headmistress, was indeed a crime.

The latter nonetheless responded with a gracious: 'You did right to come, Miss Bech. They are expecting you up there.'

'Thank you,' replied Cecilia for no good reason, and hurried past her through the doorway. The certain knowledge that they had been discussing her made her feel uncomfortable. 'They are expecting you.' Who was expecting her, and what was expected of her?

She entered a small room that looked like an office. Shelves full of suffrage literature ran the length of the walls; there was a desk under the window and in the middle of the floor stood a round table, loaded with piles of different coloured leaflets, and bundles of envelopes to be stuffed and addressed.

Around the table sat three ladies, each with an inkwell to hand. One was Dr Henning, who now got to her feet and came towards Cecilia, beaming.

'Bless you for coming after all,' she said. 'I've an inkwell and a very boring job for you right away, but first let me introduce you to those members of the Hard Labour Gang who are here. This is our Secretary, Mrs Horneman – '

A tall, slender, dark-haired woman in mourning clothes stood up and welcomed her warmly.

'And this is Miss Anna Gylling, the General's right-hand, literally and in many other ways besides.'

Anna Gylling, a pale, slightly stooped girl with tired eyes, extended a thin, hard hand to Cecilia and said something about the impossibility of escaping Dr Henning, once she had got it into her mind that a particular person should be drawn into suffrage work. Anyone marked by her was lost.

'I am not so sure the Doctor will get much in return for her trouble,' replied Cecilia, belying her own words by taking off her hat and coat, sitting down at the desk and locating a pen.

'Oh, but I'm quite sure,' responded Mrs Horneman with a friendly smile, passing her a list of addresses. Cecilia looked up at her, realising only now how attractive she was, as lovely as any woman could be, immediately turning all Cecilia's preconceptions on their heads. What could have brought such a beautiful woman to the campaign for votes for women?

'What do you mean?' enquired Cecilia.

'Well, I can see just by looking at you that once you've been with us for a while, you'll be put to use for diplomatic missions in Society, and to decorate deputations and agitate at afternoon tea parties in aristocratic circles.'

Cecilia looked in hopeless dismay at Ester Henning, who began to laugh.

'Mrs Horneman isn't aware of our agreement,' she said, 'but you mustn't be alarmed. Nobody will force you to do more than write envelopes, if you don't want to. But the fact is, Mrs Horneman thinks attractive suffragists are a gift from God, and must be used to best advantage. But let's get to work. I expect you find our premises very cramped and humble, yet a great deal of work has been fitted in here.'

'And a chapter of modern history has been written at this table, you could say,' said Anna Gylling, writing at top speed. 'Pass me some more envelopes. Oh, these city council elections! I'm starting to get tired of doing nothing but petitioning, and never making progress any other way, and not even that way, in fact.'

'Does it hurt your pride?' asked Jane Horneman.

'No, my sense of mathematics. It's only natural to take the shortest route between two points, if you have no option but to make the journey.'

'We must reach our goal whether the road is short or long,' declared Ester Henning with a firmness that brooked no contradiction. Anna Gylling smiled but said nothing, and they worked for a while in silence.

But then the door was flung open and something very small and wiry and in a tearing hurry came in.

'Ah, another historic figure,' remarked Anna Gylling, and they started to laugh, for the new arrival had little in common with one's usual image of a historic figure. Her hair hung wearily round a lean, birdlike face that looked young yet worn out; her very clothes looked threadbare from hard labour and her boots bore all the hallmarks of having worked overtime.

Jane Horneman at once got up and helped the newcomer off with her coat, a courtesy which surprised Cecilia, but clearly nobody else.

'I've found such a nice, reasonably priced skirt suit for you,' said Jane Horneman cheerfully. 'We can go and try it on tomorrow, if you've got time, and I've already finished trimming the hat, so you can collect that at the same time. You really can do with it.'

'You've been splendid, as usual, but all that's too worldly for me just at the moment,' said the new arrival, once she had shaken hands with her comrades and been introduced to Cecilia as the Hard Labour Gang's finest brain, Kerstin Vallmark, schoolmistress. 'I should have said right away, that I'm absolutely livid.' She collapsed into the basket chair, making it creak violently, a fact that she noted with a certain pride, as a measure of her rage.

'We could tell, actually,' said Ester Henning. 'What is it, then? Have the press excelled themselves again?'

'No, not that lot, but would you believe it, in Gästrikland they've gone and thrown out...'

'Wait a moment,' interjected Jane Horneman. 'Before she tells us the story, I must just ask: shouldn't we ring for some sandwiches?'

'But a suffragist isn't allowed to eat,' said Anna Gylling disparagingly.

'By rights she should eat twice as much as everyone else,' replied Jane Horneman,' who was already at the telephone. 'Well, Kerstin?'

'Yes please. Now you mention it, I haven't had a bite to eat since I left home this morning. Can you credit it, simply getting rid of her, and putting in a little headmaster, a boy with no other qualifications but his male self-importance and a basic little degree! As if she wouldn't be capable of putting students through their school-leaving certificate, when she has been running the whole lower school in such an exemplary fashion for fifteen years!'

'Do you want ham or salt beef?' asked Jane Horneman, almost apologetically.

'Both. Isn't it shameful?'

'No doubt the law doesn't allow a woman such an elevated position,' said Anna Gylling, 'and the law is right in that, you know, even if a set of interacting coincidences make it seem rather brutal in this case.'

'Coincidences! How can you call them coincidences when they decide everything men think? And does it make it any better? Was it a coincidence, eh, when I...' she broke off, for what was the point of airing her own bitter old grievances, forgotten by everyone but herself, or so it seemed.

'I think it shocking,' said Ester Henning, 'and we must do something about it.'

'Let's hope for the sake of the cause that she has a family to provide for,' said Anna Gylling, 'because in that case she will be as excellent an advertisement for women's suffrage as the sewing machine was in its day.'*

'Let's hope? She's somewhere down in Skåne now with a cut in salary, and a mother and two brothers to support.' Kerstin Vallmark gave Anna Gylling a reproachful look: there were limits to what even she was permitted to say, spoilt child of the whole suffrage movement though she was.

'Is there nothing we can do?' said Jane Horneman. 'Just a minute though, here come the sandwiches.'

'I shall ring Penwoman. She should be able to make something out of this.'

'Surely you could write something yourself? You've done it so often and so well before.'

'No, I'm *too* cross.'

'There's no such thing.'

'For *me* there is.'

She rang the *Liberal Morning News* and got straight through to Penwoman.

'Do you fancy writing a fiery indignation piece? – Oh, you're always so obliging.'

'Any idea of subject? I most certainly have. – Not this evening? – Could you pop in here on your way? – Oh, splendid. See you soon.'

They devoted themselves to their sandwiches and envelopes for a time, while they waited for Penwoman.

Sure enough, she soon appeared, and greeted them all cheerfully, but without revealing her immense surprise at seeing Cecilia, who was happy to remain as forgotten as she had been for the last hour. With a few succinct questions, Penwoman briefed herself on why she should be indignant, reacted instantly and angrily, and dashed off after a few minutes to a working women's study circle, pausing only to issue a threateningly worded challenge to the authorities in question.

'What are you planning to do now?' asked Ester Henning, once Kerstin Vallmark had finished her sandwiches. She herself had one eye on the clock and was wishing she could go home, but there were so many envelopes still unaddressed, and Anna Gylling was clearly so tired she could hardly stand up any longer.

'I intend preserving my anger and storing it away for times to come,' replied the schoolmistress, failing to interpret Dr Henning's veiled request to be relieved.

So then she asked straight out: 'Couldn't you channel it into addressing envelopes?'

'No, it's too holy for that,' Jane Horneman put in at once. 'Let her go her own way and we'll take care of this. I'm sure by the time she gets home she'll have had some brand new, highly original idea for converting Parliament and giving the poor teacher her post back.'

'In that case you'd better get going at once,' said Anna Gylling obligingly. Kerstin Vallmark noticed the sarcasm.

'Don't you think a woman can be original, then?' she asked, a little piqued.

'Oh yes, just as much as a quilt can be warm in itself,' replied Anna coolly. 'I think you should go, too, Ester,' she went on. 'The rest of us can easily finish off here.'

'But aren't you're dreadfully tired, Anna?' said Ester dubiously, getting to her feet.

'Not in the slightest,' answered Anna Gylling, bending over her paperwork so no one could see her face.

'Oh well, if you're sure...' Ester looked relieved.

'Remember that new suit and hat tomorrow,' Jane Horneman reminded Kerstin Vallmark, as they were at the door.

'You're quite right,' said Anna Gylling once they were alone, 'to be concerned about the suffrage campaign's wardrobe; it's a far greater mission than anyone realises. Our popularity depends on it, to an extent. I was going to ask you if you couldn't do something for the campaign's complexion, too. We're starting to get old and tired and grey in the face, and that will never do. People will say that votes for women is ageing us prematurely.'

'On the contrary, it keeps us young,' declared the beautiful Jane, confident of victory.

Anna Gylling smiled, and again they worked away in silence for a while. Then Jane happened to turn her head rather quickly and see that Anna would not be able to go on much longer, and asked, 'Isn't the General expecting you at home this evening, Anna?'

'She certainly is. But I thought we'd finish here first.'

'Can *I* not do it tomorrow?' asked Cecilia shyly.

'Well, here we have a case of sudden suffrage poisoning,' said

Anna, looking almost sorry for her. 'Just don't get too carried away, the whole cause isn't worth it, and don't be too willing, because any willing volunteer has had it, once the Hard Labour Gang get their hands on her.'

'How can you say that, as a suffrage campaigner yourself?' asked Cecilia, a little taken aback. 'I thought...'

'That we were all like that Flaming Torch for Suffrage, Ester Henning? Oh no. If that were the case, we would have set fire to the parliament building long since. There are plenty whose enthusiasm wouldn't so much as heat up a cold compress.'

'You are a strange girl, Anna Gylling,' said Jane Horneman. 'I don't think there's a single one of us who slaves away as desperately (no, not as desperately, thought the girl to herself), yet still you never miss a chance of telling us you don't believe in the justice and success of the cause you're working for. If I weren't as sure of both those things, as I am of the sun rising tomorrow, then I wouldn't be able to go on.'

'Oh, you have to learn,' said Anna Gylling shortly. 'But since you're trying to give Miss Bech an image of me, you must tell her that I never make a big song and dance of my heresies, even though I may feel that the women's movement is at root an endeavour to gird women's loins and carry them whither they would not.* But I never say it, except when I'm with you people, and you get too carried away.'

'And you want to be really pleasant,' said Jane Horneman good-naturedly. 'But at the risk of making you cross, I have to remind you how eloquent you were at the bank director's dinner the other evening.'

'Yes, but for God's sake Jane, the hostess herself, sister-in-law of our own beloved General, came and begged and implored the Members of Parliament over coffee not to give women the vote, because she wasn't worthy of it, so what was I supposed to do? The whole assembled company of influential Members of Parliament instantly allowed itself to be duped into applauding her as a model of feminine impartiality and modesty, poor woman. The bank director was no help, either.'

'He could hardly disown his own wife,' said Jane Horneman a little brusquely in his defence. If once, a long time before, the bank director's pro-women stance in Parliament had been attributed to Jane Horneman, it was as if she was now being unconsciously reproached for his perceptible cooling.

'Yes, why do prominent men have to be so impossible?' she asked, to make the topic less personal.

'Oh, I can tell you that,' replied Anna Gylling, who when she was very tired did not always trouble to be considerate. 'It's because they marry geese, not us!'


Cecilia and Jane Horneman walked home together.

'Do you think you're going to like it with us?' asked Jane. 'And there's no need to give a polite answer.'

'What has been astonishing me all afternoon is how different women can be,' said Cecilia, rather than answering. 'I mean, from what I can see, you are all living totally different lives, with different trials and hopes and disappointments and aspirations, from the women I know, and from myself, with no strong feelings one way or the other. Someone like me must always feel an outsider.'

'Perhaps to begin with, but not forever,' replied Jane. 'In many ways we're just like most other women, you know, but the reason you haven't noticed it is that we keep our private lives completely outside our community here. We actually never have time to talk about our own or other people's. It may so happen that we occasionally have to ask one of our comrades a favour, and she may need to be told a bare minimum. But apart from that, we all mind our own business.'

Cecilia made no reply, reflecting on this, a thousand memories running through her soul.

'And yet you tell me you are all the same as most other women, Mrs Horneman,' she said.

## Chapter 6

One day, Penwoman disappeared into her room straight after dinner, and there were undeniably those among the group who watched her go with regret. But as the company was drinking its coffee in silence, she stuck her head round the door and addressed her roommate.

'I don't think I shall be home tonight,' she said. 'I just thought I ought to mention it, so you're not surprised when I don't turn up.'

The authoress gaped and failed to find a reply, literary though she was, but Mr Tufve immediately put in: 'Are you spending the night at the newspaper again?'

The rest of Penwoman came into the room. She was wearing a long, dark blue reporter's coat, as straight and narrow as a penholder, and a crimson poke bonnet, from the depths of which a pair of wily eyes peered out as she said: 'I suggest you try to find out who with.'

Emerging from the front entrance a few minutes later, she found young architect Block pacing up and down the pavement, and with a swift glance up at the windows she bade him good evening.

'I was expecting you, see, I came prepared,' she said, taking a hammer out of her coat pocket.

'What are you going to do?' he asked, in a tone that was anything but courteous.

'Tie my shoelace,' she replied. 'Here, hold the hammer. Actually, you could come with me,' she went on, as if something had just occurred to her, 'if it's allowed. In fact, wait a minute, we can telephone and ask. Are you any good at hanging pictures, fixing pelmets and shifting heavy furniture?'

'Yes, and building houses,' he responded. Now he knew what she was talking about, but he was not going to let her off without a rebuke for her inconsiderate way of deliberately scaring people who loved her out of their wits.

'You give yourself a worse reputation with every passing day,' he said gloomily.

'Yes, and all to please you,' she said, without looking at him.

And he really was pleased then, though not, as she had implied, about her bad reputation, which he indignantly perceived as an insult to him personally, but that it was for his edification she had compromised herself this time, since she would persist in doing it anyway.

As they passed his front door, he asked whether she would like to come up: he would make coffee for her himself, to compensate for her having to run away from her own.

'Thank you,' she said simply, 'but we'll get coffee at Cecilia's. Aren't you glad to discover where we're going? I'm utterly delighted, myself. Nobody can believe it's true, but she really has got an apartment of her own on Blasieholmen, and it's all my doing. She turned out to have four thousand a year, but it just hadn't occurred to her to arrange herself a peaceful, male-free refuge until I taught her how. Imagine if it were me, oh my God, with a place of my own, completely my own, I who go down on my knees daily and worship solitude with all my heart.'

Her words, and still more her tone of intense longing, made him feel very uncomfortable.

'So you consider solitude the ideal, do you?'

'As you can well imagine it would be, for anyone who lives in a boarding house and has to share a room,' she replied cheerfully. He could not understand at the moment, just as he was beginning to be in love with her, that she, sated with human contact and hounded by contradictory impressions, longed from a pure instinct for self-preservation to process all that material in peace, and in that peace to learn to be more tolerant of people. She peered past the brim of her bonnet at him. He still looked earnest.

It suited him, but it still hurt her to see it.

'But I'm sure one can have solitude enough by sharing with just *one* person,' she said. 'I would be very happy to live with Cecilia.'

'Yes, you like *her*,' he said.

'Yes, and who wouldn't,' said Penwoman, 'but the remarkable thing is, she likes me too, though we're so different in our ways. I don't know anything about her, though: she's like a locked casket whose key has been thrown into the sea.'

'So now you've set out nets to catch it?'

'No,' she said, stopping abruptly, halfway down Kungs-backen. 'No. And if I did chance to find the key, I'd throw it straight back into the sea without trying it in the lock. So now you know. What are your sisters like?'

'Ordinary,' he said, surprised she had taken such offence, and wondering if he would ever get to know this thing called the modern woman. To mollify her, he said: 'Women can have a good time of it these days, can't they?'

'Yes they can,' she replied, her face suddenly brightening. 'But it's only fair, isn't it? Because I assume you concede that woman is the crowning glory of creation?'

'That may well be,' he said generously, relieved she was being nice again.

'Just you watch out,' came a knowing voice from the recesses of the bonnet, 'that we don't eventually start having a good time of it through our own efforts. You men have had your big chance, without being particularly remarkable, to offer us a home, and all women love that. But once we can arrange our own, what will you do then?'

'Oh,' he said, confident and unconcerned, 'we shall marry you, whether you want us to or not.'

While this conversation was in progress, Cecilia stood looking rather lost among packing cases, sacks and items of furniture, asking herself what could be the meaning of all this, happening in a life that she had accustomed herself to viewing as over. Was it the dawn of something new, or just an illusory revival?

Nothing had happened inside her, she told herself with anxious fervour, for any sign of life within her would have terrified her as much as it would coming from someone assumed dead. It was just outsiders, who had exploited her minimal willpower, dulled by much suffering, and taken her by the hand to lead her where they pleased. They wanted to provide her with a home and a purpose, and though nothing could be more alien to her than those two notions, she had followed them without demur, so why not give those kind people the pleasure of thinking they had succeeded?

Yet she had to admit, extraordinary though it was, that she had awoken that morning for the first time in her own home, without instinctively identifying herself with the usual sense of loathing. She had forgotten it in all the thoughts of rugs and curtains, and only registered this a while later, with unutterable surprise –

But her pain, which was beginning to worry that something was going on, stepped forward and made its presence felt. Here I am, it said, and you need not think I shall fail to thrive just as well in your new apartment or with your new friends. Have you forgotten so soon what happened last time you tried to set up a new home? Don't you remember that flat where you went about singing as you busied yourself with your tasks? The pair of you had rented it for three years, remember, because it had a nursery. Have you forgotten the storm and the destruction? Are you now going to let yourself be deceived into building a hut from the debris? Do you imagine I grant my life prisoners a pardon after seven years?

Cecilia's face grew smaller and smaller, sadder and sadder, and her movements more and more absent-minded, less and less purposeful, as she stood there amidst the chaos, picking up books that needed arranging in the bookshelf.

From the inner room came the sound of someone in constant

motion, moving furniture, knocking in nails, and finally lighting a fire. It was Kristin, who had arrived the day before from Simrishamn and settled in with the firm intention of spending the rest of her days there. At intervals she stopped to listen, and when it all went quiet in the larger room, she came to the door.

'I might have known,' she said, with an anxious note in her southern Swedish voice, 'that you were worn out, Ma'am. It looks quite reasonable in there now, so why don't you have a little lie down, and I'll make you some coffee, and you can leave me to put away all these books.' Cecilia obeyed her blindly, an old habit from her childhood home, partly because it was easier than objecting, partly because Kristin's orders were generally wise and always prompted by goodwill and concern.

'Oh, this looks like a proper room now,' said Cecilia with a sudden feeling of satisfaction and peace. 'You have worked wonders. How nice the curtains are: they are all it takes to make a room look like home.'

She broke off with a look of surprise on her face. On the bedside table lay an unfamiliar Bible and hymnal in a neat little pile.

Kristin noted her look.

'I thought you might like to borrow them, Ma'am, until we found yours,' she said, 'and you're most welcome to, because I've got an everyday Bible and hymnbook that I use all the time. These are my confirmation books, and I can't bring myself to use them.'

'Thank you,' said Cecilia, a little embarrassed, and went over to the sofa. Kristin immediately brought a pillow, which her mistress accepted gratefully, not having realised until that moment quite how exhausted she was.

'But what about you Kristin, are you not tired?' She regarded the tall, solidly built girl with a look of helpless admiration.

Kristin just gave an indulgent laugh.

'Well that wouldn't do now, would it?'

'Why should it do for one and not the other?' asked Cecilia, who in sharp contrast to her maidservant was a democrat in her views.

'Well you should know, Ma'am, being gentry and all, that God created maids' bodies differently, because how else could they do their duties?' said Kristin.

'Whoever made you believe such nonsense, Kristin?' asked Cecilia, taken aback.

'Oh, it was her Ladyship, my old mistress, and she was a sensible person, old-fashioned, and knew what was right, but nowadays people behave as if they've taken leave of their senses.'

At that moment there was a ring at the front door, and Kristin went to answer, albeit unwillingly. 'Visitors, when everything's such a mess,' she grumbled.

Cecilia, who was expecting Penwoman, followed Kristin out to the hall, to see her young visitor standing in the doorway with a doubtful look on her face.

'Good day,' she said. 'Admittance only for those not on business, I assume?'

'Come in and shut the door,' said Cecilia.

'No,' replied Penwoman, with a shy glance at Kristin, who stood waiting with a forbidding air, 'I can't, because I happen to have brought someone with me: Mr Block the architect, you remember, from the boarding house, the only man one can tolerate in a room. Full instructions for use will be provided. It's almost as good as engaging a porter.'

'Ask him in, by all means,' said Cecilia, 'and stop beating about the bush. We're about to have coffee.'

'Ah, so that's the new head of government,' said Penwoman, once Kristin had gone. 'She looks as if she ought to be able to steer the ship of state with a firm hand.'

The girl, seeing now that Cecilia had not been put out by her ruse, was beaming like a grateful little sun.

'Is it a constitutional monarchy?' asked Mr Block, who had taken off his outdoor things and was surveying the chaos happily, because he was going to be needed here, and for a long time.

'Yes,' said Cecilia, 'but the difference between me and other monarchs is that the power is not even nominally mine.'

Penwoman immediately launched herself into the furniture question.

'I love all this,' she said with rosy cheeks. 'I wish I could do nothing but move furniture ever again.'

She could not be persuaded to settle to any specific task, preferring to shuttle between the architect, who was fixing up pelmets, Kristin, who was unrolling the carpet, and Cecilia, who was sewing on curtain rings. She was in sheer bliss when the sofa was shifted into place, and speechless with rapture when Mr Block, perched high on a ladder, hoisted the chandelier to the ceiling. Never had she admired the political editor for his leader or any of her colleagues for their well-written reports as much as she did this wonderful architect's gift for nail hammering and furniture shifting. None of them could ever have dreamt how quickly a place fit for people to inhabit could be created, and once the last packing case had been dragged out to the hall, full of sacks, wood shavings, paper and string, and an overjoyed Kristin had borne the hammer and ladder out to the kitchen, they sat down, breathless and proud, and surveyed the works of their hands.* It all went quiet for a moment, each of them thinking their own thoughts, and strangely enough, on this occasion Cecilia's were the least melancholy.

'Kristin,' Cecilia suddenly called, 'you must give us a bite to eat after all this hard work.'

Kristin appeared at the door and made the oddest signals to Cecilia, intended to express powerlessness, despair and humble reproaches.

'That means we haven't got seven sorts of cold meat, nor omelettes, nor steak, nor even a herring salad,' said Cecilia with a carefree smile, which horrified Kristin as the height of irresponsibility. 'Nor a pudding, though wait a moment, didn't you tell me, Kristin, that you'd whipped together some kind of cake mixture to test the oven this morning?'

Kristin departed with an audible sigh, shaking her head. Would she be obliged to offer first-time guests tea and cake mixture? Penwoman followed her out to the kitchen. She had already made friends with Kristin, after all, and did not feel intimidated.

'Oh, the cake's already reached the manuscript stage,' she cried out with delight to the others.

'You might as well proof-read it then,' Cecilia called back, laughing. Then she turned to the architect to make some polite comment, but caught him staring so longingly at the door through which Penwoman had vanished, and from which her depredations in the kitchen now echoed, that she took pity on him and suggested they go and help with the supper.

Kristin was standing, hands clasped, before the gas stove, which was a new phenomenon in her simple world.

'I think I like it as much as I like you, Ma'am,' she declared.

'Penwoman's in there,' she went on, lowering her voice. Knowing no other name for the girl, she had resigned herself to it, as to all the other oddities she had encountered in this 'Sodom' that was Stockholm.

'I'm in here, in the gentlemen's room,' called Penwoman herself, from a little room off the kitchen. 'I'm looking at all these pictures of you, back to when you were little, Cecilia. You were – ' She broke off, embarrassed.

'...pretty as a picture,' said Kristin, proudly. 'And there wasn't a single young man in Simrishamn who – '

'Is this the gentlemen's room?' interrupted Mr Block, looking in on Penwoman, who was sitting on the edge of the bed, indiscreetly leafing through a plush-covered album. 'Why do you call it that?'

'Where else would the gentlemen be but in the maid's bedroom, eh, Kristin?' replied Penwoman. 'But tell me which of all these handsome boys is your fiancé.'

'It's that fine-looking chap with the curly hair, the one with the cypress sprig underneath,' she answered from the kitchen.

'Oh, is he dead then?'

'Dead? No, he's in Stockholm, and has been for many a year.'

'So won't he be happy to have you here now, Kristin?'

'Well, it won't do him much good, and he knows that, because we've been talking for years. He's an attendant at the Nordic Museum, or whatever they call it, but he knows full well that I won't marry him until he sets up his own museum. Until then I shall stay with Miss Cecilia.'

'Lucky Cecilia,' said Penwoman, only now noticing that Cecilia was no longer in the room. She had laid an improvised tea table in front of the sofa and was pouring tea, with a promise to invite them very soon to a dinner that would restore Kristin's injured pride. Penwoman and the architect exchanged happy looks. They realised that they would be permitted to come here together, that he had been accepted into the circle, and that they thus had a corner of a home in the world, where they would be able to see each other.

'Lucky Cecilia,' said Penwoman again. 'May we come one day at the end of the month, because the food at the boarding house is always worst then.'

'Can you believe it,' said Cecilia, 'in less than three days Kristin has made her Scanian accent feared and respected among the market stallholders of Hötorget? She was telling me today that the women behind the stall this morning asked her nervously whether she could see anything to suit her, and offered her their best wares, assuring her that old gentlemen generally like roast beef and cauliflower. The old gentleman is me,' she explained with a smile. 'They have not realised yet, you see, that the fussy old spinsters' century has dawned, but one can hardly expect them to be so attuned to the changing times.'

'We shall have to teach them about the vote,' said Penwoman, 'in fact, that's what was decided at a meeting recently, and the task was assigned to all the women there with households to run.'

'Well, I'm afraid enlightenment hasn't reached Hötorget

yet,' said the architect. Penwoman, instantly alert to his slightly scoffing tone, set down her teacup and prepared to deliver a heated rejoinder, but just then the door opened and Kristin, Kristin stubborn as sin, entered bearing a ham omelette.

# CHAPTER 7

It was Saturday evening, and bitterly cold after a heavy fall of snow. Penwoman, wearing her poke bonnet and her warmest winter coat, came dashing down Blasieholmen with her hands thrust deep in her pockets, breathing rapidly and taking every street corner sharply. Only once did she slow down, and that was when she paused to give a superstitious curtsey to the new moon,* which hung burnished and radiant above the Nordic Museum.

She made her wish humbly: 'Please let him be able to build that farm for the poor.'*

Kristin answered her ring at the door, welcoming her with a kind and familiar nod. She would have been very disappointed if a week had gone by without Penwoman showing her face, and she had accustomed herself to the extraordinary fact that her visits could take place at any time of day or night. One day, Kristin had presented herself at the boarding house to collect a couple of nightdresses and a change of clothes for Penwoman, having learnt from experience that the latter was prone to appear at eleven o'clock at night, wet through and worn out after hours out with the police – those whose job was to question unaccompanied women, she claimed – or after pursuing some person of sudden importance round far-flung parts of the town.

'Miss Cecilia's writing,' she said importantly, gesturing in the direction of the closed study door.

'Great heavens,' said Penwoman, 'is *she* writing now, as well? What's she writing about?'

'About the Vote,' whispered the well-informed Kristin.

'I've heard nothing but votes for women in this household recently. You'll be a suffragist yourself before long, Kristin.'

'I already am,' came the self-conscious reply.

'Oh, congratulations! Why, if you don't mind my asking?'

'Because Miss Cecilia is, of course. Oh, and I think it's shameful that we have to pay such awful taxes.'

Penwoman was careful not to laugh.

'How is Miss Cecilia?' she asked quickly.

'Well, she says she's fine, but – well, nobody can really tell with her, see, and I wouldn't rightly like to say. You know we did the laundry last week, Miss Penwoman? Well, when I took it in, five of the towels had rust marks on them. Our best towels, so I cried most of the morning, and I didn't know how to tell Miss Cecilia when she got back from school, but then she asked me what was the matter. "The thing is, Miss Cecilia, the towels are ruined," I said. "They've got rust marks on them." "Oh," says Miss Cecilia. So I say, "Oh? Is that all you can say, Miss? The marks will never come out, you know."

'"So what do you expect me to do about it, Kristin?" she asks, and pours some water into her washbowl to wash for dinner, as if nothing's happened. "What do I expect you to do, Miss? I expect you to make a fuss, of course, and tell me off and look at the towels and work out what they cost and be cross all day, because all my other ladies would have been, and your own mother worst of all, Miss, if she'd still been alive today." But Miss Penwoman, do you know what Miss Cecilia does next? She turns round and gives me a little look and laughs: "Kristin, my dear, we must mind that we don't get rusty ourselves," she says. "Think of the glorious weather out there in the city today." Now I ask you, can anyone make head or tail of a mistress like that, for I'm sure I can't. Get rusty ourselves! It's as if she's lost touch with the things of this world, and that's a bad sign.'

'Just you wait. If the suffrage gets rust on it, then you'll see, Kristin,' said Penwoman. 'Everyone treasures what is closest to their heart. I can stay until tomorrow morning and have coffee in bed, can't I? We two would rather have coffee than suffrage, wouldn't we, Kristin?'

'Yes,' admitted Kristin in a whisper, 'but don't tell Miss Cecilia.'

Penwoman went soundlessly into the big study, which she had loved ever since the day she and Dick Block had helped to make it habitable. Over by the desk, the mother-of-pearl-tinted lampshade gleamed like a huge opal in the quiet room, which with its understated colours and serene lines resembled Cecilia herself.

But the desk chair was empty; Cecilia was lying asleep on the sofa with her face turned up and a large cushion in her arms, its smooth silk pressed to her cheek. The lamplight fell on all the lines that nights of sorrow had etched on her small face, which but for them would have been young and beautiful. Penwoman stood watching her for a moment before turning away, as if she had been caught committing an indiscretion, and crept quietly to the desk, where an unfinished page of writing bore witness to the task interrupted by sleep. She read a few lines and smiled the smile of a professional writing woman at the many crossings out and painfully correct sentences. With a little nod she took up the pen and continued where Cecilia had left off. But after writing for a few minutes, she laid the pen aside and leant back thoughtfully in the chair.

'Women must show that they are interested in the outcome of the suffrage motion in Parliament,' Cecilia had written. Penwoman sat thinking about all the thousands and hundreds of thousands who would most likely remain oblivious to the debate; she thought she could hear the contented small talk from a thousand sofa corners, hear the patient lullabies sung over a thousand little beds, see the tired faces looking down at innumerable socks to be darned. A wild, impotent longing to reach in everywhere, to be heard and understood, came over her. 'Oh women, if I could make you raise your heads just for today, just for tomorrow, just for those hours when the men in Parliament are deliberating on you and your rights!' She knew it was unthinkable, that it was far beyond any human power, but the very impossibility, the resistance and coldness she felt streaming towards her, spurred her into applying her shoulder to the wheel and doing her utmost.

Her heart began to beat hard; she was suddenly acutely aware of all those who were with her, sharing her hopes and dreams, maybe without knowing it; she became but a pinprick in a vast multitude, and for a brief moment a great horizon opened up to her, and light shone on the road as it climbed and wound its way to its distant destination. She took up the pen, the words seemed to come trooping up to the tones of a celebration march; with a shiver of joy she felt a flowing sensation run like rivers of fire through her right hand and down into the pen. When she reached the signature, she rose suddenly, went over to Cecilia and burrowed her hot head into a fold of her dressing gown.

'I have been awake for a little while, dear child,' said Cecilia, 'but whatever is the matter? You are shaking all over.'

'Am I? It must be all the effort I've just been expending,' the girl replied uncertainly. 'Do you want to read it? It's more or less what you would have written, but you happened to fall asleep before you finished. A person does what she can for her friends.'

Cecilia did not answer; she was reading.

'I have never seen you write like this before,' she said when she had finished, stroking the younger woman's hair as she spoke.

'No,' said Penwoman, who was now more like her old self again. 'No, and it's just as well, because if I always wrote like this, there isn't a single editor in all Stockholm who'd want to use me. And I'm not at all sure I shall manage to place this article, either. They'd take it all right, if they thought it written by an amateur in a respected position in society, but as for one of their own getting so carried away, no, they'd be ashamed. It's that wretched sensitivity of mine, but I shouldn't complain about it, because it's what makes me unbeatable when it comes to writing about battered wives, women burnt to death in their own homes, or children with tuberculosis. I did something similar when I was adopted by the suffrage, but I keep that composition tucked away in a briefcase, and occasionally get it out to read and smile over.'

'How long ago was that, and how did it happen?'

'Two years ago, and it happened because it had to. When you have a job like mine, you gradually get to see all the capable, untiring work that women do, and you learn how restricted they are, how powerless, when they try to apply their experience on a wider scale than running a children's home or cottage hospital. And it finally dawns on you that even though you yourself might prefer a new hat to the right to vote, there are others, much better people than yourself, who have every reason to absolutely insist on having it. With a bit of luck you then realise that it's your blasted duty to help, and from then on, every step seems so self-evident. God, I remember how I was swept off my feet, the first time I was with the women's suffrage campaigners as one of them.'

'Tell me what happened,' said Cecilia.

'Well, I'd written something the General happened to like, and the clever woman had me brought forward, and solemnly laid her hands on my head to initiate me into my calling as champion of the suffrage in the press. I did her bidding at once; you must know that all hearts open to her, like kitchen windows to an organ-grinder's tune. My only regret was that I hadn't been part of it all from the beginning, and I felt rather like a warrior who gets to the battlefield only when his comrades are on the verge of victory and is too proud to share the spoils and the glory with them. I remember the General had to comfort me by telling me the worst was yet to come, and assuring me there was more than enough time for me to get my fill of suffrage work, before we reached our goal, but I had no idea how right she was, that day.'

'And I cannot deny that your words are something of a comfort to me, in my turn,' said Cecilia with her melancholy smile.

'Aren't you glad you've found religion?' asked Penwoman thoughtfully. Over the previous months, to her secret surprise and satisfaction, she had watched Cecilia becoming increasingly caught up in their work, half against her will and still with a determination to portray her contribution to herself and others as merely mechanical, as unskilled labour that had nothing to do with her personal views. But now she seemed to have decided to confess her new faith.

'Oh *yes*,' she said with conviction.

'But you never have any time to call your own any more; they're hard taskmasters, your commanding officers, and so short of willing, capable workers like you. How long did you sit up last night?'

'Oh, until two, I think, but the night flew by, I was so busy.'

'And the night before that? The same, I dare say? Do you think you can cope if you carry on like that?'

'There's no need for me to live any longer than the suffrage movement,' said Cecilia in such a dry, objective voice that Penwoman realised she had worked it all out long before the subject came up in conversation, pieced everything together and made her decision.

'I shan't be like that,' said Penwoman vehemently. 'I want to live and work for a hundred years, and then have a nice little old age afterwards.'

'But then, you will not turn out like me,' said Cecilia decisively. 'I shall ask Kristin to bring in the tea tray now.'

Once they had drunk their tea, Penwoman wanted to be feminine and help with all the jobs that were to be done, something she always made a point of on her evenings off, only to regret her offer deeply, five minutes later. But Cecilia, who thought Penwoman's skills too one-sided for words, always put some sewing task into her hands; today it was the bedroom curtains, which needed their rings sewn back in after washing.

'How lovely it is to have a bit of peace and quiet,' said Penwoman despairingly, after five minutes.

'Yes, isn't it?' nodded Cecilia, continuing with her sewing and pretending not to notice the plea for mercy behind the words.

A few minutes later: 'Cecilia, I shall write a pamphlet for you, like none you've never read before, if only you let me off the sewing. Come to think of it, I ought to ring the paper to check whether they want to send me anywhere.'

'When you've finally got an evening off, that really would be spoiling them. But let me see, it is eight o'clock, what if you were to ring and ask Mr Block...'

'Oh, you clever pedagogue,' said Penwoman, with a little smile at Cecilia, who really thought Penwoman would be sitting here, if... 'He's out of town today, as it happens, but that's frightfully kind of you, and I'm so grateful to you for letting me bring him here sometimes, you know that. It's such a good education for him to see you here, in your home.'

'Education, humph,' said Cecilia, without looking up from her sewing.

'Oh yes, you see,' replied Penwoman, letting the curtain sink onto her lap in feigned distraction, 'someone like him, with a rich, fat, right-wing mother and a couple of country cousins for sisters, and then cigar shop assistants and all that sort of thing,* he has absolutely no idea what kind of people the rest of us are, since we don't fit into any of those categories. Did I tell you he assumed that as a journalist, I must be a loose woman? Well, no one's ever made him suffer so much for anything before, so there's no need to look so disapproving. Anyway, he's busy revising his opinions now, and completing his knowledge of women, and you shall help me to make his opinions just what a young man's should be. He already has a lot of respect for you, but that's still only because your annual salary is higher than his. I want him to know about the sort of women you represent, the independent ones who organise their own lives, pleasures and interests entirely unaided by those menfolk he considers so indispensable.'

'He is welcome to come here,' said Cecilia. 'And if the pair of you,' she hesitated a little, 'if the pair of you ever needed to speak to each other alone, if you – wanted to be left undisturbed...'

'That's very kind of you, thanks, but he has a private entrance,' Penwoman replied simply. 'And anyway, I'm thinking of renting a room of my own...'

Snap. That was Cecilia's needle breaking.

She sat there without moving a muscle for a minute, aghast at the precision with which life repeated the fates it measured out to mortal children. 'My own beloved, my own entrance,' and there was nothing one could do.

'Dear child,' she said softly at last.

Penwoman threw her curtain to the floor.

'What frightened you so?' she asked, taking the sewing out of Cecilia's trembling hands. 'There now, don't you go saying, just when we were having such a nice time, that you think me on the verge of going under!'

'How carelessly you speak of it; if you only knew what it is to go under.'

'But I'm not predisposed to it, you see. Let's talk it over, and look at me for once. I most definitely reject the thought I could read in your face, namely that a private entrance would be the ruin of me.'

Cecilia looked up, relieved.

'Ah, I should have known, that you are a cool-headed and sensible girl, with many greater interests than love,' she replied. 'You must be one of those girls who can be a good friend and comrade to a man without the addition of physical relations, isn't that so, Penwoman?' There was something imploring in her tone, but Penwoman stiffened. It seemed so futile, trying to make her understand.

'But if it was more than comradeship,' she said, 'if I started to be fond of someone, would I go under then? After all, it would be bound to make me feel happier than I ever thought possible.'

She sat watching Cecilia, who blushed painfully, and saw to her utter astonishment that her friend, ten years older than herself, was squirming at the prospect of enlightening her, Penwoman, that there were temptations which, if you put yourself in their way, could prove too strong, and then you were done for, for all eternity.

'Dear girl,' said Cecilia at last, 'you are a child; you do not know the danger; you rely so much on your own resources, and it is as if you were born to head straight for your own ruin without noticing, until it is too late.'

'What do you mean by too late?' asked Penwoman, keeping her impatience in check.

'Oh, you know very well, losing your respect for the most sacred thing in life and for yourself.' Penwoman pondered briefly on the meaning of this obscure expression, but then appeared to tell herself that someone like Cecilia simply could not be expected to be any more explicit, and one was still obliged to comprehend.

'Cecilia, listen to me,' she said then, getting resolutely to her feet. 'You don't understand me in the slightest; you are entirely mistaken in me. You think it's because I haven't grasped the consequences of consorting so freely with a young man one is fond of, that I am so unconcerned.'

'But then...'

'I grasp them very well, in fact, and yet – ,' she ended the sentence with a smile. Cecilia sat in total silence, weighed down by the acute and impotent pain of a mother, an elder sister.

'How defenceless we are,' she said to herself, 'how defenceless...'

'Ask my colleagues at the *Morning News* how defenceless I am,' said Penwoman with careless complacency.

'A pure-hearted woman is always defenceless,' said Cecilia, 'and unblessed are the pure in heart.'

'Well isn't it just as I've always said, that not being the least bit pure in heart has its uses,' said Penwoman consolingly. 'Now I can get something back for having dragged my heart through all the dirt in Stockholm in the course of my duties. I do have a huge amount of self-respect, on the other hand, which I'm thinking of keeping, and no one can rob me of that but me myself, not even poor, unsuspecting Mr Block.' She brushed her hand encouragingly across Cecilia's cheek – it seemed to her that the latter, for all her years and all her pain, had never lived in the world or realised anything about it, as if she judged her own and Penwoman's fates from the strict and schematic viewpoint of a well brought up girl, fresh from confirmation classes.

'That is all very well,' said Cecilia, amazed in her turn at Penwoman's lack of worldly wisdom, 'until you give someone else any power over your fate. But once you do that, and he can depart, taking your self-respect with him...'

'I don't know what you mean by that,' said Penwoman, who was coming close to losing the patience she had indulgently maintained. 'Haven't I got my own value, quite regardless of whether a man stays or goes? Why shouldn't I be able to live and write and vote and stand for election and become famous, just like a man can?'

'Yes my child, but we are not made of the same stuff as men, you know. For us, love is different: fraught with dire consequences.'

'I should say so,' said Penwoman. 'We're the ones who have to have all those little children. We invest more in a relationship, and our risk increases in proportion. But I still maintain that I shall not lose respect for myself if – may I speak frankly, Cecilia, it suits me best?'

Cecilia nodded without looking up.

'All right, you mean if a man I had loved were to leave me and take with him the memory of my body. For that's what you're so afraid is going to happen to me, Cecilia, and there's no need to be so embarrassed about it. I'm not. That's what the new generation's like, you see.'

'Women have not changed that much in the last ten years,' said Cecilia, her cheeks flushed. 'You think a person is who they wish they were, but you have no idea, have you, that this has to do with something mystical and inevitable in women's natures, which...'

'You're wrong there,' said Penwoman. 'If the arguments for women's emancipation have taught me one thing, it's that there's nothing women have left behind them in their evolution that wasn't once called inevitable. Just think how many there must be, Kristin among them, who consider it one of the most inevitable things in women's nature to waste a whole day of our short lives grieving over a few rust-stained towels. You're as degenerate in Kristin's eyes, as I am in yours.'

'But if someone came along and said a woman could surrender herself without love and suffer no ill consequences, what then, Penwoman?' asked Cecilia.

'Well then, naturally, I wouldn't go along with that. I'd feel they had touched the very essence of me,' the girl admitted. 'But you know that would reveal a weakness in my character, along the same lines as my being spiteful and telling lies, and that is a thing inside me, to do with my innermost soul, the battlefield where it's decided whether I shall live or perish. It certainly has nothing to do with any qualities that might reveal themselves in the man I'd loved. You want the vote for women, and yet you believe we're a room with no direct light; if a man closes the door of his favour, we're plunged into darkness. In that case we might as well not bother with the vote, either.'

'That all sounds very fine,' said Cecilia wearily, 'but however brave a face you put on it, you cannot escape the fact that you are a woman. At any event, the world is the same as it was before, when it had the power to impose its own judgment on a woman. You have to remember that our sins are never forgiven and never forgotten; if you were to use Christian terminology, you might say that Christ did not die for us, though so many of us have died for Christ.'

'You're wrong,' said Penwoman. 'Christ both lived and died for us, if you want to put it that way, it's just that He's alone in that, just as He is in every other respect. I happen to think the world is changing, too, if reluctantly. Actually, I don't really care much what the world thinks in this case. I don't feel any obligation to enlighten it about what sort of mess I get myself into, as long as I don't tread on anybody else's toes.'

'Even that will offend it, as you well know; and anyway, you are a simpleton if you think it possible to keep a love affair secret. Remember, that when one of us, a girl from a good home, embarks on such a thing, it seems unprecedented to her. A girl like that thinks: I must be the only educated girl who dares this much for her love.'

'That's surely an exaggeration,' thought Penwoman, on her part.

'She believes that she has chosen an entirely solitary path, and that everyone, and most of all those closest to her, are enemies and spies. She thinks of nothing but her immense secret. And you can see, can you not, that such a woman will assume a certain look, her eyes will have a different sparkle and her voice a different ring. Soon it will be whispered in rooms and shouted on market squares: she has a lover.' She stopped for a moment to adjust her voice to a more neutral tone. Penwoman sat staring straight ahead, for she knew that confirmation of those words was in Cecilia's face at that moment. For a brief second, the girl was truly impressed, for she realised that if Cecilia had not been extremely concerned about her and had every good reason for it, she would not voluntarily have fished this key up from the depths of the ocean.

'I once knew,' Cecilia went on, 'a young girl who had a job in Stockholm, in an office I seem to recall, and a rumour started that she had a lover. For a whole year she was the centre of curious attention in the office; when she arrived at work in the morning, her male colleagues and their acquaintances would cluster round the front door to watch her go by. When she reached her desk there were whispers, she suffered a thousand little discourtesies and snide remarks, and in the end she lost her job; her colleagues were no longer prepared to work with her. She lives in obscurity somewhere, I do not know where, but I do not believe she has had a carefree moment since. Imagine having such a sullied reputation.'

'Well of course one feels sorry for her, but she's had the same chances as everyone else, hasn't she, to forget, to fall in love again, get married, if she thinks that's better, and be happy?' suggested Penwoman, her eyes still fixed stubbornly on the wall.

'Get married?' said Cecilia, perplexed. 'With her history? She cannot find a man unworthy enough.'

'That isn't normally the least bit difficult,' said Penwoman drily.

'So what I have been saying makes not the slightest impression on you?'

'No, none at all.'

'I hope you never have to admit I was right.'

'No, not even from the bottom of Hammarby Lake,' said Penwoman.

When it was time for bed, she patted her friend, who sat there with an empty face, like a piece of jewellery that has lost its precious stone.

'You needn't lie awake for my sake, I can do that for myself,' she said.

Five minutes later she was fast sleep, and remained so until morning.

# CHAPTER 8

Christmas was still not quite over and done with, and Dick was still exiled with his family in Östergötland, when Penwoman arrived back from the newspaper one day in a wretched state. She made no reply to the landlady's reproach; it probably had been unwise to go off to work with a temperature and a cough, but if the girl would insist on being unwise, it was no one's concern but her own. Mrs Bengtsson need not worry; she asked nothing more than to be left in peace.

She was so poorly and so dejected when Cecilia, alerted by the boarding house maids, came to check on her, that the latter found it hard to conceal her concern.

'She is going to fret her heart out,' thought Cecilia mournfully, 'yet it is no time at all since she was so full of herself. But I was right; no woman of breeding can cope with that sort of relationship. It will break her.'

So when the unsuspecting Dick came back a few days later, the first news to reach him was that of Penwoman's illness.

It must be said that she had made no particular effort to get well before his return, but the day he was expected to dine for the first time, she had very little patience with her bedridden lot. She sat bolt upright, trying to interpret every sound from the dining room: what was he saying, was he upset, oh she couldn't bear the thought of his being unhappy for a single moment, what sort of a person was she, to have almost looked forward to his consternation through the long hours of missing him?

If anyone had happened that day to open the door from the dining room, they would have surprised a small figure in a nightgown, listening at the keyhole in the hope of picking up her beloved's voice or a sigh from his heart, which was so close, so full of longing, and yet seemed forever parted from hers. But nobody did, and nobody had time to come and see how she was, though she waited right until she heard chairs being scraped back after the stewed fruit before dashing back to her room, light-headed and trembling, crawling into bed and shedding the bitterest tears of her life on a shaving token* that she had kept as a souvenir of Dick on his departure, and had worn on a string round her neck ever since. If you are poor and without a home of your own, then woe betide you when you are in love! But later that evening, when Cecilia came in with a thousand greetings from Dick, she found a Self-Supporting Educated Woman* who was deeply ashamed of her weakness.

'How pathetic I am compared to Susan B. Anthony* and the rest,' said Penwoman, full of remorse, 'I cried when I heard Dick ask for the bread basket.'

Once she was back on her feet again, so pale and fragile that Kristin prophesied her imminent departure to a better world, she gave notice that she would be leaving the boarding house, and embarked on a hunt for a room of her own. Cecilia was deeply disappointed by the decision; she had been hoping against hope that the period of reflection and soul-searching the girl had been through would change her mind.

One day, Penwoman was led by an advertisement up into an apartment building by the Adolf Fredrik churchyard, rang the bell, and when the shabby door was opened, found herself face to face with one of her former classmates, from her home town.

'Oh Klara, good day to you,' said Penwoman cheerily, but the other girl blushed bright red, as if she suspected a thousand other reasons for the visit than her own advertisement in the newspaper, and she only recovered herself when Penwoman asked in some surprise if she was the one with a room to let. At that she became suddenly animated, drew her guest through a little hall into an attractive corner room and began to enthuse about all the flat's advantages.

'And it's in such a good location,' she said. 'Here, please, do sit down, how nice to see you, its own front door and nobody to hear your comings and goings, or what you get up to, for that matter. But maybe you don't set much store by that?' she added, regarding Penwoman disdainfully.

Suddenly deeply embarrassed without knowing why, Penwoman directed her gaze to the street outside. She could not bear to see that expression in the pretty face that had smiled at her.

'How much does it cost?' she said.

The price was not high, and Penwoman realised her search was over.

'Fancy your wanting to move, though,' she said. 'Surely you couldn't find anything nicer than this?'

She felt utterly estranged from her childhood friend, who had turned out more beautiful than anyone could have imagined, and with her refined elegance bore a flattering resemblance to Princess Charlotte, but it was not that; there was something hard and scornful about her, which Penwoman did not recognise.

'Yes, I made up my mind in a moment of desperation, you know the way one does, when one's sick of everything and wants to start all over again,' said Klara contemptuously.

'It's best not to trust impulses like that, born of desperation,' advised Penwoman, 'and you certainly shouldn't turn them into advertisments.'

'What would you know about that?' asked Klara with a sneering laugh. 'Tell me, do you like men? You never showed any interest when we were at school.'

'I was saving myself for now,' replied Penwoman.

'Hah,' said Klara, who had planted herself in front of her dressing-glass without ceremony and was pulling faces at her image, 'I've just decided to do something useful and turn my back on them; they cause nothing but misery. Has anyone written from home and asked about me?' she enquired in a sudden change of subject, and in an entirely different tone.

'Why should they ask?' said Penwoman in surprise. 'Sorry, I wasn't trying to interrogate you,' she added, as the other girl gave a start.

'Much good may it do you,' snapped Klara. 'Listen, do you want to take over my telephone?'

In the end, Penwoman took over not only the telephone but also some of Klara's pretty furniture, and then went to Dick to tell him the outcome of her expedition with a strange mixture of happy anticipation, vague reluctance and heaviness of heart.

The following day brought explanation of her feeling in the form of a letter from her mother, with a message from Klara's mother begging her for God's sake to find the girl. She had squandered all her inheritance from her father and now, with no more money to be expected from home, had stopped writing to her mother. She lived by the Adolf Fredrik churchyard, unless she had already moved on.


It was with a joy she took no pains to conceal that Penwoman gathered up her worldly goods and moved out of the boarding house, where she would henceforth only take her dinners, and she had certainly never been happier than the first time she went to sleep in her own bed in her new abode. She and Dick had worked until late in the evening, unable to contain themselves until they could see how every last picture looked on the wall. Dick had designed and made a new bookshelf, and with her bed turned so she could see it, Penwoman fell asleep blithely unaware of the restless spirits who had inhabited the room before her. She had no idea where she was or what time of day or night it might be when she was roused by a loud ring of the telephone beside her pillow.

'Hello,' said a voice, 'do you want to come down and let me in?'

'This late?' said Penwoman, bewildered.

'It's no later than usual,' said the voice, 'and it's so long since you let *me* up to you.'

The stress on the word 'me' sent a shiver of horror through Penwoman. She had already realised this must be someone in the habit of telephoning Klara, who could not distinguish between their voices, since both girls had the same regional accent.

'I don't think there has been anyone else,' she said quickly, thinking of Klara's mother.

'Don't lie there talking rubbish, come and let me in.'

The voice sounded impatient and imperious.

Penwoman thought for a moment, and looked at the clock. Half past one, so there was little risk anyone else would open the front door and admit the voice, and it was surely a risk worth running to solve this particular mystery.

She threw on the bare minimum of clothing, then an evening coat and her deep poke bonnet, put a torch in her pocket and went down. She was careful to leave the key to the main entrance on her bedside table. The entrance to the building was secured at night with an iron gate, and as soon as she reached the bottom of the stairs, she saw a male figure pressed against the other side of the bars. When he caught sight of her silk bonnet in the gloom, he raised his hat, only to give an exclamation of astonishment as she came forward into the glare of the streetlight.

'What do you mean by ringing me in the middle of the night?' asked Penwoman, who was feeling completely calm, but rather chilly.

'The same as you, whoever you are, mean by coming to let me in,' said the figure on the other side. 'I must have got through to the wrong number, but I'm not fussy. Just open up, and we can come to an agreement afterwards.'

'I daren't,' said Penwoman. 'Klara's away, and I'm on my own up there.'

And yes, there was no mistaking the way his ears instantly pricked up at the name.

'Where's she gone?' he demanded violently.

'If she hasn't told you herself, I'm sure she doesn't want you to know,' replied Penwoman, digging her hands deeply into her pockets.

'It's that damn actor, of course,' the figure swore between his teeth, 'but no matter; admittedly I can't see you very well, but you've the voice of a young and, I hope, charming woman. Get that key out; I don't care who you are or what you're like, just open up.' And as Penwoman remained immobile, he shook the bars with both hands.

The girl took out her torch and all at once was looking the man straight in the eyes, but she equally quickly switched it off again: oh, she would still never, as long as she lived, forget that face.

'Go, for God's sake,' she said, horrified, and with the iron bars rattling wildly behind her and an angry voice calling her back, she rushed upstairs and cried herself to sleep, shedding tears for Klara and the whole world, but most of all for Klara.

Now that Penwoman was renting her own room and had her own spirit stove and her own saucepans, she began to feel the urge to invite the whole world to tea. She dutifully asked her landlady if she was allowed visitors in her room, but the former merely shifted her fat half a turn in Penwoman's direction and declared, 'You may do as you please, Miss, as long as I don't get into any trouble for it.' This signalled the start of a series of odd parties at Penwoman's, and Dick often found himself helping with the drying up after visits from Social Democrats, Salvation Army slum-sisters, and fallen women.

'Interviews should only ever be conducted over tea and toast,' Penwoman would say, 'but I can hardly invite round the likes of Mrs Skogh,* or the Crown Prince's chamberlain.'

Everyone shared her delight in her lovely new rooms, and said how lucky she had been; not even Dick knew how many times she was jolted out of sleep at nights because she had dreamt someone was rattling the door, trying to get in. Dick had, however, been commissioned, if he happened to meet a tall, beautiful girl with auburn hair, a black fur coat and a black hat with white feathers, to follow her and find out where she was going, but Klara had vanished without trace, and Penwoman would often brood on the girl's fate, hers and Princess Charlotte's; the two looked so alike.

The only attempt at social interaction on the part of better society ended most ignominiously.

Penwoman was having dinner one day at the boarding house, where she was now considered irrevocably lost, when to her astonishment the textiles girl, seizing the opportunity of her mother Mrs Bodin's absence, came over in an unguarded moment and announced she was intending to visit Penwoman's new home. What was more, she actually did so: there she sat one afternoon, and once she had studied everything around her, she said: 'Don't you think it's hard to divide yourself between work and love?'

Penwoman flushed, but when she saw the other girl's vapid expression and her innocent delight in the phrase, she laughed.

'No, do you?' she asked, with a mocking look at the girl, sitting there in all her Arts and Crafts splendour, in a loose-fitting, hand-embroidered dress with huge pieces of silver jewellery under her chin and all down the front.

Nothing could describe Penwoman's astonishment when the girl suddenly buried her face in her hands and whispered: 'Yes'.

'Yes?' repeated Penwoman in amazement. 'I would never have thought it.'

'It's dreadful,' said the girl. 'It tears your heart to shreds, whichever you choose.'

'Oh,' said Penwoman, 'you're making matters far too complicated for yourself; just don't worry about that sort of thing.'

'If we take our work and our love seriously, all we women who devote ourselves to art find that sooner or later we are faced with a choice,' said the textiles girl somewhat indignantly. 'And I thought you, of all people – '

'But I'm not an artist,' said Penwoman, with as straight a face as she could muster.

'No, that's true of course. It does make things a bit easier for you. But you may be attached to your work, even so. Don't you think you might feel reluctant give it up? Can't you even imagine what I shall feel?'

Penwoman concentrated on that thought for a moment. 'No,' she said.

The textiles girl looked most surprised and crestfallen. She had been expecting something quite different, was greatly put out, and remained mute.

'Are you getting married?' asked Penwoman suddenly.

'That's precisely the thing I can't decide,' replied the girl. 'It's true there's nothing to stop – '

'Well then, you can be glad of that, since – '

'But I've asked for a little time, to wage this hard battle with myself. Tell me though, don't you think I would regret it, if I abandoned my art?'

'Don't be absurd,' Penwoman persisted.

'What do you think happens to a person who abandons their object in life?'

'Aren't you ashamed to be talking such rubbish?' Penwoman burst out impatiently. 'Take yourself off and get engaged, and give thanks to God that somebody wants you!'

That was the Art and Craft girl's first and last visit to Penwoman's flat.

# CHAPTER 9

It was a blue and bitter spring evening.

Cecilia hurried through the little streets in the north of the city without looking round, without so much as raising her eyes to God's bright, springtime sky. A person should be grateful to suffer for the cause for which she is fighting, only not this, not going out to meet the spring, not being forced to witness a springtime evening drawing in once more, exactly as it did back then.

The summer rally committee, reminded by the early spring weather that time was going by and summer was on the horizon, had held its first meeting, and Cecilia had been elected as its secretary. This past winter had taught them they could count on, and make use of, her loyalty and willingness to work, and when this began to dawn on her she felt a sense of pleasure. In the course of the meeting she had even caught herself saying 'we' in a totally new and intimate tone of voice, and she thought she must be starting to understand what the others meant by 'The Cause', as they called it at rare and solemn moments. But she had not counted on the lively afternoon deliberations up at Lästmakaregatan going on so long; evening had come, and it was spring.

It was spring. For the seventh time it was a wretched spring, there was no way round it. She walked as fast as she could, avoiding the sun lying in wait for her at the entrance to every street, scarcely daring to breathe in the young, blue air. Look, every window pane was gleaming with gold and rubies, like young hearts on which love shines, only to be snuffed out as quickly as them. The years grew as transparent as the spring

97

evening light; they rose into the air and vanished like mist, so a person could see straight through them into the past, and feel again, with inexpressible anguish, that it would follow her to the end of her days.

At Regeringsgatan, someone called Cecilia's name. It was the schoolmistress, Kerstin Vallmark, who had been slow to leave after the meeting.

'Do you really think we should discuss tactics at a public meeting like that?' she asked breathlessly.

Cecilia stole a glance at her bright, happy face and wondered what sort of person it could be, who was man enough to spend an evening like this rejoicing that she could stand in local government elections,* but this woman was doing just that.

'Do you not think there is a melancholy beauty to this evening?' she asked, with a sudden wish to talk of life's cruelty with another single, middle-aged woman.

'Yes,' said the schoolmistress, 'but who do you think should make the opening speech, in that case?'

Then Cecilia sighed an envious sigh and obediently talked suffrage all the way down to Kungsträdgården, or rather, listened as the Kerstin Vallmark took both friends and foes to task.

Finally Cecilia was alone, and hurried along Arsenalsgatan to turn down to Blasieholmen Quay and reach home at last. The quayside was empty, but on the pavement outside the front entrance to her block she spotted two distinctive silhouettes. It was Dick and Penwoman, nowadays as inseparable as a pair of ducks in spring. Cecilia was not surprised; this evening she had been half expecting this final straw.

When they caught sight of the solitary figure, Dick unlinked his arm from the girl's, and they came towards Cecilia.

'We've been up to mend that table, you know,' said Penwoman, the words pouring out of her without embarrassment, 'we were invited to, you recall, and Kristin fed us lots of sweet things, no indeed, we weren't offended, because we'd been told you were at a meeting, you see, and I insist the suffrage must always take priority.' This last was said to annoy Dick.

They all stood there indecisively. Cecilia realised full well that these two, of all the people in the world, needed only an invitation from her before coming up to be happy in her apartment this evening, and she clenched her hands.

'It would have been lovely to invite you up,' she said with her unfailing politeness. 'How annoying that I have agreed to get a particular task done for the morning. But if I may call you on the telephone – '

'Yes, you do that,' said Penwoman. 'Please don't worry about us, and try not to work yourself to death.' Cecilia nodded with a slight smile and hurried up the steps to the door.

'That makes me very sad,' said Penwoman. 'I'd been imagining that she...' she broke off and walked in silent contemplation for some time. Finally she said:

'Let's go to Gärdet,* it's easier to breathe there.'

There, in the darkness under the big trees that shaded the military cemetery he brought her to a stop; there had been something in her face that needed kissing away.

'Are you happy again now?'

'Yes.'

'Right, let's go on then.' After a while they left the path and crossed the open field, which lay silent and deserted in the dusk.

'Look round', he said, when they were at the far side of a small hill, 'What's happened to the city, eh?'

'Oh, it's gone,' she said, 'all at once it's hidden, just like the future.'

'The future, my little love, aren't you happy?'

'Yes,' she said in answer to his question, 'but please tell me: will the day come when spring drives me to despair like that?'

He did not really know what she meant, and she gave the answer herself.

'No, because I'm stronger, and you – ah you, my love, are not like the rest?'

'How do you mean, not like the rest?'

'Going off or getting bored, or forgetting...'

'Oh, I'm like the rest all right,' he replied humbly, 'but the difference is that you aren't. Anyone who has started loving you, will love you forever.'

'That's all right, then,' she said, and contented herself with that, 'but let's go on, it's cold.' He obeyed, though he would much sooner have stayed behind the hill, kissing her.

'Oh look, there's the city again,' he said, 'first its brow, then its eyes, see, so many eyes, looking at the two of us.'

'Just think of the time when we've been in love so long that we have a whole city of memories to walk in. I'm longing for our love to grow old,' she said. 'How old are *you*,' she added, suddenly.

'I'm not telling you.'

'Are you shy about your age? You can scarcely be thirty.'

'Yes, because I'm already far too old only to have met you now.'

'You can kiss me once for each year,' she said.

'I thank God for every one of my years,' he said, and kissed her a hundred times.

They paused by a signpost, from which three paths led off into the darkness, shining white in the evening light.

'Which way should we go?' asked Penwoman. 'You must know, being the man.'

'For a suffragist, you're quite reasonable,' he said jokingly. 'And if I'm to choose, I say we turn to face our destiny, and go home. Haven't you anything to do for the paper tonight?'

'Good heavens above, I'd forgotten the paper, for the first time in my life! Actually I'm meant to be sitting in the Victoria Hall right this minute, but I'll have to slip down there in a while and find out if there's to be a resolution; it's bound to drag on, because it's morality. I told the deputy editor I was going to a meeting, and so I have – ,' she gave a happy laugh.

She was quite anxious about her neglect of duty, all the same, and it took some persuasion on his part before she agreed to board a tram at Narvavägen and go home with him.

'Morality always lasts longest, you know that,' he said, to calm her anxieties.

'In that case, I'm afraid our story will be a short one,' she replied.

As soon as she had taken off her outdoor things, she curled up in the corner of the sofa and rested her head on his shoulder.

'And now darling, tell me what made you start loving me,' she said.

'Have I got to tell you all over again?' he asked, flattered, 'I've told you so many times.'

'I want you to tell me again, even so; it makes me happy.'

It was true, for as he was speaking, she remembered much more vividly all those things she so was so fond of calling to mind. The bolt of lightning that had struck her soul when she saw his face for the first time after their serious talk, a new face, older, more manly, quite an ordinary face from among the crowd, deepened and ennobled by a strong, new emotion: the boy who had grown up in a single day.

They had not exchanged a word – they were surrounded by people in any case – but when one of the elderly women, thoughtlessly inquisitive, had begun lamenting, 'What's the matter with you, young Mr Block, looking so pale,' it was she who had been embarrassed, not he. 'What have I done,' she thought, horrified, 'and what will happen now...?'

'Go on, you were going to tell me.'

'Ah yes,' he replied. 'You were so pretty.'

'Am I still pretty now? I'm never anything else.'

'No, never,' he said in affirmation. 'I've said so from the first moment.'

'That's what you think now. But I'm not so sure. You soaked up all the evil rumours that were flying around about me, and took quite a delight in doing it.'

'Yes,' he said, in precisely the remorseful tone she had hoped to provoke, because she loved it so dearly. 'Yes, but you have to remember I wasn't used to your way of talking. "Are you coming to our ball next week, Miss Penwoman?" "No, my husband won't let me." That's just one example which has stuck in my surprised head. And as regards my delight, it was nothing but simple economy, as I've explained so many times before.'

'Damaged goods are cheaper,' she suggested. This interrogation interested her just as much, every time.

'Yes. You see,' he justified himself, as patiently as ever, 'I had no idea about loving. All I knew, was that it was easier to kiss girls with bad reputations and morals.'

'Have you kissed many?'

'No, I assure you I haven't. This Christmas just gone, I was still able to keep count.'

'Well, thank God for the whole host of them,' said Penwoman after a moment's reflection, with a certain smile that for her was synonymous with tears. 'If you'd only had *one* falling in love with *one* woman behind you, then I'd die of jealousy, but I feel better able to cope with this unsophisticated polygamy of yours. Tell me, did you enjoy all that random kissing?'

'Now I know what loving is, I think it was nauseating. You're trembling, my little darling. You've gone and caught a cold.'

'No, just a little sorrow. But go on. Did you think you'd get me just as easily, on the cheap? Did you think it was worth it?'

'Yes. You see,' said Dick, self-consciously searching for the right words, 'a young man like me, who – who can scarcely earn his own keep – it simply doesn't occur to him that he has any choice but damaged goods. He's well aware he has nothing to offer a girl, and presumably you wouldn't want him to go dreaming that the loveliest woman in the world will give him her love and become his, without money and for nothing? My debt to you is so great...'

'Yes, yes,' she broke in, 'we've been through all that and settled it.' And she smiled a little at the memory of her own eloquence, and the admiration it had aroused in Dick. 'But now, tell me how you came to find out that I wasn't what you believed.'

'I met you at Tegelbacken,' he went on readily, 'I invited you to dinner, you agreed and I thought: now's my chance to let her see I've nothing against a little fling.'

'As if you hadn't let me see that long before!'

'But you bridled, my little love, and I was a bit surprised, but I didn't give up...'

'No, you certainly didn't...'

'No, I thought: we'll take a stroll along Skeppsholmen then; that usually helps. But you were so sweet, and told me your views and explained them so intelligently.'

Penwoman quickly leant forward, to see if there was any hint of mockery in his expression, but he looked entirely sincere.

'I was horribly embarrassed,' he admitted frankly, 'because I'd been such an idiot, but then I forgot that, too, and as I was walking home, everything inside me began to change. I lay awake for ages that night, and I've loved you ever since, it's just got worse and worse. If I hadn't initially had such careless, casual thoughts about you, I'm sure it wouldn't have hit me so hard.'

'Beloved Dick,' said the girl, 'how strange it is. For me it's not like that; I can't remember the exact day when I started loving you, but I'm afraid it was much later. It started with my being touched, and thinking it was nice to have an illiterate poodle – for a change – who faithfully and devotedly followed my orders and never begrudged me my ten öre a line, or a better slot in that day's paper. Well, it served me right, because now I love you.'

'Do you?'

'Need you ask?'

'No, but it's so lovely to hear you say so.'

'I've given you everything I can,' she said gently. 'Prime position on the front page, I've no more to give.'

For an instant she felt a shiver run through her: what have I done? What will my life be like now?'

But Dick said, close to her ear and holding her trembling form tightly to him: 'Do you know, when I'm expecting you, my heart beats so fast that I jump up, thinking it's your dear footsteps on the stairs.'

'I'm satisfied with you, too,' she said, as if he were a little schoolchild. 'Are you satisfied with me, as well?'

'With you, yes,' he said. 'If only I could be with you always and watch over you every day and every moment, if I could say to every lout who looks at you: hands off, she's mine – there must be lots of them wanting to prey on someone so glorious. Why can't I earn enough for both of us, why must it take so long before I can? When I think of the possibility of losing you, I go utterly cold with fear.'

'Cold, you go utterly cold?' asked Penwoman eagerly.

'Yes,' he confirmed.

'Good,' she said gravely, and gave a nod. 'But just at this moment, my love, you're anything but cold –

'Perhaps I should go down to the meeting, after all?'

'Oh no, it's too late,' he begged in alarm.

But she freed herself.

'If I hurry up, I'll still get down there for the resolution.' She gently pulled his head close to her and contemplatively stroked his shoulders, as if trying to preserve the memory of him between her hands.

'Are you going to miss me?' she asked.

'I already am,' he said.

# CHAPTER 10

Baron Starck of the Upper House was sitting in his rooms, waiting for an interviewer from the *Liberal Morning News*. The deputy editor had asked for the interview the day before, and in his astonishment he had agreed to receive the reporter and was now a little curious as to the topic of the interview.

The clock was just striking half-past ten, the appointed time, when a knock came at the door of the outer room.

'Come in,' said the Baron.

But he heard nothing – 'I crept in like a misprint,' Penwoman said later – and he was just repeating his 'Come in' in a louder and somewhat irritated voice, when the half-closed door of the inner room where he was sitting slowly opened to reveal a young lady, dressed in an elegant, pale-grey suit, with a black sombrero on her pale blonde head, standing on the threshold.

'I'm from the *Liberal Morning News*,' she said, in answer to his look of dismay.

The Baron, who had got to his feet, now recoiled a few steps.

'My God, a woman!' said the Baron.

'Yes, isn't that nice?' asked Penwoman, with a reassuring smile. Then she fell silent and waited quietly for him to recover. In the meantime, she appraised him with her thoughtful eyes; he was an imposing elderly gentleman, going grey and tending to corpulence, and not without a certain conservative bearing, which suited him. She decided to like him, and he was to like her, because, she thought, if he wants to, he can help give us the vote.

'But what do you want of me, young lady?' the Baron finally asked. He had now recovered his poise enough to gesture an invitation to his guest to take a seat.

'I should very much like a statement from a representative Conservative,' explained Penwoman, 'on the Upper House* and woman's suffrage, now we've reached the end of this parliamentary sitting, you see, my Lord.'

'Are you, young lady,' with a most impolite emphasis on the last two words, 'intending to conduct a political interview?'

'I've been practising on the Lower House, as you may perhaps have seen in my newspaper in recent days, my Lord,' said Penwoman a little shortly.

'Do you understand politics then?' asked the Baron, not remotely aware of Penwoman's series of interviews in the *Liberal Morning News*.

'No. Do you, my Lord?' Penwoman let slip, and was instantly terrified, but the Baron was obviously far too taken aback to be angry.

'So you write in the newspapers, young lady?' he said, taking his time.

'Yes, I'm what they call a journalist,' explained Penwoman.

'I thought the women only wrote about clothes, and how to blow children's noses and cook, oh, and love stories, of course,' said the Baron honestly.

'Then it really is high time you became acquainted with one of us professional girls, my Lord,' replied Penwoman, and smiled. She was in no hurry, either; it was still so early in the day.

'Are all, er, women journalists like you?' he carried on his line of questioning.

'Oh yes,' she said, 'more or less. But if everyone I had to interview was like you, my Lord, I wouldn't get anywhere.'

At that he realised she meant to get down to business.

'Well do start, then,' he said with a sarcastic smile.

On the tram ride there, Penwoman had crammed her head with facts from a booklet of parliamentary proceedings, and was now quite well versed in the Baron's contributions to the previous year's suffrage debate.

'Your view, my Lord, is that one should wait to see the effects of male suffrage reform, before thinking of giving women the vote. Could you inform the suffragists, my Lord, roughly how long this new waiting period ought to last?' she asked, pulling out a minimal notebook.

'Well,' said the Baron, now speaking in complete earnest, as if he had forgotten he had a woman in front of him, 'first we shall have new elections...'

'In the autumn,' said Penwoman.

'Yes, that's for the Lower House,' said the Baron, 'but it will take a little longer for us to achieve that in the Upper House, and then of course we shall have to see how the new Parliament goes.'

'I thought,' said Penwoman, 'that the Upper House was in absolutely no doubt about that during the big debates on universal suffrage. If I remember rightly, you yourself painted a very bleak picture of the future, my Lord.'

'I did indeed,' he said with satisfaction. 'We shall see if I am not proved right, we shall see.'

'If, against all expectation, it turns out well, will we get the vote then?' Penwoman persisted.

'Ah,' said the Baron with a shrug, ' I am not omniscient, but I expect your prospects would brighten, in that case.'

'But if it all goes wrong? Will we have to suffer for your stupid laws?' asked Penwoman in the same polite tone of someone determined to increase her knowledge at any price.

'You are certainly very impatient for that vote,' the Baron retorted a little coldly, 'though I do not think you have much to complain of.'

Penwoman sent a little thought to all those in the ranks of the suffrage movement, and to the multitude of others behind them, who had still not even discovered the route to better conditions, who could merely sigh under their intolerable burdens; no, he would not understand the reality of it, she thought.

'If you had worked for a cause for many years, my Lord, constantly rehearsing the same arguments to prove the justice of your demands, constantly being rebuffed with the same excuses, and in the end had to ask yourself how to keep people's interest alive during the long period of waiting, then you would be impatient, too,' was her simple answer. 'But I will send you our literature, if I may.'

'Yet in actual fact there are so few of you asking for this,' he said.

'Yes, but the brightest and the best,' asserted Penwoman confidently, openly meeting the Baron's eye, because, as she said to her friends afterwards, 'the General had ordered me to do my very best'.

The Baron was now in an excellent mood, and their conversation proceeded most amicably.

'If you were my daughter, young lady,' he said, 'I would be in no doubt that I wanted to preserve you from political life. Believe me, you are made for something quite different.'

Again Penwoman thought: oh, he won't understand what we are or what we want, but since he had sounded genuinely kind, she could only thank him for his concern.

'Just think,' he went on, in a paternal and instructing tone, as if hoping to bring his young guest round to a more appropriate way of thinking, 'of the effect it would have in our homes. You know a husband does not like to be contradicted in questions he is used to deciding; if his wife or daughters were now to take a different view from his own, there would be constant battles and no end to the discord. And if the running of the household were to be neglected into the bargain, I am afraid he would be so incensed, that he would demand a divorce the day after the election.'

'I think that only goes to show that a man shouldn't marry, until he's learnt to control himself a little,' came Penwoman's unexpected answer.

'Hm,' said the Baron, shaking his head.

'After all,' she added, looking earnestly at the Baron, 'we two are political opponents on every point, but we get on splendidly together, don't we, all the same?'

The notion of Penwoman as a political opponent struck the Baron for some reason as so irresistibly funny that he burst out laughing and carried on for some time, while Penwoman regarded him with mild, imperturbable gravity, thinking that the time might come -

'It's a pity,' Penwoman told her friends later, 'that a journalist never dares let his paper print the best bits he experiences; we had such a nice time together, the Conservative Baron and I.'

'May I ask you for one thing, my Lord?' she said finally, once he had calmed down.

'Of course, what is your Ladyship's wish?'

'Your picture, Sir,' said Penwoman, with an appealing look.

The unexpected consequence of this was that the Baron blushed, his face red all over.

'Can a young lady like you really want the picture of an old man like me?' he asked.

'Yes, our vast readership and I would simply despair otherwise,' she replied, too magnanimous to take advantage of his mistake.

Painfully embarrassed, the Baron quickly bent to rummage in a drawer, and finally produced a cabinet-photograph.

'Perhaps I could have it back eventually?' he said, to show he understood.

But Penwoman could no longer resist: 'Couldn't I keep it for personal use?' she said, and got to her feet.

Surely she did not need to go already, could she not tell him a little more about her working conditions, the events of her working day, what she thought of her profession, and so on.

Penwoman sat down again and tried, in the course of the ensuing conversation, to get over to the Baron a few simple facts about the working woman.

But the Baron took very little interest in the working woman in general.

'Have you ever thought of marrying?' he asked.

'Certainly,' said Penwoman. 'But it's easier said than done, let me tell you,' she added mysteriously.

'Surely not, for a someone like you,' he said courteously, 'so young and...'

'Yes, but there is one obstacle,' she interrupted him. 'The fact is, I – but good Lord, here I am, taking up your valuable time!'

'No, I assure you. The fact is, you were saying?'

'That I've sworn to marry no one but the leader of the majority party in the Upper Chamber,' she said.

'Has nobody else a hope?' he asked thoughtfully.

'Well yes, if he becomes the leader himself, of course,' said Penwoman generously... 'Anyway, thank you so much, I really must be going now,' she said. 'I shall make a long interview out of this, enough lines to add up to a pretty little sum.'

'The *Liberal Morning News* is liberal, it is true' said the Baron with a slight ring of disdain in his voice, which brought Penwoman up short and put her on the defensive, for woe betide anyone who attacked her newspaper, 'but I hardly imagine they will let you write about votes for women the way you want to, and I fear for your pretty little sum.'

'They'll have to,' said Penwoman, beaming. 'I'm part and parcel of their political programme!'

## CHAPTER 11

With considerable difficulty, Penwoman had saved one evening for her beloved, and was now hurrying through the streets with that evening in her hands, as if it were a precious pearl in a bowl.

She was still on a lower flight of stairs when she heard him opening the door.

'I knew it was you,' he said. 'I haven't been able to work; I never can when I'm expecting you. Oh, come on in, quickly, it's an eternity since we saw each other.'

'It's 158 hours,' she answered, and started taking the hatpins out of her hat. But suddenly she stopped, stood immobile with arms raised and, without a word but wearing a radiant expression, regarded the young man before her.

You might have suspected anyone but Penwoman of having struck that beautiful pose deliberately, but Dick saw at once that her thoughts were far away.

'What are you thinking about, my little love?'

'Come and sit down here, and I'll tell you,' she said. 'About how happy I am. Do you know, when I was walking home from the protest meeting last night...'

'How late? Did anybody bother you?'

'Half past one, yes, of course they did. I was in high spirits; you know how we whip ourselves up at the big rallies, when there are a thousand of us, all wanting the same thing; we had speakers from all the parties, and I was wild with enthusiasm, oh, I would achieve great things, it was such fun to be working, to be living, to be part of it all right now – and then, when I started thinking, that you

111

would be coming back home, and that I could be with you this evening, I and no one else, and you were so fond of me, then I felt I was so rich and happy, and it was so glorious to be alive, that I couldn't bear it.'

She sighed. In one hungry, yielding movement, he nestled in against her shoulder.

'At last, thank God! That soothes my breast a little, being able to hold your darling little body again, and feel your warmth against my cheek. In a little while, you can tell me about all the amazing things you've been doing, but first, oh, let's just sit here and say nothing at all, my God, you're so sweet and lovely, it takes my breath away.'

'No, mine,' she replied in a happy voice.

An hour passed, and they still had not uttered a rational word.

'Look,' he said, extracting a little white feather from his wallet, 'you've had votes for women and goodness knows what else while I've been away, but I've only had this.'

'That's from my boa,' said Penwoman, touched, 'where did you find it?'

'Lying on the boarding house steps. It had blown into a corner and – it was like you; I wish I could put you in my wallet. See how soft it is, no one would believe it belonged to a suffragist.'

'You don't really like me being one, then?' the girl asked.

'I don't understand it,' he said, 'but I'd like to know why. You mustn't take this amiss, but I think, like all other men, that woman's place is in the home.'

'Whose home?' asked Penwoman. 'What do you think would happen, if I – ? My brothers have never had anything spare to help Mother,' she added.

Dick, for his part, was thinking he would have given the whole world to be able to say, 'My home', and was thinking in his heart, that if a fellow's will and intentions meant anything -

♦

'Well, as I say, I don't understand it,' was all he said, for he was not one to make lavish promises, 'but I do know that for your dear sake, all the women in the world can have the vote, as far as I'm concerned.'

'Thanks, that's very kind of you.'

'But you've got to love me just as much as before. And no other man may so much as breathe on you.'

'I have only one pail, sir, and I have already set my dough to rise in it,' replied Penwoman proudly. 'But I reserve the right to make eyes at the Upper House.'

A lively discussion ensued on the subject of how accommodating Penwoman should be to achieve political aims, and she told Dick of her meeting with the Baron, which had taken place in his absence.

'He's in love with you now, I suppose,' said Dick, spoiling for a fight.

The room was now dusky, and the stove, lit in Penwoman's honour, shed a restless red light from its open grille onto the rug. The girl got up and opened the door to the little balcony. They were on the top floor, and the buildings on the other side of the newly developed street were low shacks, so you could see out over the city, which lay there like a width of dark cloth, pierced by golden stitches. If you turned to the end of the street in the west, you saw it beyond a pale, curving line of lamps, shining on rough, uneven façades, finished off against the sky by two massive ends of buildings, heavy and grey, as erratically shaped as two gigantic boulders, the cleft between them filled with a yellow light, pale yet intense, a golden gateway to paradise.

The hum of the street came into the room, and with it a breath of chilly spring air. She suddenly remembered that she was not at home, that she had to walk the length of that street and several more, before she reached her home, and felt a surge of disinclination. She quickly closed the balcony door and curled up in the corner of the sofa again.

'What are you doing over there by the stove?' she asked.

'I'm thinking about how much I love you.'

'Can't you come over here and think it? Do you believe you always will?'

'Yes, I do believe that.'

'Sometimes I think,' she said, 'that I, that we all, that I am nothing but a little insert in the lining of my beloved's coat. And it's as natural for you all to change us as to change your coats...'

He had never heard her sound so affectionately miserable before. Something inside him felt sorry for her, but at the same time he rejoiced, because no one is that afraid of losing something they do not hold most dear.

'I don't believe I could ever tire of you,' he said, and she was content with that, for she knew he was not one for solemn oaths. 'For me you are a thousand women, you know, a new one every day. You are one for my work' – and Penwoman felt a sudden satisfaction in all those times she had talked about arch vaulting and asked precocious questions about ground plans.

'You are one for my work,' he went on, 'one for my festive mood, one for my hopes and one for my bad temper. You're one for my tenderness, too, one for the heat in my blood and one for the simple boy, who sometimes longs to be at home with his mother.'

'And one for sewing your buttons back on,' supplied Penwoman, stroking his long, architect's hair.

He took hold of her hand. 'How dreadfully cold you are!'

'Yes, my extremities are getting chilled,' she admitted. 'Come on, let's warm ourselves up by talking about the summer.'

'We shall both wear our student caps,'* he said.

'Yes, and rent a cottage in the skerries together, among the vegetables – '

'Do you think that's the done thing?'*

'Oh yes, I shall hem towels on our ferry trips every day, to preserve our reputation. And it will be warm and green, and we'll be so happy.'

But that was not enough for him; he needed to see if she had changed, grown pale and thin, and he turned up the electric light.

It gave him a shock to see how thin the girl's cheeks were; her neck, too, disappearing into the white, turned-down collar, seemed more slender than he remembered.

A thought like an arrow barbed with pangs of conscience gouged its way into his heart. Is she secretly grieving over having given herself to me? Can such a sensitive and guiltless girl as this bear the thought? Or is she anxious in her heart of hearts that I will abandon her? If she had only asked me; in such matters, after all, a man can speak for himself.

'Tell me all about it, my little love. How are you? You can tell me everything, you know that.'

'Thank you,' said Penwoman, glad to be fussed over a little, 'but you already know everything about me, that is,' with a look expressing both jest and melancholy, 'everything that concerns you! No, don't look so horrified. I am a happy person, it's just that I'm burning for so many different things at the same time, and that takes its toll, you see. But wait for the summer and the holidays.'

'You need to ration yourself out, it's still a long time until then,' he said anxiously.

'You know I can't do that.'

'No, you think you have to be like a Marcus Larsson* painting: thunder and lightning, moonlight and wildfire all at the same time, you little spendthrift.'

'You've got to take me as you find me,' she said, 'but since we're talking about appearances, something much worse has happened to me than losing a couple of kilos: I've got my first wrinkle. Don't you feel sorry for me?'

'How did you get it?'

115

'It's the Seven Farewells from you every week,' she replied.

# CHAPTER 12

'So I said, you see, that I'd be most grateful if they could send the car for me at eleven, then we could come round and pick you up afterwards.'

Penwoman was on the telephone, excitedly delivering this message to Cecilia. But the latter, who had received the Sunday invitation to the General's with more modified rapture, replied with a question: would it not be better for Penwoman to come to her on Saturday evening and stay the night, and then they could go out to the General's together?

Penwoman laughed.

'No Cecilia, thanks all the same,' she said. 'I have a meeting to go to, and even if I hadn't, I wouldn't want to ruin my reputation unnecessarily by being away over Saturday night.'

'Well, I thought that was the last thing you were worried about.'

'Yes, that's how I used to be, before I really had a reputation to keep up I scattered it to the four winds, but now I'm loath to give away any more of it than I can directly benefit from,' replied Penwoman in a businesslike manner. 'We must be worldly, Cecilia, and help ourselves, if we are not to perish. Perhaps those who come after us will be able to steer a straighter course.'

Over on Blasieholmen, Cecilia looked horrified, and even Penwoman put down the receiver with a little sigh.

Sunday dawned blue and beautiful, and Penwoman beamed to match the sun as she dressed, folding her prettiest dress into a flat cardboard box to change into for dinner, and putting on a practical skirt and jacket, tall boots and a tam-o'-shanter.

117

As the car whisked them along the road, Cecilia sat studying her friend, which she could do without hindrance, as Penwoman had forgotten everything for the intoxication of speed, air and sunlight.

She looked at every line in the young face, wondered whether that cheek had always been so thin, the angle of that chin so sharp or the eyes so deeply shadowed.

The girl had her face turned upwards, her hands clasped, and such a concentrated expression of life and energy in her features that they appeared drawn tight, as if in some perilous horseback ride. From time to time she cast a quick glance at Cecilia, as if to convince herself the latter was as enraptured as she was, and gave a fervent, trembling smile. With stinging heart, Cecilia smiled back.

Now they were turning into the park, and there was the General's house, with the lake shining through the birches beyond.

Anna Gylling came out to meet them and gave orders to the chauffeur, who was to pick up some dinner guests from the centre of Stockholm. Penwoman looked most alarmed when she heard that they were expecting the General's brother Mr Veber, the bank director, and his wife, but when Anna Gylling added: 'and another old parliamentary buffer, Baron Stark of the Upper House, who has begun taking an interest in the women's movement, God only knows why', she burst out laughing.

'It's my very own Baron, Cecilia!'

As they were taking off their coats in the hall, however, she whispered to Cecilia with a worried look, 'Do you think that's the only reason I've been invited?'

Cecilia, grasped at once that 'that' meant the Baron, assured her that long before the Baron began 'taking an interest in the women's movement', the General had been talking of her wish to entertain Penwoman for her valiant work for the suffrage, and it was assuredly just a coincidence. She was wrong about that, as it happened, and the Baron knew very well what lay in store.

'How nice that it's turned out fine,' said Anna Gylling. 'Last

Sunday, when the party leaders were here for lunch, it poured with rain. We've been unlucky whenever we've invited the politicians this spring.'

It did not take long for Penwoman to realise that she most certainly had been invited in her own right. The General was so charming that you forgot she was really meant to be revered from a distance; she remained a cathedral, but you could talk to it, and what was more, it liked it. She took charge of Penwoman and gave her tea; she made her describe her daily life and work, and was so evidently amused, that Penwoman plucked up the courage to tell her about all the constantly changing succession of assignments and situations which make up a female journalist's life: from the hat show in the morning to the seventieth birthday celebration in the middle of the day and the report on the evening meeting.

'That's all I have to tell you,' she said finally, 'although perhaps there is one other thing, General, that is, if you'd like to hear about our molestation fund.'

The General, who in her own distant youth had dreamt of being a journalist, wanted to very much.

'Well,' said Penwoman, now as bold as brass, 'we once had a debate in the paper about women's right to be left unmolested in the street. You know, the sort of feature you resort to when you're at a loss how to fill the space. We men and women on the staff wrote most of the pieces ourselves, and one of my colleagues, male of course, said that women shouldn't be so namby-pamby, so quick to take offence, and that kind of thing. But the very evening his article was published, I was pestered on my way home from work by a smart gentleman who wouldn't leave me alone, and quoted my own paper's views as the reason and the excuse for his behaviour. That was three years ago, when I was still seething with indignation. The next afternoon, I got hold of the article's author, assembled as many of our colleagues as I could, and said: look, this has happened; what shall I do with him? Somebody suggested the culprit should pay for my cab home from the paper, every time I was so late that the trams had stopped running. And out of that, the molestation fund grew, because I suggested the obligation to contribute should be extended, so only those who knew they had never bothered a woman at night be let off. So then they agreed to join in, virtually all of them,' she added gravely. 'Now the fund is so large, that my female colleagues and I get a tidy sum each, divided in proportion to our age and our likely appeal to pests.'

Anna Gylling and Cecilia observed with wry interest the General's venerable face beneath her white hair; a mischievous look had come over it and she, usually so white, with such mournful eyes, had a touch of pink, like the flush of a young girl, on her cheeks.

'Penwoman's going to be her favourite out here, and the funny thing is, she hasn't a clue how close she is to success,' said Anna Gylling with a smile.

But Cecilia's face darkened, and she said nothing.

It had been enjoyable to sit chatting on such familiar terms to the General, who was so much nicer and understood so much better than one could have dreamt possible, and Penwoman sighed at the sound of the car pulling up at the bottom of the steps. She went quiet all of a sudden, and the General could not get another word out of her.

As the guests entered, she drew back into a window alcove and decided to steal out into the grounds at the first opportunity. The General's brother was admittedly not an unknown quantity to her; he was one of those elderly gentlemen who always like to inaugurate the better class of charitable enterprise, and she had spoken to him at many crèches and sanatoria. He was a fine-looking man, as imposing as the General, and moreover to be respected for his pro-suffrage motions, which was why one had to swallow one's irritation when asked to introduce oneself for the twentieth time. The only diverting thing about the guests was Baron Starck, who was both surprised and delighted to see her, saying: 'My dear young lady, I had no idea I would meet you here today, but I have read your suffrage brochures, even so!'

'Has it helped?' enquired Penwoman with interest, while

Anna Gylling muttered: 'Now we understand his miraculous sudden interest!'

The General's sister-in-law surveyed the young journalist with an amused smile, and pitied her a little for her blouse and boots, while congratulating herself for her own tact in selecting her oldest dinner dress in order not to stand out too much among the suffragists. Mrs Veber did not like them; she thought women would plunge themselves and the country into misfortune if they got the vote, but she knew, too, that her polite and amiable husband had never loved her the way he had once loved Jane Horneman, many years before.

Penwoman drew back from the circle. 'I'm just going out for a little walk,' she said.

'What for?' asked the Baron.

'I'm going to see if I can find any hepatica,' replied the girl.

'I wager you won't find any. It's a long time since we had such a cold spring, and they tell me in letters from home that the lakes are still frozen,' said the Baron, wanting her to stay in the drawing room.

'Yes, let's make a wager,' responded Penwoman without embarrassment, 'but if you lose, my Lord, you must promise me something.'

'By all means. I only wish your prospects of winning were better. But what?'

'Well,' said Penwoman, who had moved towards the door, 'if I win, my Lord, you must promise to put votes for women – '

'And our eligibility for election,' put in Anna Gylling.

'And our eligibility for election on your political programme, and always speak in favour of it in Parliament.'

'Yes,' said the Baron, caught off his guard. 'Yes, yes... I shall do that, as I have promised, but how will I account to the House for my change of attitude?'

'I'll help you with that, my Lord, I promise,' said Penwoman with a nod, and was gone.

'Don't stay out too long,' he called after her.

Mrs Veber gave her husband a look; he was sitting there with furrowed brow, for this joking with legislative authority was beyond his experience.

What was the Baron thinking of? Had the old bachelor fallen in love with the girl?

She asked Anna Gylling at the earliest opportunity.

'Well if so, does it come as any surprise?'

'There is not normally a queue of barons and Members of Parliament at the suffragists' front doors,' retorted Mrs Veber with a slight sneer.


Penwoman, meanwhile, had left the open parkland and found her way onto a forest path, where she luxuriated in walking on the deep, black earth, intoxicated by its intense fragrance and the scent of the spruces all around. On the sunny side of the path it was so warm that she unbuttoned her jacket; it was glorious to be free and have space to stretch. 'My darling,' she said softly, 'how lovely it is to be alive!'

The Baron's flowers, she thought suddenly, the wager! She turned off the path and began hunting among the clusters of overwintered leaves that protruded from the moss. Nor did it take long before she had found a whole clump of hepatica, which she carefully loosened with her penknife. Then she picked up the clump of flowers tenderly in both hands and turned to walk back.

They looked like a group of little women, she thought, huddled together, bending into the wind in their downy grey clothing, modest but bold, with whole flocks of little beginners down at the hems of their skirts, and only one of them had as yet had the courage to turn her calm, blue gaze to the sky.

Just like our own pioneers, she thought, and it was as if they only now came alive and could be taken to her heart, all those who had dared to make a start, when the frost was still biting, and the drifts of snow lay hard-packed in the forest. To her own surprise, tears came to her eyes; they were all dead, and they would never know how much we now understood, remembered and revered. She amused herself childishly, extending her original notion by giving them names: Fredrika Bremer, Mrs Olivecrona, Mrs Adlersparre...*

Back in the park, she came across the rest of the party, taking a gentle stroll in what appeared to be a rather lacklustre mood.

'There is no escaping it now, my friend,' said the bank director as Penwoman, trying very hard not to look triumphant, came up and handed the Baron the plant.

The Baron, not really knowing whose side to take, stammered something, but the General said gravely: 'Spring is with us, and truth will out.'

For Penwoman, the smile that accompanied those words was a greater reward than all the compliments she had ever received.

Anna Gylling was delighted.

'Well done,' she said. 'Come here and start calling me Anna immediately.'

'I'll be happy to,' said Penwoman, not a little flattered, 'but if he turns out not to keep his word,' she added scrupulously 'you've still decided to dispense with formal titles!'

'If you don't make sure he keeps the promise he has made you in front of all these witnesses, we will most certainly be back on formal terms,' threatened Anna with a laugh. 'Go and be nice to him, my girl!'

'Yes,' replied Penwoman obediently, and before long, she and the Baron were to be seen deep in eager conversation, turning along a solitary path that led across the park, while the General, clearly determined not to notice anything, continued entertaining her brother and sister-in-law.

Cecilia and Anna Gylling went on with the conversation interrupted by Penwoman's return. Anna was not generally the communicative type; most people considered her reserved, and would have been astonished to hear her today. She could not explain herself why she suddenly felt such a strong urge to unburden herself to Cecilia, of all people. She was too tired and dispirited to resist it, though she was annoyed at her own weakness, foreseeing she would come to regret it bitterly. She had sworn, had she not, that she would be burnt unread? She was white in the face with neuralgia, but when Cecilia uttered a few words of sympathy, she held up a hand to ward them off.

'No, don't pity me for my pain,' she said. 'I've reached the point where I find the physical affliction invaluable as opium to dull my loathing of life. The way it is now, the pendulum swings between the painful and the pain-free days, and I wouldn't at any pirce want to miss the rare and heavenly sensation of feeling the pain loosen its grip and leave me weak and numb, without thoughts, without a future, without a past, just luxuriating in the physical pleasure of my nerves keeping quiet in my body.'

'You pay a high price for that pleasure,' said Cecilia.

'Nothing comes free of charge,' replied Anna Gylling. 'And anyway, strictly speaking it would be worse to have the time and the energy to curse one's life.'

Cecilia walked in silence for a while, and Anna Gylling's fear that she would open her mouth and say, 'Oh, surely it is not that bad,' grew with every passing second.

'I have been at rock bottom, too,' replied Cecilia at last.

'So I wasn't wrong,' said Anna Gylling, with evident relief, 'I thought I recognised the signs. That was why I felt such an urge to talk to you, I suppose.'

'But since then, the suffrage has helped me to live,' Cecilia went on, slowly and a little hesitantly.

'In my case, on the other hand, it has been the ruin of my life,' said Anna Gylling, with a faint smile when she saw Cecilia's shocked expression. 'I bought the right to work for it with my possibility of personal happiness in life, and that decision haunts me. Now that there's nothing to stop me working day and night, I hate it.'

'But that's not the fault of the cause, you know,' Cecilia put in amenably.

'Yes it is,' said Anna Gylling darkly, 'or no, naturally not, if you prefer. It sounds ridiculous and affected, but it really is true, that our work took me over too entirely and too hard. I was so young, and the movement so huge; it was half of humanity on its way to light and freedom, the advent of God's kingdom on earth. If the choice had not been presented to me just then, when I was going about quite drunk with the women's movement, burning with suffrage fervour, but oh, that's when it came, and I was a traitor, three times a fool as I was. I was fond of the boy, and had been for a long time, though all these new ideas occupied my thoughts too much just then. Some time in the distant future we would marry, of course, but I didn't need to worry about that yet. Then suddenly, one day, he had taken a job out in the wilds of furthest Norrland. "Do you want to come with me?" he said...'

Her face and voice expressed such utter despair that Cecilia, who had pretty high standards in that department, was impressed.

'I let him go alone,' Anna Gylling went on, with a shudder of shame, 'I could not give up my women's movement work for the ordinary sort of hard, simple women's work. I thought, but God has punished me, that I was absolutely indispensable among the few workers we had, and that I, who had been given the fire and the enthusiasm, should not desert them right at the very start, when there were so many others who could do the work he was offering me, and bring his child into the world. I suppose I thought he would wait for me, would beg and implore and persuade me, but he didn't say a single word; he left, and I realised I was dead to him, and he would find another woman for his life. And then they all disappeared: my belief, my conviction, my happiness; there was not even enough left of my great dreams to cover my misery...'

'Oh, you poor thing,' said Cecilia.

'So now do you understand how I can be the Anna Gylling who works for something I believe will intensify the conflicts in women's lives even more, and pull their hearts apart, however they choose? The General says I can't see clearly and my own fate makes me blind; I hope that's true, but the General has children and grandchildren of her own, and has no idea, God bless her, what it is to taste eternal death.'

'Suffrage work found me,' said Cecilia, after a pause, 'battered and bloody at the roadside. I have sacrificed nothing for it, but when I realised what it was that lay behind all this writing, speaking, petitioning and agitating, this new way of thinking taught me to live, and walk more calmly towards eternal death.'

'Or to put it less poetically, it is for you what the neuralgia is for me,' said Anna Gylling bitterly, 'opium to reduce the dread and dull the longing.'

'No,' said Cecilia with sudden intensity, coming to a halt. 'No, for I have learned, or started to learn, that there is some meaning in my own miserable fate, if I can carry but a single stone to the great building, and I want to teach myself to believe, that it grew so,' her voice trembled, 'so empty around me because...'

'You want to give it your all, yes,' said Anna Gylling pityingly. 'How many are there, existing on that lie?'


Anna Gylling lent Cecilia and Penwoman her attractive set of rooms upstairs, so they could change for dinner. Anna, who was lying on a sofa to rest for a while and take some revitalising poisons, was so enchanted by the results of their efforts that she almost forgot her neuralgia. Penwoman was wearing a stylish blue dress shot through with matte, blue-tinged gold, which went beautifully with her vivacious blonde hair, and Cecilia's outfit, 'the colour of the tears she once shed,' thought Anna, was a most becoming reworking of sackcloth and ashes.

'It serves Mrs Veber right!'

'Don't you think we're rather smart for suffragists?' asked Penwoman, childishly delighted at having access to a mirror that reflected all of her.

'You both look simply enchanting,' Anna readily confirmed. 'I should like to dub you our Lady Patricia,* and Penwoman – no, you can never be anything but Penwoman of the Suffrage, my funny little bud.' She gave a friendly nod, her smile so dazzling that they both suddenly realised what Anna Gylling had once been.

'Let us go down now,' she said, getting to her feet, 'hand in hand and singing some song suitable for the occasion. Ideally we should have had our Votes for Women banner, too, but since it isn't ready, we'll just have to do our best to trump them anyway.'

And she told her friends how the calm, quiet evenings the General treasured so highly were spent reading aloud from tendentious literature, and sewing the new suffrage banner, which had to be ready for the summer rally. It was a routine only broken if the General saw fit to summon out to the house some guest who was to be inspired to take a leading role, or prevailed upon to use their influence in aid of one of the General's schemes, or persuaded not to commit some act of stupidity.

'You can have no idea, how many wills have been transformed and how many orders have been given in that room,' said Anna Gylling, as they passed the library on their way to the dining room, where everyone was now gathering for dinner.

'So you are thoroughly converted now, I suppose?' was the first thing the bank director said, once they had taken their places. And he divided his mocking smile between the Baron and Penwoman.

'I would be ashamed of myself otherwise,' replied the Baron. 'In this company, any prejudice one could possibly have had against the suffragists is bound to evaporate.'

'I am starting to feel positively isolated.' This from Mrs Veber, cutting in a little sharply after a whole morning spent biting her tongue. 'Everyone here is such a believer except me.'

Penwoman stopped herself from making an unkind remark about the many hidebound women of good families who sat at their well-stocked tables dishing out abuse, because they neither felt the ill effects of bad wages and laws, nor had anything new or good to contribute to the life of society. Naturally she maintained a polite silence, but her look was so full of undisguised, childlike animosity that Mrs Veber could not resist replying, as if she had in fact been reproached. 'Well just you wait, little miss sitting there looking so affronted, until your blessed suffrage has caused you as much vexation as it has me.'

'It has come at the cost of hard work for us all,' said the General gravely, 'and Penwoman has done her share, too.'

'The young lady can hardly have found her social life inconvenienced by it,' Mrs Veber put in hotly, 'but *I* know how it feels. They blame me for Klas's pro-suffrage motions, you know, as if I were the one forcing him to put them at the top of his agenda! "Oh yes, Mrs Veber must keep her husband on a tight rein, to have made such a ladies' man of him": do you think a wife likes to hear that sort of thing?'

'No, of course not, if she knows in her heart that she isn't worth the compliment,' conceded Penwoman.

Mrs Veber gave her a little look.

'But I have managed to get him to the point,' – she simply could not deny herself this piece of spite, especially as she knew he would not be able to oppose his wife in public – 'where he will not propose any more motions in this parliament. We have had quite enough trouble already. It is Baron Starck's turn now.'

The Baron appeared discomfited. He knew as well as Mrs Veber that it would take courage to shoulder that particular burden, and he lacked the deep ethical commitment required. He, too, had naturally poked fun at the ladies' man on numerous occasions.

The General looked dejected. It always made her feel uncomfortable when her sister-in-law could not conceal the ill feeling she felt towards her for the influence she, the General, had on her brother. She knew she had an enemy who sought to thwart her efforts, and it distressed her to find this opposition coming from the very direction from which she should have had the steadiest support. This brother of hers, with his deep and lucid intellect, and a naive idealism where women were concerned, had gone and fallen in love with lovely hair and a captivating smile that concealed nothing but irredeemable small-mindedness, instead of all the beautiful things he had written in poems!

'Well, standing up for women's rights doesn't exactly make you popular,' said the bank director, breaking the awkward silence and coming to his wife's aid with unerring courtesy. 'Women laugh at you, and men are full of something halfway between bitterness and scorn; I am aware of it, though they rarely dare to voice it in my presence. But a man takes no notice of all that, of course.'

'I fail to understand,' said Cecilia, quietly and meditatively, 'why men are as embittered, that is to say, as I hear that they are, I encounter so few; I live my life among women. Perhaps I am very stupid and incapable of imagining the true state of affairs, but I feel they should be glad, impressed even, to see us striving to be cleverer and stronger and better informed. I think that if I were a man, my impulse would be to bend down and hold out a helping hand.'

'There's nobody as naive as you,' said Anna Gylling, regarding Cecilia with a smile of contempt and pity.

Everyone seemed to be expecting the General to say something, but she sat in silence, her gaze fixed on something way beyond the conversation.

'One really cannot expect them,' said Mrs Veber, 'to be happy, when they see women inundating the areas of work that have been theirs since time immemorial, and that are most suited to them, say what you will. Men liked things the way they were and did not want them to change, I find their reaction only natural.'

'So do I,' said Anna Gylling grimly. 'I mean to say, it must be splendid always to have a handy group of people who work and suffer in silence. It is women who are stupid, for wanting to improve the world. No, they should say as the farmer's wife did, when they came to tell her the farmer was lying at the bottom of the well: "Father is master in his own home, and can lie where he wants to!" That's how it was in the old days, but these are different times.'

'We worry about the drinking water these days, of course,' Penwoman put in.

A fleeting smile crossed the General's lips. 'I have met so few,' she said, 'capable of seeing that there is something tragic and touching about this striving of souls who have grown aware of their shortcomings to rise, and move forward. I have spoken to many men about the women's issue, and I have heard many points of view, but I have still heard far too few say: "They are human beings, too."'

'But my dear General, it takes a great deal of willpower and magnanimity for any of them to say that,' said Anna Gylling.

'Well they could at least say: *poor wretch!*'

Penwoman said this with such pathetic earnestness, that none of them dared smile, not even Mrs Veber.

A momentary silence descended. Then the General suddenly rose from the table.

'Those that come after us will be greater than we,'* she said unexpectedly, as if answering a question from her own soul.

# CHAPTER 13

Once, hundreds of years before, the sea had come right up to where they were sitting today, close together. But now the rock lay exposed, grey and naked, polished by innumerable medieval waves, and far below them, so far that Penwoman felt giddy when she looked down, the water nestled its smooth cheek against the rock. This was their favourite retreat on summer evenings; you could, as it were, command the whole archipelago from there, looking out over islands, bays and sounds, way out to sea, but tucked right away to the west, swathed in its own smoke as if in a thin, grey coat, lay Stockholm.

'This is where one ought to come,' said Penwoman the first time she discovered the place one clear, spring evening when they were searching for a suitable summer cottage, 'this is where one ought to come and learn to write leaders, so people see far and clear, get the big picture, unclouded by details, and a profound perspective on the future.' And so it was that, for as long as those happy summer visitors had it to themselves, the place became known as The Leader and was never called anything else.

It had been an eventful day, but now evening was drawing in. Shadow and sunlight were fighting it out in the west, and their battle had flowed crimson down to the horizon. The air was still, the inlet lay glassy and grey, in the dappled shade of a tree of cloud, but from time to time a little breeze floated by on its back, thinking to reach the open sea. A boat slipped past with limp sails:

'See,' said Penwoman, 'that's how slowly the hours pass, when I'm waiting for you.'

She was sitting under a sturdy little pine tree, her back resting against its trunk; Dick lay with his head in her lap, looking up into the air. He said nothing, but now and then he found her hand and squeezed it.

Their souls still trembled with the memory of the great moment of confession they had just been through, and when she at times gave a quiet and preoccupied smile, and the very next minute he felt that smile against his lips, he knew each time, just as if she had said it aloud, what she was referring to.

Penwoman had taken a week off to go and see her mother, whose birthday it had been; she was to start work again on Monday, but today was Saturday. Dick had had to go into the office as usual, with the greatest reluctance, but they had agreed to telephone each other at least every couple of hours. How they had laughed and joked that morning, when Dick came in to wake her and found her in bed with her international women's suffrage badge pinned to her nightgown, writing under an open parasol, while the curtains flapped like taut sails, so you thought you were aboard a ship, since there was nothing but water to be seen through the windows. How she had toiled and hummed to herself to make sure she and the coffee were ready when he got back from his dip; how funny it was to serve breakfast on the front porch of Villa Borgis* and then, just like a married woman, see the family breadwinner go off to work, while you did your morning chores and fetched water from the well, all at a leisurely pace.

'This is what it will be like, later, always,' she thought contentedly, 'but sometimes I shall simply have to go to the paper and get them to give me an article to write, otherwise I shall die.'

When everything was pristine enough to satisfy even a professional housewife, she took a walk inland and soon found herself in a sloping meadow, where the baking sun shone generously on her and on all the flowers of the field as she lay on her stomach, not, as Dick would have said, to listen in on the effects of votes for women in the Antipodes, but to imagine and dream about the thousands of things that have absorbed every young girl of every era.

At twelve she was back home, filling all the vases with flowers and waiting for Dick's call.

There it was: 'Hello, all's well here. And with you?'

But before Penwoman could answer, she felt a painful stab at the back of her neck, gave a violent shriek, clapped her hand to it and received another sting from an angry wasp, dropping the receiver in her alarm. Dick, on a telephone in Vasagatan, went cold with fear: a cry of fright, and then nothing, utter silence! He did not stay on the line for long; one look at the clock told him that if he really hurried he might just catch the next boat, and when Penwoman, remorseful and somewhat more composed, picked up the receiver again, no one answered. She had to tend her little wounds in apprehensive silence and solitude, and the worst of the smarting had just about subsided when she saw Dick coming up the hill with an expression on his face that made her heart almost stop in her breast.

'Well thank God,' was all he said, 'my darling' – there was nothing more; he was groping to find words, and the only part of him not shaking was his arms, which pulled her to him hard, as if he and she had been walking on the edge of an abyss together, and it was a good while before she could make out what he was mumbling with his head against her breast.

'I can't imagine life without you, do you hear?'

'Yes, thank you,' said Penwoman, with a little smile, because she might never have heard him say that if it had not been for the wasp, and thank God it had not stung her in the face.

But she suddenly caught sight of an unfamiliar look, filled with anguish. Oh, she had never known, that Dick -

'Don't be afraid,' she said lovingly, 'I shan't leave you, nor you me, ever, will you?'

It was so like the old Dick, that he took a moment's pause for serious thought, for this was a promise that had consequences for his whole life.

'Not until I die, Penwoman,' he said finally, and then she knew that nothing on earth would shake his resolve.


She sat there smiling, aware of the blood still coursing fast and hot through her body. Who could have known that love was so dizzying when you descended into its depths? No one had ever told her, she had had to discover for herself that in her own person she had tremendous power over life and death. It made her feel somehow solemn, but as the emotion threatened to overwhelm her, she leant over Dick and asked in her most matter-of-fact tone if he wasn't hungry after all that.

'You suffragists are terribly prosaic,' he said, but straightened up immediately and with some relief, as if glad to be back to a more everyday train of thought. 'I'm becoming ever more aware,' he went on, frowning, 'that public interests take away that lovely, rosy, feminine bloom that we men prize above all things. You may laugh, my girl, but it's like the bloom on the cheek of a peach: once gone, it can never be restored. Now up you get, I could certainly do with a pipe and some coffee.'

'I can tell you one difference between a woman and a peach,' said Penwoman, as they were walking up to the cottage, arm in arm, 'and it's that a woman can become as rosy as you wish, if you just give her five minutes to herself – '

While she was grinding the coffee, he suddenly said – and she realised that this was what he had been thinking

about, when she interrupted him to ask if he was hungry –
'If the love carries on growing at this rate in my heart, I
truly don't know how there will be room for it in the end.'

'You'll have to take it up to the loft, the part you don't
need for the time being, but you're not allowed to give a
single bit to anyone else.'

All right, he would not do that, and they also agreed to
feel dreadfully sorry for all those who had not 'got each
other', as Dick put it.

'Like Cecilia, for example,' he said a little hesitantly,
not sure how Penwoman would receive his words.

'Why Cecilia, in particular?' asked Penwoman quickly,
looking up.

'Well, she isn't young any more, and she's so alone, and
I sometimes catch her looking at us with such a strange
expression in her eyes. Has she ever said – ?'

'Cecilia never talks to me about things like that,' said
Penwoman, 'but sometimes she reveals it all, even so, in a
gesture or a tone of voice or a silence, but anyway, I don't
like discussing with my lovers what I as a friend know
about my friends!'

She said this so earnestly and looked so funny, telling
him off with her nose in the air, that he immediately felt
obliged to kiss her.

'You little modern woman of principle, you! I thought it
was a known fact that women always betray their women
friends to their lovers and vice versa.'

'Not us,' said Penwoman proudly. 'Talking of my
friends,' she went on with a roguish look that concealed an
element of apprehension, 'I've got news for you: we're to
have neighbours from midsummer.'

'What's that?' he instantly looked genuinely appalled.
'People you know? Does this mean a sudden end to our
freedom and domestic bliss? It really was far too short, my
love!'

She let him look miserable for a minute, while she

attended to the coffee.

'So you think you've had a nice time here with me?'

'I never knew anything could be that nice.'

'Well now I've got you to admit that with a knife to your throat, I can tell you there's no need to look so unhappy – pass me that little red bag of isinglass* – because, you see, the people planning to set up camp at the Söderbergs' place are all suffragists.'

'It's a fair step from here, it's true, but that doesn't really help, does it?' he said gloomily, for Penwoman might say what she liked, but he only half trusted them. 'In fact, it just means you'll know every last one of them, and we shan't get a moment's peace. It might as well be Mrs Bengtsson's boarding house.'

'But why should you be worried, love, when I'm not? I know the whole lot of them. They won't ruin our domestic bliss. They won't notice us.'

'Watch that coffee, it's about to boil over,' he said morosely. 'Won't notice us. No woman in the world could fail to realise – '

'In our circles,' replied Penwoman with the same pride as before, 'in our circles, if we're not supposed to realise, then we don't. Come and have your coffee on The Leader. You bring the pan, and I'll bring the tray, but don't shake it about now the grounds have settled. Dear me, how anxious you look! I'm convinced it would never occur to them to go inquiring into things I haven't told them.'

'If you're all so admirable even *before* you've got the vote – '

'It's the fact of not having it that gives us so much else to think about, of course. Our only interest in people's doings is in how they might impinge on the suffrage. If they noticed I was behaving in any kind of way that could bring the cause they're fighting for into disrepute, then that would be another matter. Then they would be implacably stern. Luckily I have no position within the movement; I'm a devoted little freebooter, as they know, who will brave the flames for them if need be, but no one identifies me with The Movement.' Dick said nothing and his expression was still suspicious.

Penwoman went over and sat down beside him.

'Don't be sad,' she said lovingly. 'Look how well our page layout works!* My chin reaches just to your shoulder. There now!'

'It's you I'm sad for,' he said slowly. 'I'm thinking about what you're laying yourself open to because of me. You'll be the one, after all, who has to suffer the pinpricks and knowing smiles. At this moment, I feel as if I've acted with no backbone at all, damn it!'

'Oh no you haven't! Shame on you for the thought. I'm sure everything will be fine, but even if I do have to take the odd pinprick, I shall still always be glad, for as long as I live, that I've had this chance to show you how I love you,' she said.

'You could have had that anyway.'

'Yes, but not like this. If you had been rich and able to provide me with a good home straight away, then you would inevitably have ended up thinking, if I ever happened to be nasty to you: perhaps she only took me because I could support her. So that's why I'm glad I had a chance to love you in my youth, not for advantage or prestige, but for love's own sake. Which won't do anything to stop me being very happy when I one day become the wife of a certain young and highly capable architect.' She smiled and looked up into his face; he had to smile back, but with a pang of pain in his heart.

'I wish,' he said earnestly, 'I could make you as happy as you deserve.'

The battle in the skies was over, the clouds were on the run, and the sun sank bright and gold into the sea. The flames of sunset licked about the earth and sky for a long time, but even after they had burnt out in the turquoise-coloured air of the summer night, the two of them sat there on The Leader, entwined in each other's arms, saying nothing.

## Chapter 14

Villa Borgis had stood empty for a few days, the sun searching in vain for familiar faces behind closed windows. But if it had been able to penetrate the dense foliage of the treetops of the Adolf Fredrik churchyard, it would have been able to get straight in at the open window of Penwoman's room, where the girl sat at her desk with her fingers stuck in her hair, reading softly to herself from long sheets of proofs, while Dick lay on the sofa, smoking. Whatever he was thinking about, he found himself interrupted time and again.

'You simply must hear this,' she said, gravely quoting what struck her as a particularly felicitous phrase from her manuscript, which made the case so eloquently for women's rights of citizenship.

'What do you say to that, Dick?'

'Yes, that seems very reasonable, my little love,' he would invariably answer, in an absent-minded tone.

'Huh,' she said finally, running out of patience, 'you aren't listening to a single word I say, are you?'

'Stop showing me your darling little hands, then.'

Penwoman looked offended.

'Am I supposed not to show my hands now, just so you can think about serious things? You are behaving like a downright Turk. What if you were to bring your drawing board round here, to cool you down?'

'If you mean you want me to go home, just say so – '

But that naturally made her leap up from the table with streamers of proofs fluttering all about her, and come straight to Dick's side: 'No, but come and dance with me – '

139

It might seem scarcely credible that, under such conditions, Penwoman would meet the deadline for her task of making up and proofreading the newspaper that was to be published in time for the long-planned summer rally, yet the day before the rally opened, a huge parcel of copies, hot off the presses, lay on the table in the campaign office. Beside it stood Penwoman like a proud mother, handing a copy to everyone who entered, be they friend or stranger. There was a constant stream of people coming up to hear all the latest news, to find acquaintances who were expected from all over Sweden, and to offer to help with whatever needed doing.

Jane Horneman was in a corner, eagerly discussing something with Kerstin Vallmark, who was looking rather troubled, as usual.

'Dear child,' she said, 'you must have a new hat. You will be seen quite a lot at the rally, and as press committee you will have to speak to all the journalists. Can you really justify it to your suffrage conscience if the press goes home associating the movement with that awful, ugly old hat? How much do you want to spend on a new one?'

'Any amount,' said Kerstin Vallmark with a generosity born of despair. 'But let's go at once. Once we've got the vote, I shall go back to my dear old hat.'

'Now I come to think about it, we really do need to get you a smart blouse, too,' went on Miss Horneman mercilessly. 'I'm so glad the skirt suit we got you last year has worn well.'

Jane Horneman, immaculate in an expensive white outfit with a black, Rembrandt hat,* ushered the poor schoolteacher out of the door.

'Hurry back,' Penwoman called after them, 'and you can help sell newspapers later.'

'Now there's a treat to look forward to, if you're good,' Jane Horneman consoled her charge, and Kerstin Vallmark brightened a little at the prospect.

'Who were *they*?' asked a voice with a pronounced Dalarna accent. Penwoman turned and saw before her a tall, plump, red-cheeked lady, whom she immediately recognised from pictures and accounts as Mrs Kjell, one of that band who kept the suffrage flag flying all round the regions, and whose cheerful energy had won over many enthusiastic new supporters. The girl accordingly curtseyed low and gave the desired information, adding her own name – after a moment's thought, for she had almost forgotten it. It then transpired that Mrs Kjell was similarly very much aware of Penwoman's existence, and they were soon chatting away merrily. Penwoman found herself meeting a whole series of apostles from various parts of the country; they were all very nice to her, all happy to be with their comrades; they were not as spoilt for like-minded company as the Stockholm women, after all. As soon as Cecilia arrived, Penwoman was eager to include her in the happy circle, which kept expanding as the little room gradually filled up, and the sound of excited voices carried right up to the Central League for Social Work* on the floor above.

'Right, I'm off,' said Penwoman finally, taking a bundle of newspapers. Mrs Kjell and a few of the other rally delegates followed her example, along with Kerstin Vallmark, Ester Henning and, to some people's surprise, Cecilia. Jane Horneman declared a preference for completing some less lethal task while she waited to hear how they got on. Mrs Kjell and Penwoman initially stayed together, the former touting and selling her wares with as much confidence as if she had been an itinerant newspaper vendor on the streets of Stockholm all her life.

The first thing Penwoman saw as she came down Sturegatan was Dick, and she made straight for him.

'Have you got any change?' he asked.

'No, I forgot about that.'

'I thought as much. Here you are,' and he smuggled a handful of coppers into her coat pocket. 'Don't I get a paper, then?' He was duly given his copy, and stood there with it in his hand, gazing after Penwoman as she, after a quick glance around her, headed for a couple of older women, greeted them politely and offered each of them a paper. It was all to no avail, for they swept past with cold smiles and not a single word, but by then she had already collared a young man, who at once developed a fervent interest in votes for women. When Dick saw this, he decided to shadow her. Who knows, he said to himself to justify his action, she might be needing my manly protection. Penwoman soon noticed him, and beamed. He imagined it was because she was having fun in her street urchin guise, and he was quite right, but there was more to it than that.

Many a time, on the tram or walking along streets and across squares, she had wished she knew what all these people going about Stockholm and constituting the population thought of the suffrage campaign, and it suddenly struck her that now she had a chance to find out!

She therefore made no efforts to avoid anyone, even those to whom she clearly had no hope of selling a paper. If she could not do that, she could at least put in a good word that perhaps one day might bear fruit, and if nothing else, she would be repaid with some instructive taunt. For it was only very well-bred ladies who confined themselves to passing by and pretending they had seen and heard nothing.

'Is it for me to blow my nose on, this paper?' asked a voice from a group of young men, as the rest of them jeered.

'Oh poor you, can't you read?' said Penwoman sympathetically, and as the young man made to reach out for the paper: 'No, no pearls for those who only blow their noses on them.'

Turning round, she was met by two smiling, good-natured faces, belonging to the kind of Stockholmer often seen on the ferries to the archipelago with briefcases and newspapers.

'So you want the vote at any price?' they said.

'That's the idea,' said Penwoman. 'Let me sell you a paper, gentlemen, then you can acquaint yourselves with the question a little better.'

They were both quite willing to buy a paper, but they would much prefer some personal instruction: what on earth was going on, since ladies were out selling papers?

'We're having a summer rally,' said Penwoman, 'and if you gentlemen want to do me a favour, tell your wives to come to the public meeting tomorrow evening, it can only be to their advantage.'

'Can we come, too?'

'Yes, of course.'

'Will we see you there?'

Penwoman looked round. Dick was approaching.

'Well, goodbye for now,' she said hastily.

Along came a beautiful and elegant lady. Penwoman felt extremely plain, but addressed her anyway.

The lady looked a little taken aback, but she did stop. 'What sort of paper is it?'

Penwoman explained it all in a few words, and the lady listened attentively before saying: 'Well I have to admit that I am not very interested in the goal of women's suffrage, but if you are prepared to go round selling these, the least I can do is to buy one. What do they cost?'

'How kind,' said Penwoman. 'Ten öre – '

'I've already had one old battleaxe to contend with,' said a cross voice.

Penwoman laughed: who could it be? She looked around and spotted one of her comrades ahead of her: it was Cecilia!

The cross voice sounded far from promising, but here were a pair of young girls: 'Of course we must have the vote,' they said, 'no question about it. Isn't it good fun going round selling papers?'

'Well, moderately,' said Penwoman, 'but if you two go up to Lästmakaregatan and get some copies, the pleasure can be all yours.'

Next she encountered a labourer, but he pre-empted her and spoke first.

'I suppose you're just doing it to get yourself married?' he suggested.

'I already am,' said Penwoman.

'Then you must have a henpecked husband, seeing as he hasn't given you a good hiding and made you stop all this vote nonsense.'

'Yes, he's not up to much,' replied Penwoman, 'but at least he's better than the honourable gentleman who last spoke.'

She decided to do a circuit of Berzelii Park, where people were sitting listening to the afternoon concert on the terrace at Berns.* Look, there was a well-to-do married couple who didn't seem to be locals; this would be fun. But she had never ever seen a person look as self-satisfied and scornful as the woman did when she realised – though it took a little while – what was at issue.

'Here's my right to vote,' she said, putting a hand on her husband's solid shoulder.

'But what about those who're not married?' objected Penwoman humbly.

'Well they should see to it that they soon are,' said the woman. 'Then they'll have other things to think about. If they can't even manage that, they can't run the country either.' And that was that. Penwoman moved on with the scent of every coffee party in Sweden in her nostrils. A little further on, a kindly-looking old gentleman was sitting on his own. But when she explained her purpose, he leapt up from the bench, purple in the face.

'Women have rights without making us suffer all this suffrage, young lady,' he said, and Penwoman beat a rapid retreat, to avoid being the cause of an apoplectic seizure.

'Let's hear what women without men in tow have to say about that,' thought Penwoman, and headed for a couple of old maids who were sitting over their crochet work at the side of the main walk. At the very word suffrage, they began to hiss and spit like angry cats, and Penwoman could not deny herself the pleasure of staying to provoke an argument. But they refused to engage in conversation with the girl, addressing

only each another: 'Such ill-bred, impudent hussies, Amalia.'
'Yes, my dear Sofie, they stop at nothing to make themselves
seem important. In our day, that young miss would have got
the treatment she deserved. And if she still will not go and
leave us in peace, we shall call for a police officer.'

'I can do that for you,' said Penwoman obligingly. 'Did you
want one particular officer, or would any of them do?'

A loud and lively group of men and girls came strolling past
Berns, and one of them asked Penwoman: 'What sort of paper
is it?'

'*Votes for Women*,* she replied stoutly. The girls began to
roar with laughter. 'We vote for the men,' they said.

'I'm afraid you ladies can't even do that,' Penwoman
answered gently.

'Oh yes we can,' and there was a great deal of laughing and
joking, but Penwoman was already out of earshot.

Emerging from the park, she saw Mrs Kjell a little way off,
and went over to her with a sigh of relief. 'You know what,'
she said, 'I was so touched to see a genuine suffragist that it
brought tears to my eyes.'

'The longer one lives, the more touching the suffragists
seem,' responded Mrs Kjell. 'Now come on, let's go and get
fresh supplies of papers.'

They were the first to be welcomed back by Jane Horneman
and to hand in their takings, but before very long, the whole of
the initial wave of newspaper sellers had returned.

'I have done all I can for now,' said Cecilia. She looked pale
and exhausted.

'Yes, wasn't it diverting?' said Ester Henning. 'What do you
say to my cousin, who I ran into and tried to tempt to the
meeting tomorrow evening, since she's always so keen to be
known as interested and well-informed, so I thought it would
be easy. "Well thank you very kindly, it would have been a
pleasure, but I couldn't possibly not have time,* I have so
much to do." I suddenly worried that there must be some vital
task one had to do at home at just this time of year, so I asked

what it was: "Your children are in the country, aren't they, so are you getting new maids, then?"'

'"No no, but there are some things one simply cannot entrust to maids." My trepidation grew: what sort of things? "Well, I have started a new piece of sewing work, and I am hiring the tapestry pattern." "Oh well, in that case I understand," I said, but what do you say, girls, a pattern costs ten öre, one might almost think she was lying?'

'I'd believe anything now,' said Penwoman, 'but this past hour has certainly brought me to my senses. We get used to being among our own, among the enlightened and the outcast, and before we know it we've forgotten that great wall, which we tend not to notice because it says nothing unless spoken to. But it's there, all the same, and it's as well for us to know it.'

'As if we didn't, anyway,' smiled Jane Horneman, who was made to suffer ignominiously for her beliefs every day among her own circle. 'If only our enemies opposed us with reasoned argument, rather than mere feelings – '

'And scarcely that,' put in Mrs Kjell. 'They do it from some instinct, composed of a host of different ingredients, and not always the best kind. But we shall get the better of them.'

'But they are so many, and what are we?' asked Cecilia somewhat dejectedly.

'The Few who prepare the way, and we *will* succeed, for ours is real love,' said Ester Henning in her emphatic way.

'Oh yes, you know, I did feel in spite of everything that there was hope, on the whole, for – the men,' said Penwoman reflectively.

# CHAPTER 15

The next day, the first big rally day, Cecilia awoke with a headache that no poisonous powders could help to alleviate. But when she rose from her bed anyway and announced her intention to go to the rally, where she was entrusted with the sale of newspapers and pamphlets, a panic-stricken Kristin telephoned Penwoman, who came straight round on an empty stomach, convinced her friend was at death's door, for it really was that serious, according to Kristin.

She found Cecilia very pale and wan, but seated at the breakfast table, and smiling.

'You should really be in bed,' said Penwoman, and took a seat herself, for now that Cecilia was not going to die, she suddenly felt hungry.

'I must get up there and see to my publications,' Cecilia said firmly.

'Well I'm glad you realise how indispensable you are,' replied Penwoman, pouring herself a cup of coffee. 'That's a sign of life, at least.'

'Indispensable, no; it's true I've become naive and childlike all over again, but I have not taken leave of my senses. If I had been in a state like this a year ago, I would have been lying immobile in bed with the curtains drawn and eau de cologne compresses on my brow, but since then I have acquired a certain amount of ambition. It exasperates me that it can so truthfully be said of us, that we are dependent on our physique. If I stay at home in bed today, and on other important days, there will always be people who will say: see, that is women for you; when it really matters, ten to one their headaches will keep them to their rooms. So I am coming with you.'

Penwoman realised there was no point trying to make her change her mind, and in any case, she could not but agree with her. But it remained a mystery to her how this iron-willed individual that Cecilia was increasingly proving herself to be could once have lost both her will and her spirit so entirely to a man, that it had taken years, and a powerful external stimulus, to rouse her from her stupor.

'And what was it that was so wonderful and unique about that man, I wonder?' Penwoman asked herself, but her question remained unanswered, for how could she, who had never herself awoken from love, have any idea that what is wonderful and unique about the one you love so often turns out to be something within yourself, yourself and the love that transforms everything.

'It's like I said, the suffrage does help,' she thought. She dared not admit, even to herself, a suspicion that had been coming and going: that it had been a hollow boast on her part, when she claimed there was now something for a woman in the world, to help her get over losing Dick if she ever needed to.

There was no suffrage in the world, however, that would have made it possible for Cecilia to eat anything just then, which was why Penwoman and Kristin, in strictest secrecy, made a pack of sandwiches to be produced if she felt better a little later in the morning. Then the two friends set off for the rally at a gentle pace, with Kristin's dismayed gaze following them from the window. Her belief in the benefits of votes for women had been seriously shaken and would remain so for some time.


It proved a hot and exhausting day, but interest in the subjects under discussion at the rally served Cecilia better than any headache powders could. For her, thrust headlong into the work of the movement, oblivious to the bigger picture of its origins and methods, it came as a revelation to see the task in the context of the developments of the age and women's part in them, and to learn of the many and varied interests that lay behind the enforced concentration on this single issue: suffrage for women. Her despondency of the previous day had been exchanged for boundless amazement that she had not always and of her own accord appreciated all these things, which now seemed so simple and self-evident; that she could have spent year after year teaching French verbs and the most correct English pronunciation to her girls without thinking that they would become women, who would need the full legal rights of a citizen all too well. Why had hearing them talk of their future studies and professions prompted in her only a profound sadness as she contemplated all the disappointments and difficulties and poor rewards for their pains that lay ahead of them as women, without for one moment thinking: something can be done about that, if we band together? In the end, all these thoughts threatened to overwhelm her, and she felt she simply must voice them. So when the discussion turned to how the host of indifferent individuals could be won over and retained, she stood up, very pale and shy, and testified to her new faith, simply and in too quiet a voice, but with such warmth underlying her few words, that no one could fail to be moved. And as she ended, suddenly confident and smiling, by declaring that becoming a suffragist was the best thing to have happened to her in the last ten years, she was interrupted by spontaneous applause. Penwoman clapped frantically, with tears running down her face; but from the corner where Miss Adrian and the anonymous letters were sitting, a sneering whisper was heard: as far as that was concerned, she hadn't exactly had much to look forward to, with her broken engagement!

By the end of the morning's proceedings, it was the end of Cecilia, too; she hurried home and did not join the others for a meal, or to sell any more newspapers in the streets. But when she set out again a few hours later, somewhat recovered, she encountered massed ranks of women making their way to the meeting in the cool of the evening, chatting together as fellow citizens.

It was to be an open meeting, with various well-known speakers, male and female, and a large venue had been hired in the expectation of a good turnout from the public.

Penwoman was already wandering round the as yet sparsely filled auditorium selling papers and pamphlets, and Ester Henning was adjusting the flags decorating the platform, when Cecilia appeared in the doorway. They exchanged perfunctory greetings from a distance, and Cecilia went over to her table by the door, where she found a pile of coins and a scribbled note saying: 'Have sold 100 *Votes for Women* papers, 50 "Why Mrs Håkansson Joined the Suffrage Society" and 45 "Why Should Women Wait?" Penwoman. P.S. The overpayment is all from gentlemen.'

Ester Henning came over and was impelled by the morning's events to shake Cecilia energetically by the hand. Cecilia showed her Penwoman's note, and they laughed as they looked over at the girl, who was at that moment engrossed in conversation with a gentleman, as keenly interested as he could possibly be.

'Thank you very much,' said this unknown and surprising fellow seriously, 'I already have your newspaper. It was purchasing it yesterday evening that made me come here. But I did not buy it from any of you,' he hastily added. 'I decided that since I was free this evening, I could at least come and find out what you suffragists have to say for yourselves, and see what you look like at close quarters.'

'You were quite right,' nodded Penwoman. 'One has to keep up with the times. And we are "the times", you see. It's beyond me why not everybody realises that we're actually awfully exciting, every bit as much as the socialists.'

'How do you mean?' he asked in amusement.

'Because though they are more powerful and there are more of them, people know a lot less about us and what we are going to get up to. The socialists have already told us everything about themselves, of course, but ask the *historici** if there are any analogies to our movement. Now I must get on; there are people sitting here, simply hungering for knowledge. It would be a very good thing if you let yourself be converted.' She gave him a friendly nod and moved on to the next man.

The serious gentleman watched her go.

So that pretty little head concealed plans to transform the look of the whole world? She really did seem to have no thoughts of anything beyond this utterly new and fascinating game. But what of women's mission in life, he thought, bewildered. When does a woman like that have time for loving, for us, for our joys and sorrows, our food and our socks? Now admittedly, it is when men love that they most intently believe themselves destined to change the face of the earth, but surely it could not be the same for women?

Penwoman, meanwhile, continued along the rows with considerable success, but even as she sold, counted, gave change and canvassed with indefatigable zeal, she kept glancing towards the door, which opened to the street outside.

The closer it got to eight o'clock, the more distracted she became, and when she had sold every last paper and pamphlet, she did not arm herself with fresh supplies but stood against one wall, constantly scanning the audience, which had begun to swell, filling the rows of benches. Every male figure silhouetted against the light evening sky in the doorway was, shamefully enough, the object of her eager interest.

She kept looking at the clock, her brow furrowing into a frown, look, the General was going up onto the platform. But suddenly she beamed, full of sunshine, gave a sigh of relief and went over to her place at the reporters' table.

Well thank goodness, Dick had finally arrived. She had caught a glimpse of him, and they had exchanged a look over the heads of a thousand suffragists.

After a few words of welcome, the General had introduced her brother, the bank director, who to the great surprise of everybody except one person had volunteered to speak that evening. But Penwoman had still not managed to collect her thoughts enough to focus on what he was saying, and when she

151

awoke to her obligations to the *Liberal Morning News*, the speaker was well into his stride.

She leant across to the reporter next to her, the one who had expended so much pencil lead at meetings without the faintest idea what he was reporting.

'While women have come to realise the worth of citizenship and to feel their lack of voting rights as an evil, yet we continue to deny them what they desire, then every day is an insult (bravo)', wrote the man beside her with boundless indifference. Now wide awake again, Penwoman made a hasty note of what she had missed and then devoted her full attention to the bank director, who spoke with unusual warmth and forcefulness, and was quite unlike his everyday self. She could not resist taking a quick look at the General's face, which was as white and unmoving as a statue's; what might she be thinking? Anna Gylling sat there smiling. No one could be in any doubt that she was thinking about Mrs Veber, with malicious glee.

The bank director was followed by Ester Henning, who had one of her best days, and her audience were in a state of high excitement when she spoke of spirit of self-sacrifice and told her listeners they could be certain that women's cause would not become dear to women until they had all made sacrifices for it, and not just small ones, either.

'We should make a collection now,' thought Penwoman. 'We mustn't waste the inspired atmosphere of this evening's meeting.' And she put the idea to Jane Horneman, the treasurer, only to discover that Jane for her part had not heard a word since the bank director had left the podium and sent her a look as he went to sit beside the General.

Last to speak was Miss Morgonvind,* the Social Democrat. A few people who had got up to leave after clapping Ester, sat down again or loitered at the door to see a small, thin, blonde figure, so ludicrously young, almost childlike, but with the composure and confidence of a seasoned speaker. Penwoman tried to start a round of applause, for she certainly deserved one, and had looked a little bitter, but it did not really get off the ground; she was obviously not so well known to this audience.

People whispered to each other: 'She must have started young,' which made Penwoman smile. She knew, of course, that Miss Morgonvind's earliest memory was of Axel Danielsson* in his student cap, speaking new words to the crowd, speaking until she fell asleep in her father's arms, to be woken by cheers and applause. Knew, too, that Miss Morgonvind had grown up surrounded by speeches and debates, that it was many years since she had made her first public appearance, and that she had never simply lived, like other young people, but had always lived for her Movement.

In her speech, Miss Morgonvind took up where Ester Henning had left off. She looked a little stern as she quoted Ester's words about a cause only becoming dear to one's heart if one had made great sacrifices for it.

'We know what it means to make great sacrifices,' she said, and by 'we' she meant the Social Democrat women. 'Think what it is for us, working hard all day to earn a basic living – I am a factory worker myself, so I know what it means – to try to save enough energy and courage to work for an idealistic goal that lies far in the future! We really have made the big sacrifices. But then we are also the ones who have everything to gain,' she continued, and her pale cheeks took on a hint more colour, 'we are the ones who feel the yoke digging into our shoulders every day, and that yoke is what stops us forgetting and falling asleep, what gives us the strength to make sacrifices. We who work in unhealthy factories for poor wages, we who see our working hours and labour market regulated by Parliament, without that same Parliament lifting a finger to compensate us for the loss of earnings it is imposing on us out of "consideration for us and our children". Our children!' and she raised her voice higher, 'we are barred from working and earning money until they are four weeks old, but what are we to do to avoid starving to death in the meantime?* What thanks do we get, for bringing new children into the world for factories and armies? If a mother goes to the maternity hospital to have her baby, the help she is given there counts as poor relief! If we ever get the suffrage the middle-class movement is working for, which is to say, suffrage on the same terms as men,* then the logical consequence will be that a mother like that, who does her duty as a citizen and brings a new human being into the world, will immediately lose her right to vote, as will the widow who receives a meagre state allowance in her struggle to provide for her children and bring them up!'

Some Social Democrats applauded. Miss Morgonvind closed her eyes and tried to recapture the train of thought from which she had digressed to talk about maternity care.

'So you see,' she went on with complete composure, 'it's hardly surprising that it takes so little to persuade us working women to join the suffrage movement. There's no need to make speeches to us about rights and duty, or stir us up with talk of the insult we suffer,' – at this the bank director smiled an ambiguous smile, and many eyes swivelled in his direction – 'for we know from bitter daily experience that we must have the vote, that we must have shelter and food, better skills, wages, places to live. And for that reason, our men understand very well that our demand is justified, and they campaign for us – yes they did, as soon as they had the chance,' she added a little hotly in answer to a violent shake of the head from Kerstin Vallmark, whose honest soul could not quite reconcile itself to Miss Morgonvind's words.

By the time the meeting was finally over, it was almost ten o'clock, and Penwoman's report would be a long one, but even if it meant working past midnight, she must have a word with Dick before she went down to the paper. If only he realised, but he did, because there he was, making his way quickly and a little carelessly through the crowd. As she stood waiting for him, the elegant lady from the previous day came up.

'I am one of you from now on,' she said, extending her hand.

Penwoman beamed at her. It was all such a joy: the whole day, Cecilia, this evening, the heightened atmosphere, which was vibrating within her in Carl Larsson's words: 'Now is the time to set great, clear bells ringing – .'* And now this, all the more gratifying for being so totally unexpected. Dick had to wait while she took the convert over to Jane, to have her name officially registered with the treasurer. The two ladies clearly knew one another, and Jane seemed astonished, despite her best efforts to conceal the fact. As the lady entered her distinguished name in the register in her noble hand, Jane whispered to Penwoman: 'Are you the one who – ?' and when the girl shook her head, said 'Well whoever it was, this is a day for celebration.' Penwoman would like to have lingered, but there was Dick, looking impatient.

'Well then Dick, what did you think?'

'Oh,' said Dick in his laconic fashion, 'it wasn't as bad as I'd thought.'

'What, darling?'

'You lot wanting to change everything and take our jobs and give us yours, and just brush us aside,' replied Dick, a trifle provocatively. 'In fact, you want the vote because you're all so very, very feminine and all that. You could have said so sooner, instead of going in for starched shirts and men's ties, and smoking and – '

'So was that all you wanted to tell me?' said Penwoman darkly.

'No, actually, what I came over for – was to ask – can I join the suffrage association, too?'

'You are only joking, aren't you?' said Penwoman incredulously. At that moment she caught sight of the earnest gentleman, who was hovering nearby, looking as though he had something to say to her. And since it seemed so appropriate after what Dick had just done, she went over to him.

'Is there any way of showing you that I have been convinced?' he asked, regarding her intently.

'You can convert your wife, for a start,' said Penwoman, and smiled.

'Anything but that,' replied the earnest gentleman, with a hint of a smile himself.

'Oh, it does them nothing but good,' put in a jovial, elderly gentleman who happened to hear their exchange as he passed by. 'The suffrage has made an entirely different person out of my wife. All her whims and ailments have gone, now she has something to interest her. So the best of luck to you.'

'A male friend of the suffrage campaign is always a help, by his very existence,' went on Penwoman, as the earnest man was looking despondent. 'And all our friends will have the chance to do us a good turn at the polls this autumn.' They shook hands cordially, and the earnest man somewhat enviously watched Dick at once pick up Penwoman's papers and follow her out of the hall into the dusk.

'She seems to have time to think about love between meetings, anyway,' he sighed.

# CHAPTER 16

This was a summer unlike any other. For the Hard Labour Gang, there was no question of taking a holiday and bidding farewell to each other for the summer as usual. And if any Gang member catching the ferry to the archipelago bumped into a civilian acquaintance, as they had come to be known, and the latter remarked how nice summer was, a chance to laze about and enjoy life, though there were always the mosquitoes to contend with, she would have to concentrate hard for a moment before remembering that there were real, live people taking time off, regardless of that autumn's elections to the Lower Chamber. But if she then said: 'Yes, that would be lovely, if it weren't for the polls,' she would be reminded, by a blank look failing to comprehend which poles were meant, that such strange people really did exist.

Ever since the Hard Labour Gang had made the house at Saltsjö Bay its campaign headquarters after the summer rally, everyone had been extremely busy.

'Though they don't deserve any praise for it, because they're having such a good time,' said Penwoman. Not a week went by without one of the Gang going off on a preaching tour; one day Jane Horneman returned from Gästrikland, moved and delighted, another time it was Kerstin Vallmark from Skåne or Ester Henning from Halland, or her sister, who had become such a fearless suffragette in England, from Blekinge, and so on. Or their headquarters would play host to people from the regions who were passing through on the campaign trail, such as Mrs Kjell and other well-known preachers, and for two days their flag was flying for Frigga Carlberg.* All of this kept them in constant touch with the whole country; whenever good news came in, it was cause for particular celebration that evening, with everyone gathered after work on the verandah overlooking the sea, and Kristin's bill of fare – for she was the fixed star among all these restless planets, whirling about the country – Kristin's bill of fare, then, changed to match the political situation in the land. The Executive Committee met a couple of times a week; its main problem was finding enough people to do all the canvassing they considered vital. Experience showed them, every day, that it was a matter of teaching women their political ABC, and they were realising what a short time they had left for such a huge task.

'Well we've helped to spice up the election campaign, at any rate,' Kerstin Vallmark would say, emerging from her room with inky satisfaction at dinner time, for she was engaged in controversial dialogue with newspapers in virtually every part of the country.

'This is supposed to be their summer holiday,' said Kristin crossly. 'They just slave away and take no time off, getting browner and skinnier as summer goes by. I'm only standing for it as long as my own Miss Cecilia doesn't have to go on one of them there tours.'

And Cecilia was indeed chained to her desk, dealing with the vast amounts of correspondence generated by the arrangements for all the tours, answering letters and enquiries from every quarter, some from suffrage associations, others from voters' groups and parliamentary candidates, some from simple farmers, who sent 'brotherly' requests for a speaker to come and talk about the suffrage in their local district, 'and if she happened to know anything about politics, then so much the better if she could refer to the current situation'.

Her colleagues often suggested that she might like to vary her work by undertaking a tour, but she always declined, on the pretext that she did not feel any inclination to explain the workings of the vast system she had now mastered to anyone else. The truth was, she liked her part of the work, which brought little glory, if that had been what she sought, but was uniform, steady and demanding. She liked her workplace by the window, with the great, windblown pine just outside and the roar of the sea, which would fade away in the evenings, once the last streak of sunshine had fled the room. The evening's walk and conversation, the hard-won night's rest were all she felt she needed in the way of refreshment. Who was she, to have any pretensions to inspire an audience, and, to think of herself for a moment – it was not such a simple thing, a heart; it contained so much, that might spill out at dusk at a silent railway station, as one waited for the train to Värnamo.

Penwoman, who had kept her distance for the first week, turned up more and more often as the summer wore on, appearing in the evening when she knew she would not be disturbing anyone to hear the latest news from the battlefield, and nobody asked her where she had come from or where she went when she left. Sometimes they would send for her, if they needed an instant article on the mood in Norrland or women's electoral duties; Cecilia was the only one who knew the telephone number, but nobody found anything strange in that. Dick had contributed to the political campaign by making a kind of primitive speaker's rostrum, which was used at a couple of open air meetings at the village nearby, and it was naturally from that very rostrum Penwoman delivered her maiden speech.

This took place one Saturday evening in August, but it was a debut that had caused Penwoman some soul-searching in advance. The thought was expressed first by Kerstin Vallmark, who had once met Dick and Penwoman together and later referred to him in her innocence as 'your brother'. Penwoman was so delighted that she forgot to pay any attention to what the rest of the Hard Labour Gang thought on the subject, and the possibility of reservations did not even occur to her, until one night, one night when she was sitting in bed, watching the dawn break, and thinking about the demands that the motto 'The Suffrage Can See You' might make on her personally. For a few days she said nothing, and that continued to be the case on the day she asked the deputy editor for some time off to deal with some personal business and made her way quietly to the General's house, agonising over the possibility that she was about to make a fool of herself.

But once she was seated in the library, alone with the General and ready to talk about her life, for which she had never felt obliged to account to anybody before, she found that her instinct had guided her wisely, and it would not be so very awful to do the right thing as she had thought.

'It is never an entirely private matter, how we run our lives,' said the General, who seemed instantly to understand everything, 'least of all if we wish to stand up publicly for a cause that is also espoused by others. But the fact remains that we are not obliged to let ourselves be judged by just any old body.' So Penwoman told the whole story, while the General listened, thinking with a grave smile how strange it was that she, the recipient of so many confidences, had never been faced with this problem before, but presumably it had not arisen for those women busily working away for her so competently all over the country. She asked a few questions, which Penwoman answered without hesitation, then embraced the girl and sent her away, relieved of any reservations about speaking for the suffrage, but burdened with a debt of gratitude to the General that she would never be able to discharge.

Dick knew nothing about any of this. It was as if he had forgotten his own misgivings at the start of the summer, and he took Penwoman's hesitance for beginner's nerves, natural for anyone who had never spoken in public before.

'Well,' he would say, 'when are you going to stand up and let your voice proclaim words of truth to station hands, boarding house guests and the women who work in the baker's?'

In the end she tired of his teasing and made up her mind on the spot: 'I shall do it on Sunday!' Dick was very pleased to hear it. 'Then we can have a bit of peace and quiet,' he said.


Penwoman was in a very solemn mood as she parted from Dick outside Villa Borgis and made her solitary way to the suffragists' camp, brooding as she went.

When Cecilia, glancing out of her window, saw Penwoman coming across the grass, she could see her anxiety even from a distance. She knew how it felt; it was not that long, after all, since she had been in the same painful situation for the first time, and she hurried down and took her into the dining room on the ground floor. All traces of activity had been cleared away that evening; the only item on the big table, usually covered in letters or leaflets, was a bunch of stocks in a copper jug, and in the window lay a worldly novel, the property of Jane Horneman. Only the huge map of a Sweden on which they had expended such effort, covered in marks and underlinings, showing routes and indicating places already taken, hinted at what happened here in the mornings.

Jane Horneman rose after one look at Penwoman, a look that took in both her blue and white sailor dress and her miserable white face, and went out to get a glass of wine, but in the doorway she met Kristin, who had seen Penwoman for herself and had already fetched a bottle from the cellar.

'Well, what are you going to tell our friends in Klaravik?' asked Kerstin Vallmark, emerging from her room in waxcloth sleeve protectors, inky-fingered as ever. She was in the middle of an article, for though everyone else was taking an evening off, she had never rested since joining five years ago, and nor would she, until she lay beneath that gravestone on which the inscription was to read: '*Equal pay for equal work*'.

'I shall say,' said Penwoman, shaking, 'well, you know, I shall say – that it isn't a question of imposing some new order, or dragging women by force, as some people are claiming, out of their homes – '. Penwoman raised her head just a little, and there was Kristin, standing staring from the kitchen door in such a state of petrification that she convulsed with laughter and forgot all her carefully thought out phrases.

'Go on,' commanded the schoolmistress strictly.

'I've forgotten, girls, no, wait a minute, and that therefore those who imagine they are fighting to preserve good old customs are merely fighting against what is being done to assimilate into society the new conditions that are already a fact – and that, – please go Kristin, – that our opponents are behaving as foolishly as if they were to try to stop a builder putting in floors and papering walls, when he has already built the walls and roof. Will that do?'

'Splendidly,' said Jane Horneman kindly. 'That bit about the house – '

'Don't be afraid,' nodded Cecilia encouragingly, 'I shall prompt you.'

'Good Lord, it's your first time, when all's said and done, and nobody expects miracles,' added Kerstin Vallmark, which was easy enough for her to say, given the nationwide acclaim she had enjoyed.

By the time Penwoman was on the rostrum, all her nerves had vanished. She glanced around and saw Dick at once; his look was that of a worried mother, which instantly put her in a good mood. The audience was small enough for her to be able to pick out all her friends, and she felt safe knowing they were there. The crowd looked good-natured, a little taken aback but intrigued enough; the evening sun was shining into the depths of the forest before her, making it look endless, filled with peace and security. She checked in her mind, and found everything mapped out there, right up to the resolution, which was to be her final point.

It went better than she had expected; not everything she had to say was understood, of course, and many of her painstakingly devised images and well-constructed phrases went to waste, much as she had feared, but *nobody walked away*! Her childlike seriousness and her slender little form, silhouetted against the evening sky, were in her favour, though she did not know it it.

She had had a few bursts of applause, initiated by Dick and seconded by Kristin, who had been practising for a whole week and was growing warm and red in both heart and the cheek, when the circle was suddenly broken by a gaggle of young people, far from reserved and not inclined to respect the gravity and importance of the moment. They were panama-hatted young men smoking cigarettes, and girls in white with walking sticks and big hats.

Penwoman raised her voice a little:

'Women have awoken,' she said sternly.

'Yes, but on the wrong side,' quipped one of those who had just arrived.

Penwoman stopped, leaned forward and looked at the man who had spoken.

Ah, it was none other than the Scanian from the boarding house. All at once she felt as much at home as if she were in Mrs

Bengtsson's parlour.

'Well, that side is too good for the likes of you,' she retorted, without stopping to consider whether it was advisable or not, but a short silence followed, and she went on speaking, apparently quite unruffled.

'This would be a good place for dancing the boston,' said a young lady in a loud whisper after a minute or so.

'Yes, and the band would have to be up there.'

'Let's ask her to stop then, shall we?'

Penwoman, who dared not improvise for fear of losing her thread, was suddenly beside herself. Who knows whether her whole talk might not have dissolved into wild disarray, but then she recalled that there was always the *Liberal Morning News* to fall back on! The thought restored her equilibrium, her brain supplied the sentences and expressions she had memorised, but all the while she had a depressing sense of two worlds confronting each other, full of hostility and contempt, and there was nothing that could build a bridge between them.

She had very little idea of what she had said in the preceding five minutes, when she stepped down from Dick's lectern to sarcastic cheers from the reprimanded Scanian.

'I shall have to get Dick to hit him,' she thought, and laughed at the fact that she, a modern woman, God help her, should be obliged to take refuge in such an outdated tactic. How often through the ages had Dick been told to hit out, and Dick had hit and been hit back, and it clearly made not the slightest difference, whether or not Dick's woman was a member of the suffrage association.

By the time she had received her friends' congratulations and a few words of advice for the future from the schoolmistress, who was not a teacher for nothing, Dick was just finishing with the Scanian, who had been told what a bad lot he was, and they set off home together.

She said nothing for a while, but suddenly turned an agitated little face up to his.

'Dick, there's simply no limit to how much I want you to spoil me and kiss me!'

'You're a clever girl,' said Dick comfortingly, 'and that's why you're going to be married to me before long.'

The girl was glad that Dick would never know how for a second her soul, which was just dreaming of making itself into a great orator, closed itself to his words and his hopeful joy.

'Oh Dick,' she said quietly, 'dear Dick, but that can't happen for a long time, can it?'

'Who knows,' said Dick, and had she been a little less distracted, she would have noticed he was in possession of a few ideas he was not yet ready to share with her.

'I want us to talk about our home,' he went on suddenly, a little impatiently, as if he could read her thoughts after all.

She was seized with remorse.

'Yes, let's, Dick,' she said.

'You don't know,' he said, pressing her arm close to him, 'what building a house is like. First visualising it, and then seeing it turn out as you imagined. When it's time for us to build, I want to dig the foundations in the ground myself, I want to hew the timber, I want to build walls, log by log, I want to see it rise, and we shall take delight in every inch. I want to raise the roof truss and top it off with the wreath myself, but you will have made the wreath. I want to be involved in every detail, and not a single nail will be banged in without me knowing about it. And every evening you'll come with me, and we'll see it looking more and more like a place people can live in, us, you and me, and there won't be a better house anywhere.'

'Beloved,' said Penwoman, moved by this long speech, 'beloved, our home – '

She felt a vague dissatisfaction with herself for having been so absorbed in her own affairs when he had been speaking of their home to the end of their days. For a single moment her clear young eyes caught a glimpse of something that had never worried her before: the hint of a conflict, for which there was not usually any room in her distinct, somewhat programmatic interpretation of life.

But Dick went on telling her about his vision and his plans for the future, and soon she was simply Dick's beloved, settling into the home his thoughts were building for her.

# CHAPTER 17

'Well Dick, here's something for you to contemplate in your solitary state: a year ago, we didn't know each other; we could have met on Drottninggatan without any draught from the wings of fate telling us we were about to attain the fulfilment of our lives, and now look at us! I carry a permanent warm feeling in my heart, and it's the memory of the happiness I've had and the riches that are waiting for me. And the best thing about this happiness is that I needn't worry about having used any of it up in advance; it's all ahead of me, and here I am craning forward to our reunion, the same as I lent forward for your first kiss. It's limitless, isn't it, this joy we've been granted the privilege of giving each other?

You're right, Dick, your Östergötland is a fine place, and yet you can have no notion of the splendour and glory all around me. You'll remember that for the two days that my suffrage crusade took me to Fredevi, I was to stay with the WSA chairman, who is also the teacher at the elementary school, and you'll be wondering, despite your local patriotism, if it's possible that even suffragists in this land of Goshen* live in great pomp and luxury. That's not the case, however, nor am I using the expression because I want to flatter you. But I find myself staying at the Manor, and now I shall tell you the whole story from the beginning.

I was met off the train by the aforementioned teacher, with whom I was to stay, plus a lively little photographer girl, who's the association secretary, and the county law officer's wife, their treasurer. We'd hardly had time to shake hands before a man in livery came up and asked for me. Yes, here I was, and he gave me a letter; I pretended not to be curious, and held it unopened for a few moments, until I saw that none of the suffragists would take the least notice of what I was saying until they knew what the letter said. As my esteemed reader will already have guessed, the letter was from Baron Starck, and the Baron's entailed estate* dominates that part of the county. He wrote: "Dear Miss Penwoman, I have seen from posters about the town that you are to address the suffrage association this evening, and that the constituency's parliamentary representatives are invited to speak about their respective stances on votes for women. Although we are in other respects 'political opponents', we are nonetheless united by our fervent interest in women's rights, and it would give me great pleasure if you would be my guest at Fredevi Manor while you are conducting your political campaign in Fredevi. It might interest you to see the house, and I can offer you the company of some young women of your own age."

I read this very slowly, while making up my mind to stay where I'd originally been invited, even though I thought it rather aggravating, since I'm only human.

"Madam Chairman," I said, "the Baron is inviting me to stay at the Manor. Can I ask this footman to pass on my reply, or do you think I need to write and tell him you have already offered your hospitality?"

Naturally she couldn't just answer my query, but started bombarding me with questions: did I know the Baron, how come, good heavens above, and so on.

"I shall tell you all the details when we get to your house," I replied, "but please advise me what to do, first."

"My house?" she said, "Whatever are you thinking of, now the Baron has invited you to the Manor! You don't seem to realise that the Baron can make us or break us, as the whim takes him. Think what it will do for our just cause round here when word gets out that the speaker at the WSA meeting stayed at the Manor!"

The county law officer's wife and the photographer said the

same, and I didn't deny myself the pleasure of letting them persuade me, but then I went off to the Manor in the Baron's car, and it was most agreeable for a democrat to feel she was using that aristocratic mode of transport for the benefit of the people. Or to put it another way, I was naturally exhilarated, very curious, and a little bit flattered. I knew nothing of what lay in wait for me, of course, but I soothed myself with the thought that I had clean, white clothes, a clear conscience and a terrific amount of cheek. You get a long way with those, and Dick, I *have* got a long way, I can't keep it from you any longer!

As the car turned in and stopped at the base of the steps leading up to a beautiful old house in what I took to be Dutch Renaissance style, the Baron came out, dressed in white, friendly but a bit nervous, whether of me or on his own account I can't say.

"Allow me to introduce you to my ladies," he said, as soon as I was out of the car.

"Yes, let's get it over and done with," I said, because you see, he'd have been disappointed if I hadn't behaved a bit oddly, but I hadn't the heart to refuse altogether, with him having invited me and everything.

We went straight through the house – I'll tell you later about all the lovely old tapestries and things – and found four ladies on a terrace, one older, who seemed to me to be as angry as a bee, though not quite so busy, and three younger, sitting there all white and freshly in bloom on their elegant stalks, waiting to be picked. They were the Baron's sister-in-law, who was once mistress of the Manor, when the estate was her late husband's, and her three daughters, who were now guests of their uncle in their former family home – which you might imagine would have made feminists of them, but they don't think that far. Simply going round thinking I should have been sons would definitely have been enough to turn me into a suffragist, if I hadn't been one already. I was naturally very well received, because they were a better class of people and I was their guest, despite being ten times over "an unfortunate idea of Karl

August's". But it seemed to me so awfully strange, that I was there as a young girl keeping company with those over-cultivated roses – an infinite distance divided me and my life from them and theirs. It's not that I'm so much older than them, because I think the eldest and I have both experienced equal slices of our lives; no, it's more that the similarity in age makes it all so astounding. When I hear them talk, it's like listening to a fairy tale; I knew such people existed, of course, but every time I set eyes on them, I realise I didn't really believe it! I don't think they find the contrast as funny as I do; they can't see it in enough perspective for that, all they see is the outward appearance; but that's not where the tremendous distinction lies, though they have breeding and cambric where I'm self-made and homespun. I'm not trying to deny, of course, that to some extent I despise them, but on the other hand I can see that this luxury girl is the logical product of prevailing conditions. She's lazy, while we collapse under the weight of our work, and she doesn't thank us for it, she looks down on us, but then she's never learnt or needed to do anything else, and how many of us have sufficient resources within ourselves for work to grow from us spontaneously, as a natural release of the force of our nature? She's a little unsympathetic and indifferent, hardhearted one might say, but she has never had a chance to experience the hardship and suffering that teach people to know any better; she seems a bit empty and dull, but then God didn't give her a goal to live for or light a fire in her breast.

Can you picture me in the middle of all this, consigned to maintaining a balance between the Baron, who's dancing attendance on me – and it's only now I can really understand his insuperable astonishment at me – and the ladies, who only put up with me because they are so well-mannered, but who look as if they are expecting this strange insect to spread its wings and fly round the table or utter weird cries. Be that as it may, only the old lady stayed at home when it was time for the meeting. Word had spread among the locals that the WSA had the patronage of the Manor, and the place was packed when we arrived. I suppose we must have caused a sensation, but I was so scared that I couldn't see or hear a thing. I obediently gave my talk, though, and there's no need for me to tell you what it was about, since you tested me on it until you knew it better than I did. The Baron was the first to start clapping, so naturally a rousing round of applause followed, and I was as happy as a schoolgirl put straight up to the next class.

Then it was supposed to be the parliamentary candidates' turn, but the existing old incumbent hadn't turned up, so only his younger rival went on stage to testify, and he, by contrast, had had the sense to attune himself to the mood, so he promised to work positively for women's suffrage and eligibility for election. But the high point of the evening was the Baron, who "though aware he was not addressing his electorate, still considered this a suitable moment to express his sympathies with women's struggle for citizenship and wish Fedevi WSA good luck and great success."

That's what you call a man who keeps his word, wouldn't you say?

In short, it was a most blessed meeting, many souls were saved and entered in the suffrage register, and the committee was so touched it was almost embarrassing – I couldn't let on that it was all because of my bet with the Baron!

When we got back to the Manor that evening, there sat the dilatory Member of Parliament with the dowager Baroness – he'd been invited to supper. "I assumed you would come to the WSA meeting," said the Baron with a fearfully knowing look.

So not even triumph over our enemies was denied us on that eventful day, a triumph as complete as anyone could wish. We did everything we could to be subtly unpleasant to him, and all young girls are equally good at that art, whether they belong to the upper crust and have been presented at court, or like me have to turn their intelligence into underclothes and daily bread.

No one must blame the man for wanting to be unpleasant back, but it was a shame he landed himself in such trouble.

"Yes," he said, for naturally we were taking about the

suffrage, "you ladies are so keen to have it, but you should not be so angry with those of us who are holding things back a little, because presumably all the time you carry on campaigning, there are quite a few of you making a living from the suffrage?" He obviously thought he had trumped me with that, but then the most remarkable thing of all happened, the thing he least expected: the Baron piped up and rebuked him, with what? With my own words, with everything I had said about the campaign being run by self-supporting women, who have nothing to give but their overtime labour, but they give that to the very last scrap.

It went very quiet round the baronial table, the women looked at me, I maintained my composure right to the point where the Baron's speech ended in a toast to me and the suffrage, and then I blushed like a schoolgirl.

At the risk of you sending for me by telegram, I have to tell you that the day ended with the Baron showing me the garden in the autumn moonlight. He is my latest conquest, but the fact only dawned on me when I was back in my room.

I assure you, my darling, *I* don't want him, but I'd be very happy to see him married into the suffrage movement!

I'm glad I shall be leaving here in a few hours, with the prospect of the remainder of my trip going as smoothly and dispassionately as a suffrage lecture tour should.

Until we meet again, my beloved.

*Penwoman*.'

CHAPTER 18

'The suffrage has never had such a busy social life before this autumn,' said Anna Gylling.

'And never have such foreign customs been allowed to creep in among us, either,' added Kerstin Vallmark, with a reproachful look at Cecilia, who was looking very guilty in her capacity as hostess for the evening.

'You know what, girls,' came a voice from the corner where Ester Henning was curled up, 'I for one see nothing to regret in the extravagances of the past few days. As a doctor, I see them as springing from a natural instinct for self-preservation; they have quite simply prevented us dying of election nerves. If we, now the campaign is over and there is nothing to do but wait for the results, had sat at home in our rooms brooding about one thing after another that could conceivably have been done to stop our candidate losing in Filipstad or Vimmerby, then we'd all have been fit for the sanatorium. And even as things stand, I am not so sure how Penwoman is feeling.'

The girl had not joined the suffragists for their meal; she had just arrived, and was sitting over by the door in an oddly strained and listening pose that was not at all relaxing.

'It is just as well that it will soon be over, then we can all die,' Kerstin Vallmark said comfortingly, looking abnormally small and worn out as she sat there in Cecilia's best chair, smoking a lot and saying little.

Silence descended. Penwoman got up and went out but immediately came back in again, as if she had changed her mind, and resumed her place without a word. The silence continued. No one had the heart to say for the hundredth time:

'How do you think it's going?' and they knew it would be another hour before there was any point ringing any of the papers or making their way to Gustaf Adolf Square.*

It was election day, and things had been hectic.

Kerstin Vallmark had been called to the telephone during her morning lesson, for an urgent, indignant voice to inform her of a mean and unforeseen electoral trick discovered by the informant at one of the polling stations, which with every passing minute was harming the interests that were also the suffragists'. The student teachers, to whom she had transmitted her interest in politics, exchanged looks as she came back into class from the telephone, pale with pent-up anger and energy.

'There are twenty minutes of the lesson left,' she said, 'but you will have to take care of yourselves. There are great things at stake.'

'Can we help you, Miss?' the girls asked with one voice.

A mischievous glint came into her eye, but was extinguished in a second. No, you did not send the top class out as sandwich-men, however much you wanted to, and however badly you needed them in that capacity.

'Well yes, actually,' she said after a minute's thought, 'you can get yourselves into pairs and go on patrol, cover all the polling stations between you and report back at once how things are going. You'll have time for that before your next lesson.' The girls set off, beaming with delight and importance, while Kerstin Vallmark spent the next half hour on the telephone, working in that hard and focused way that her concentrated energy sometimes allowed.

First she rang Anna Gylling: 'We need to borrow the General's car for the whole day. Come at once and I'll tell you the details when you get here.'

Then Ester Henning: 'If you are prepared to spend twenty kronor and your morning on it, then get some people to the polling stations and tell them to stay put and watch out for foul play. You say it's hard to get away? Well, I haven't missed work for a single day in five years, except twice: when I was summoned to attend on the King, and later the Prime Minister. But I'm doing it today.'

Then Penwoman: 'Sit straight down and write a warning to go in the evening papers, and see if you can get a few thousand flyers printed too, but quickly. Ring Cecilia and tell her that her dinner will have to be a supper, try to get her to come along and then don't budge from Östermalm, because that's where it's worst. I've already put the drawing teacher to work: she's making a huge poster we can take round in the General's car. Jane, Anna and I will do it. There, that's the entire Hard Labour Gang set to work!'

Now, however, polling was almost over, and there was nothing to do but wait. Someone suddenly broke the silence with the suggestion that they look in the evening paper to make sure the warning had really been printed.

'I'll go,' said Penwoman quickly, and vanished from the room. But they had all got to their feet, as if at a signal.

'I can't bear sitting here any longer – nor I – let's all go together.' Cecilia caught Penwoman in the hall, about to slip out of the door.

'What's wrong?' she whispered.

'It's Dick,' said Penwoman, looking at her for a moment with desperation in her eyes.

'That's why I've thrown myself into polling day,' she added with a sort of smile, then pulled gently away from Cecilia and was gone.

The group had come to life again; only Cecilia walked in silence in the midst of all their chatter and election anecdotes, watching Penwoman scurry up the empty quayside like a swift, sorrowful rat and disappear in among the trees of Berzelii Park.

'Now, Penwoman,' she thought, 'the time has come for you to be put to the test.'

They decided to take a walk round all the polling stations, but there was not much to see; the focus of interest had plainly shifted to Gustaf Adolf Square.

Their route took them through the area where Cecilia had lived when she was twenty and ought to have been happy. Up there in a window, where a solitary orange lamp flame was now burning, she had sat at dusk after dusk with her head in her hands and her eyes patiently fixed on the point where somebody, if he had time and so on, would come into view and stroll briefly up and down, waiting, while she, who was supposed always to be ready, put on her coat and came down in a state of pure bliss. Back then, she had always imagined that the sharp corner of the brick wall would gradually be worn away by her gaze, and as they passed, she unobtrusively pulled off her glove and ran her hand experimentally up its edge, now, eight years later.

Outside the windows of the newspaper offices on the square, people were already standing in small clusters like bees outside a hive, but within a very short time the crowds were so thick that the news had to be passed from those standing at the front, out to the peripheries. By the time the first voting figures came in, the small clusters had fused into a mass, alive at every point and with various cores of energy from which a burning fire of interest spread over the square in the icily cold, damp autumn night.

One of the most charged of those energy cores comprised a small group of women, providing their animated and, as news trickled in, ever more hopeful commentary on the situation.

From up in the window of her paper, Penwoman had seen and recognised her friends, and now she cut her way through the masses like a thin little knife to reach them.

'We've just won ward five,* she said breathlessly, her whole face alight with emotion. 'It's going up in the window any moment.'

There was no helping it, they simply had to shake hands with each other.

'See, what did I tell you, there are the figures, and there's their defeat.'

'Their figures are poor.'

174

'They "thought too highly of women", and great was their fall,'* said Anna Gylling grimly.

'Another victory, listen to the cheers!' Ester Henning produced her handkerchief and waved it enthusiastically. The moment after, her comrades followed suit, and soon there were handkerchiefs fluttering like a cloud of butterflies above the black crowd while boys, out at night without permission, let out gratuitous yells, and the occasional hissing and whistling at an objectionable name merely added to the variety and exhilaration of the atmosphere.

'Are you off again, Penwoman?'

'Yes, I want to get back to the office. You should see the menfolk in there, all at their posts and working non-stop, exchanging nothing but figures with each other, steely-eyed and taut with energy – the air is totally charged in there; it's the only place on earth I can bear to be tonight, Cecilia.'

Minutes passed, hours passed, midnight came. Still everyone stood in the square, and did not feel tired. The mist thickened and the great bronze statue appeared more and more like a grey shadow you ought to be able to look straight through, and the electric light from the arc-lamp blurred like some ghostly halo about the dead king's head.

Penwoman scurried back and forth through the night between the newspaper offices and her friends in the square, who teased her for her impatience.

It was two in the morning when they left the square, but they were too happy, too exultant to part just like that, so they all went back to Cecilia's, where Kristin was waiting with the hottest coffee in the world. She had whiled away the time with some baking, and the result was immediately christened Election Night Cake. Wine arrived, they were flushed with victory, and the mood grew jubilant. They had worked so hard and here, they felt, was their reward. On this night, the prospects looked so hopeful and bright; they felt they could reach out their hand, and victory would be placed in it.

'How I look forward to some rest,' said Anna Gylling. 'I

shall make lace.'

'How I look forward to starting work in earnest,' said Kerstin Vallmark loudly.

All their hearts were open; out crept all their private little dreams, which otherwise remained hidden in the depths of those hearts. They had come from all directions and united around the suffrage, but now they had come so far, they felt that it could do no harm to discuss what to do with the oceans of time and energy they would have at their disposal, now they no longer had the vote to work for.

Only Anna Gylling, observing the assembled company, so pale and exhausted, said: 'I don't think there will be enough left of the suffragists to do much good once the day comes when they are no longer needed. No, you'll all just have to get used to the idea that you have generously sacrificed your lives to it, and now it's too late to have them back.'

'Nonsense,' said Kerstin a little disdainfully, 'I am 39 years old. Are you telling me I'm finished, once I get the vote? No, I have to have something to campaign for. I shall throw myself headlong into politics and it's my guess that a feminist will not need to worry about lack of occupation for the next hundred years.'

'I shall move to the country,' said Jane Horneman, her eyes sparkling.

'So you think keeping hens an appropriate and happy way of rounding off your career as a feminist?' Kerstin Vallmark put in a little vehemently.

She had not really meant anything by it, but Jane Horneman, who was dreaming lovely dreams of applications to Parliament for big grants for vocational schools for young women, felt snubbed and said nothing.

There was a pause.

'Beloved,' thought Penwoman, her hands clenched together, 'o beloved, I have boasted, I have been a hypocrite, I have been wrong. Nothing in the world can compensate a woman for losing the one she loves, I have learnt that now, and if I get you back, I shall always remember it. I shall be a very meek woman, my beloved, a very meek woman – '

'We shall all miss this time, even so,' said Jane Horneman at last, and as she spoke, they all suddenly realised there was a different mood in their hearts. 'All of us, who have been united by a single great and tangible goal, will go out into the world with our enterprises and pet projects. Each will choose her own patch to cultivate; we shall meet and try to interest one another in what we sow and reap, but it will never be like before.'

'We have our memories to sustain us,' said Cecilia in a melancholy tone, which made the whole group think of the time when they would gather round the tea table with tired, grey heads and talk of past times, of which they would recall only the pleasure they took in the work, the comradeship, the enthusiasm, the sweet sensation of hoping and waiting, not the fatigue, the dejection, the monotony and the defeats.

Cecilia, tired to death, thought for her part: I cannot face starting anything new, once this is done. But it seemed too shameful to say it out loud.

Penwoman had crept out to the gentlemen's room and was crying with her head propped against the corner of a bureau. Kristin, who had been fast asleep in a chair with Scriver's *Spiritual Treasury** on her lap, was woken by a sob, looked at the poor child with infinite sympathy, asked nothing but at length said, with the experienced resignation of an older woman: 'Dear Miss Penwoman, it's our destiny you know, for men to give us grief.'

It was three o'clock by the time the party broke up; they were in reflective mood, saying little, for at the very bottom of this day, full of so many different moods, they had found sadness, sadness at what they had believed to be victory.

'But where is Penwoman?'

They looked everywhere for Penwoman, but she had gone; no one had noticed her opening the front door and creeping out into the night.

And yet, when all was quiet and the lights were out, Cecilia stood alone at her bedroom window and looked out into the darkness, envying Penwoman for having someone to whose door she could go, to cry and beg to be let in.

CHAPTER 19

Emerging onto the street, Penwoman stood for a moment looking along the deserted quay, then hurried towards the city centre, telling herself she was on her way home, but determined deep down not to stop until she reached Dick's front door. Streets and squares were littered with soiled and crumpled bits of paper, ballot papers* and all kinds of appeals to the electorate. She trampled them scornfully into the dirt; what did she care who had won or lost! Just the day before yesterday, no one could have been more interested, but by nightfall she was sitting at Dick's bedside, praying to every forgotten god for his life. It was a case of acute appendicitis; how dreadful it had been to see him suffer, but at least she had still been allowed to be with him then! It came back to her now that they had scarcely spoken to each other, that she had not uttered a single word of gratitude and love, but there had been so many practicalities to see to. First undressing him and putting him to bed, and then that doctor, who was so disinclined to get up once he had finally been woken, and the time it took for him to get there!

She could surely never have greeted anyone with such a furious look on her face as she did that doctor on opening Dick's door to him. She thought about it as she walked up through Roslagsgatan; it was easier being angry, because then you forgot for a moment that you were the unhappiest person in the whole world.

The doctor comes in, and looks at her.

'So-o?' he says.

'Hurry up,' she replies urgently.

He slowly removes his coat.

'Are you Mr Block's sister?'

'No,' she answers, and her voice is as sharp as a knife; Dick,

179

lying in the inner room, does not recognise it and gives a start. 'No, I'm his lover, but be quick, don't you realise he could die?'

Then the doctor finally takes a few steps towards the door, and the light from Dick's room falls on his face.

'Well, I say,' and he gives a sneering smile.

Penwoman stands there with her arms at her sides and fists clenched, clenched tight.

'You didn't stand on ceremony like this that night you were outside my front gate, shaking the bars to make me let you in,' she says, going ahead of him into the room.

She still dared to think as far as that, but there she tried to stop. It was too awful to recall how the doctor, having made his diagnosis, took his revenge on the girl by offering to telegraph Dick's relations himself, and how Dick, after a moment's interminable tension, said yes, and how, when the reply telegram announced that his mother and sister were to be expected, Penwoman was sent away, and there was no helping it, though she begged like a dog at Dick's feet.

'I dare not, Penwoman,' was all he said, 'they would never understand or forgive, and this will pass, you must be sensible.' And by then he was so ill, of course, that she could not argue, barely cry, only obey, since he thought he was being wise and strong.

'Won't you send for me if you get worse, Dick?'

'Yes, but I shan't get worse.'

'Weren't the two of us going to be together until death?'

'Yes, but we shall live together for a long time yet, if you will just be sensible, my little beloved.'

That was the last word she had heard him say, but how was he now? A night and a day had passed, no, more, and she knew nothing; his landlady answered: 'Oh, quite poorly, I think,' whenever one asked. He had shut her out, and she would obey to the last, but no one could stop her keeping watch from the street outside.

There was light in his window, a narrow strip; someone was keeping watch, so he wasn't dead, oh Dick, beloved, can't you hear my footsteps, isn't my love forcing its way through the walls?

She started pacing up and down, heedless of the comments addressed to her by solitary passers-by. A policeman approached and scrutinised her, but since she was not drunk, he let her alone.

It was still blackest night, and the light still shone constantly and mutely, while the rest of the building was in darkness and at rest.

Then a woman came into view under the street lamp.

'Look, it's Princess Charlotte,' Penwoman thought yet did not think; she let her go by without lifting her eyes to her face, and had already forgotten her when the woman stopped and began to follow her, and when Penwoman turned, there stood Klara, not two steps away.

Penwoman woke up; Klara's face in the lamplight had woken her. It was a face she knew: she had encountered it many times, spoken to it, listened to it, and she knew the story it had to tell.

'You're sick,' she said.

'You could be right,' said Klara in a hoarse voice.

'You should go home. Where do you live?'

'I don't live anywhere. I've been kicked out.'

'Me too,' replied Penwoman.

Klara started to laugh, 'Well, we're a fine pair, getting ourselves in this mess.'

Penwoman cast a final glance up at Dick's window, her lips moving in a silent farewell.

'You come with me,' she said.

'Where to?'

'To my room by Adolf Fredrik, of course.' She took the girl's arm.

Klara suddenly stopped.

'That place, ugh,' she said, but then continued walking. How stupid could she be, good God, as if it made any difference where she went.

The two girls did not exchange many words as they walked the streets, but Penwoman noted that Klara was well known there. Klara realised what Penwoman was thinking, but did not care.

As Penwoman unlocked the iron gate she remembered the

doctor, the one allowed to minister to Dick.

Various men of indeterminate class and age passed by, hurling handfuls of abuse after them; it somehow gratified Penwoman that they applied to both of them. Hadn't she, Heaven help her, with her rather eccentric lack of prejudice, invited up the girl from Tegnérgatan and her colleagues to give them tea and books in return for the knowledge they gave her, and yet she had never known, never imagined, never understood until now.

'Are you hungry,' she asked when they were indoors.

'Starving, but have you got anything to eat?'

'In the cupboard, you know where, there are some biscuits and jam. You get those, and I'll put the water on for tea.'

When they had had their tea, Klara suddenly said, 'Oh, it's morning already,' and went over to switch off the electric light. They had not let the blinds down, and the infinitely desolate light of day, cold and thin, fell over the room.

Penwoman, light-headed with exhaustion and tears, mumbled Dick's name. It felt to her that such a day could only dawn when one's beloved was dead.

'Barbro,' Klara said quietly at last, 'let me sleep here on your rug with a cushion for my head.'

'Sleep?' asked Penwoman, taken by surprise. 'Yes of course, but we can both do it properly; I've got a bed and a sofa, as you know.' She began bustling about at once, producing sheets, blankets and towels, making up beds, filling the washbowl.

'Why are you doing this for me?' Klara had not asked her hostess a single question until then.

'Good God,' said Penwoman absent-mindedly, *'you're a woman, aren't you?'* Klara contented herself with that; the situation just now was so schematically simple, and she could see why Penwoman felt no need to explain further.

'I see, yes of course. God help us then, good night.'

'Good night, try to sleep.'

They lay there for a while, listening to each other shift restlessly in their beds; first one gave a huge, heavy sigh, then the other, and they both fell asleep.

## CHAPTER 20

Cecilia had not seen or heard from Penwoman since election night, when three days later the girl appeared at twilight, came over to Cecilia and threw her arms round her neck.

'Oh my dear child, you cry by all means.'

'Thank you,' said Penwoman, and stopped it abruptly. 'It's silly, I know, I'm so happy. Do you know what it feels like to have been in despair, the very depths of despair?'

'Indeed I do.'

'And then suddenly to have all the pain taken away, so instantly that you think you must be dreaming?'

'No, I have never known that, but what is it then, dear child, have you quarrelled?'

Penwoman gave her an account of what had happened, mentioning in passing, as if it were the most natural thing in the world, that she had been banished until further notice, but it would not be long before she was allowed back, as the worst was now over.

'How wretched you must feel,' said Cecilia gently after a moment's pause, 'my poor child, how wretched you must feel. But I knew, of course, oh I knew, that you would be put to the test, too.'

'I'm not wretched,' sobbed Penwoman. 'Dick's going to live, oh yes, and I don't take back a single word of what I've always said, do you hear me, Cecilia!'

'Yes, it's plain to see how happy you are, poor thing.'

'I'm not a poor thing. I shall prove it to you, oh yes I shall.'

The next day, Penwoman was back, with a glitter in her eye that Cecilia did not entirely like, but just as cocky as before.

'I'm here so often,' she said, 'it must get a bit monotonous for you, but it's wonderful that it offends no one's sense of propriety. Look what I've got to amuse me while I wait.'

And she tossed a letter to Cecilia.

'It's just as well I can be sure you won't go and do something stupid out of sheer desperation,' said Cecilia abruptly, looking up from the letter.

'I'm not desperate, but would it be so stupid?' asked Penwoman, looking away.

'I assume you are only saying that to make mischief?'

'Would it be so mischievous to marry the Baron?' asked Penwoman a trifle petulantly.

'Well, it is probably no bad thing,' replied Cecilia with an imperturbable calm that annoyed Penwoman just as much as the opposite reaction would have offended her, 'that this letter has arrived just now. You'll have something to pretend to get your own back with, and Dick will have something to forgive you for, once you have totally and utterly forgiven him – if you can?'

'If I can? Forgive the person I am so fond of? Don't you know I simply must love Dick, even with a little ache in my heart?'

A few more days went by, Dick's mother and elder sister, those mute security guards whom no one had seen, were still in Stockholm, and Penwoman said she had heard that they were taking Dick home to Östergötland to convalesce. She offered this news quite calmly.

'That will be nice for Dick,' she said.

At her words, Cecilia was suddenly seized by fury with that Dick, who conceded so willingly to his family's prejudices.

'Doesn't he realise how much he is hurting you?' she exclaimed with unusual passion.

'He isn't hurting me, and he doesn't understand that he's doing it – I mean – I've made my choice, and though I may not have realised – no, stop looking at me like that – that convention counts for so much in this world, it's a very good thing for me to learn.'

Cecilia stood looking at the child who, with such a princely gesture and such proud joy, had given herself to another. Her cheeks had grown thin and pale and her voice, which used to reverberate like an over-tightened string with a happiness too much to bear, had, she thought, taken on a tone of fatal disappointment.

'What we need here is the old spinster who pokes her nose into other people's business,' she mentally resolved, and when Sunday came, she went straight up to Dick's. Penwoman would never have forgiven her, but if all went well, the girl would never know.

Cecilia had that dignity and urbanity that helped her to meet with composure the undisguised astonishment and discourteous curiosity of the young girl with Dick's features, who opened the door. She presented her visiting card with a faint smile, and asked if the architect was well enough to receive her. It is unclear what view Dick's sister would have taken on the matter, had he not recognised Cecilia's voice from his room, and decided the question with an eager: 'Yes, of course I am.'

As Cecilia had calculated, his mother was at church, and his sister was instructed to keep out of the way. With a little giggle, she closed the door behind her, and they were left to themselves.

Cecilia could see at first glance that Dick was well enough not to require any leniency.

'Have you brought me a message from Penwoman,' he asked brightly, not remotely anticipating trouble. 'How is she?'

'That is what I have come to tell you,' said Cecilia. 'Things are bad enough, but now that you, thank goodness, are on the mend, let us hope that everything can be as it was.'

He gave a sudden exclamation that brought his sister to the other side of the door.

'As it was? But I couldn't help being ill, you know – and – '

'But she was sent away, when she wanted most of all to be with you, Dick.'

He lay silent for a while, as if overwhelmed, his brain working away.

'But don't you see, it was for Penwoman's own sake,' he said in surprise. 'You may not believe me,' he flushed, looking to Cecilia like a child lying there in his bed, 'but I care more for her wellbeing than for my own, otherwise I certainly wouldn't have, – it hasn't been easy for me either, you know. She's going to be my wife, that's definite, and I can't bear the thought that people might find anything to remark on where my wife is concerned, might cast the slightest suspicion on her honour. For our future,' he faltered slightly again, 'it's so important, you see, that we can live on good terms with my parents.'

He leant forward, as if trying to read approval in Cecilia's face, but she sat immobile.

'So I can't understand Penwoman's desperation,' he went on a little uncertainly, 'because I've actually told her all this myself.'

'Dear Dick,' said Cecilia, and smiled, 'how can I make this clear to you: it is precisely because you told her all this, that she is so desperate, poor little thing.'

Dick looked extremely wary:

'Has she said so?'

'No, she hasn't *said* it.'

He brightened up.

'Then she hasn't thought it, either. She must know better, of course. You probably can't understand, but she must know. I shall soon have her here again,' he added confidently. 'The hard times are almost over, and we can forget them, but if my mother had found out, she would never have forgotten.'

'Well, you can certainly try,' said Cecilia somewhat sceptically. There was nothing wrong with Dick, but he clearly had not understood this.

'Like I said,' he went on, as if to justify himself, 'it wasn't that easy for me either, I can tell you. If it had been anyone else but Penwoman! Have I told you about her encounter with the doctor? That was what decided me.'

'With the doctor, no.'

Dick told her what had happened. 'You should have heard her tone of voice, when he was trying to establish her relationship to the patient. "I'm his lover, but be quick, he could die." What's one to do with a girl like that?'

'I think I would have behaved exactly as Penwoman did,' said Cecilia pensively.

'What?' he looked as if he thought he had misheard.

'I believe coarseness should get the punishment it deserves.'

'Yes, but at that price? What do you think I should do now? I have my people here; they know nothing, and want me home as soon as possible; I have no earnings, won't be able to work for some time, short of cash – But as soon as I'm better, then – '

'If you can get better without that girl, you are not the person I thought you to be,' said Cecilia. 'I understand your way of seeing things, naturally, but I also think you are paying too high a price for that harmony with your family.'

They heard the front door opening, then footsteps and voices. It was Dick's mother arriving back.

'What do you think I should do?' he asked hastily, embarrassed.

'You should talk to Penwoman, before you leave for Östergötland,' replied Cecilia firmly. 'You can always lie on top of the bedcovers fully-dressed,' she added with a little smile. 'Goodbye Dick, let us hope everything turns out well.'

'Do give my fond regards to Penwoman,' he said eagerly, as she rose to leave. 'Tell her that, well, I'm sure she understands completely, without me telling her – '

'I dare not pass on your message,' replied Cecilia, shaking her head. 'You must never let her know about this.'

He said nothing, and it was only when Cecilia had departed that the words began to flow. If she only knew, he thought, how much I love her, how I have cried tears of longing, how I am pining, how I dream of seeing her, and nothing else.

The door opened and his mother and sister came in to take a look from the window at the elegant lady who had passed them in Dick's hall and bidden them good day, as if it were the most natural thing in the world for her to visit Dick.

'Who can she be, Mother?' asked the girl.

'I shall ask Fredrik,' replied her mother, not without dignity. 'Fredrik, who was that woman?'

'That was a suffragist,' answered Dick, looking exhilarated and much preoccupied.

His mother drew herself up: 'Well that's most odd, I must say.'

'Oh you know, Mother,' said her daughter, who after her five-week stay in the capital had developed a distinct Stockholm accent, 'it isn't really that odd, for I have heard say that they live entirely à la Strindberg.'*

She failed to notice that Dick was now sitting upright up in bed.

'You could thank your God, if you were as they are,'* he said earnestly, 'and if you dare say another word about those people I have the honour to call my friends – '

The two women exchanged a look: clearly not even their Fredrik had emerged unscathed from all the perils in which Stockholm was so rich.

'I think I must have a talk with you, Fredrik,' said his mother severely.

Dick sighed. He was not used to moral sermons of any kind; on the contrary, he was used to Penwoman, spoilt by her tenderness.

It transpired that Dick's landlady had dropped hints about a young lady who had been in the habit of visiting Mr Block on an almost daily basis, 'but since you came, Mrs Block, she has only telephoned'.

'Is this true, Fredrik?' said the elderly lady, sitting straight as a ramrod, still holding her hymn book in her hand and wearing her hat.

'Yes Mother, but you can't imagine – '

'Right is right and sin is sin,' his mother brusquely cut him short, 'and I would have expected you to know better.'

'You can't imagine, Mother, how much we love each other,' began Dick diffidently.

It pained him beyond words, having to speak of Penwoman to his mother.

Mrs Block pretended not to have heard.

'I must say, the best thing would be for you to earn a proper living and get married,' she declared.

Dick was overjoyed to hear this; he had not expected his mother to be so reasonable and conciliatory about it.

'We wish nothing more fervently,' he said happily.

The lady drew herself up on her chair.

'If any decent girl will have you now,' she said.

'What do you mean, Mother?' said Dick, nonplussed, 'After all, we've, I – '

'You heard me, I said a decent girl.'

Dick was accustomed to Penwoman and her friends, who held women's solidarity and loyalty to one another sacred. It filled his soul with bitterness and shame to hear his good mother, 'a paragon of piety', counselling him to leave the woman who loved him and was his, to marry a 'decent girl'. His clever, self-sacrificing, sweet little Penwoman!

'Mother,' he said, 'only spare a thought for the hurt I would then be doing to the girl who – loves me.'

'Oh,' said his mother harshly, 'anyone who gets herself into that sort of situation must have a fair idea how it will end. She may be used to moving on to the next one, anyway – Well – I am just a simple, old-fashioned woman – '

Dick was not in the habit of standing up to his mother, still less of rebuking her, but he was not a boy, he was a man, and a man did not tolerate hearing his beloved insulted.

'I don't let anyone speak that way about the one I love,' he said emphatically. 'She's going to be my wife and bear my name, and I know I'm scarcely worthy of her. Tomorrow she's coming here, if she can forgive me for having kept her away so long, but I thought it was for the best. If you want me ever to come home or be in touch with you again, Mother, then receive her nicely, but if you can't do that, it will be best for you to go home now, so the two of you don't meet. She's going to be here every day, if she wants to.'

He sank back onto the pillow again, a little feverish and agitated, but very relieved that the conflict was resolved, and that there was now only one way for him to go. At that moment he could not fathom why he had been so anxious about his family's disapproval, why it had seemed more important to keep them happy than to have Penwoman with him. He felt he had been as foolish as Penwoman had probably thought him, and wondered how he would make her understand, when he no longer understood himself. He did not realise that here they had two generations' concepts of right and wrong colliding, and that once the younger one triumphed, the tie which had hitherto given his mother power over her son was broken.

But the old lady, still sitting there with her hymn book in hand, understood well enough.

'In that case, we will leave in the morning,' she said dully, and left the room without looking at Dick.

# Chapter 21

The excitement of the election campaign had been so great that it was scarcely a surprise for it to be followed by a period of reaction among the suffragists, taking the form of a decided aversion to public interests. It was said that the entire Hard Labour Gang, except of course for Kerstin Vallmark, who had no idea how to hold a needle, had embarked on major needlecraft projects, and it was even whispered that gang members had been seen not once but several times at the opera and theatre.

'We have got to wait,' they said by way of excuse, 'until this blessed parliament that we slaved so hard for is in session and reveals its true intentions.'

Cecilia had not heard from Ester Henning for a long time, though she did not normally tolerate anyone being left unoccupied, but then one day she telephoned to ask whether Cecilia felt like standing for election to the committee the following week.

'Haven't you anyone better?' asked Cecilia in turn, but she could not stop her voice revealing how flattered and pleased she really felt.

'Anyone better? If I had, I would not be asking you. So that is decided. Thank you. One of us will nominate you, and I expect everything will proceed without a hitch.'

But she was wrong.

The committee met that evening at Ester Henning's house, and she announced that filling the empty place would not present any difficulty, as Cecilia Bech had already agreed to join them.

'That's excellent,' was the heartfelt reaction of Jane Horneman and Kerstin Vallmark, and they seemed to be expressing the general opinion of the committee. This made it all the more unexpected when Miss Adrian was suddenly heard to say: 'Madam Chairman, this must not be permitted to happen.'

Surprised faces turned to Miss Adrian, who met all their indignant expressions with an ominous calm.

'It is a matter for the association to elect its committee, Miss Adrian, as you may recall,' replied Ester Henning, with equal composure.

'But I oppose the nomination,' repeated Miss Adrian, as if that settled the matter.

She appeared to think she was at a staff meeting, awarding conduct marks.

'But why?' asked Kerstin, who had not noticed Ester Henning's warning look.

'I had imagined my word would suffice to prevent a regrettable error of judgment. I do not oppose Miss Bech's election without good reason.'

'Madam Chairman,' said Kerstin Vallmark. She was very agitated; a situation like this made her old wounds start bleeding once more.

'Miss Vallmark,' Ester Henning acknowledged her ceremoniously.

'Miss Adrian has done great services to our cause by her energy and untiring efforts when it comes to obtaining' – 'frightening', thought the others – 'money and other things from our opponents, but even so, I must state candidly here that it is unfair to cast aspersions on a person by virtue of one's authority and then refuse to give reasons.'

'Agreed,' said everybody; only Jane Horneman and Miss Adrian's impersonal friend on the committee said nothing.

An awkward and universal silence followed. Miss Adrian, still red in the face, stared straight ahead, profoundly insulted.

Finally, her friend overcame her fear of publicly supporting an unpopular cause, thanks to her fear of Miss Adrian herself, and said in a somewhat faltering voice: 'Could we not find someone, whose name arouses fewer misgivings, someone whose – in whom we could be confident – that she would not compromise the way the movement is perceived – by the more particular – '

'Well, some explanation at last,' said Kerstin Vallmark quickly, 'Miss Bech is considered likely to compromise the movement. I wonder whether the last speaker is aware that that is the most serious charge that can be levelled at anyone in our circle?'

'We can't be too careful,' said a voice, which the schoolmistress found to her extreme astonishment to be Jane Horneman's.

'You once managed to bring down one of our best workers, because her husband was serving a sentence for breach of the press laws,' said Kerstin, struggling hard to maintain her composure. 'But I thought we had made a little more progress towards liberalism and fairness since then, we who are, after all, supposed to be among the more enlightened.'

'Miss Bech has sinned *personally*,' the deeply wronged Miss Adrian finally replied, folding her arms over her stomach, as if by these words she had declared the matter finally and irrevocably closed.

'Is there anyone with anything to add?' put in Ester Henning quickly, with a look that Kerstin Vallmark finally recognised and understood.

Since the meeting was now officially over, Kerstin turned to the chairman and asked whether she had any objection to her speaking to Adrian privately.

'I ask you as a favour between friends,' answered Ester Henning with a merciless little glint in her eye. 'I know you understand that we are not in the habit of discussing gossip in our meetings.'

Kerstin immediately rushed after Miss Adrian and caught up with her in the hall. Before the dumbfounded old lady had time to resist, she steered her into the empty consulting room.

'Now, Miss Adrian,' she said firmly, as if the overbearing schoolmistress were accustomed to no other treatment, 'I am not letting you out, until you have given me chapter and verse where Miss Bech is concerned.'

'I would much rather not,' replied Miss Adrian, but in an unusually docile manner, for she wanted nothing better than the chance to tell what she knew.

'You just sit there and tell me; there's no need to beat about the bush, now I've asked you straight out.'

'I take Heaven as my witness that I was forced – !'

'You do that; it's a silent enough witness. Come on, hurry up.'

'I thought the suffrage movement was supposed to be led by women of unblemished character,' began Miss Adrian.

'So there is another piece of information: Cecilia is not an unblemished woman. That's splendid; we shall soon have the whole truth.'

'I would not call anyone unblemished, who has secretly lived with a man.'

Kerstin paled a little; she had not expected that.

'It has only very recently come to my attention,' said Miss Adrian, very much aware of the impact she had made. 'It was during her time at training college, just imagine, when she was enjoying tuition provided at the state's expense to qualify her to guide and instruct the young. Well, that – that – person left her soon enough, which was hardly surprising, for he could certainly have had no respect for a woman like that.'

'Why didn't she get married?' asked Kerstin Vallmark clumsily. In her book, a woman was either married, which was remarkable enough, or she was like Kerstin herself.

'Let us say,' said Adrian, sensing accurately that she had the upper hand, 'that had she been employed at my school when I found out about this, I would not only have turned her out on the spot, but also given her such a testimonial that she would not have been able to apply for another post anywhere in the country, and now you want her on our committee!'

Kerstin Vallmark could not reply; she was far too taken aback. Good Lord, here she was among educated women, and yet –

In Ester Henning's own consulting room sat Jane Horneman, along with Anna Gylling who had just arrived, awaiting the outcome of Kerstin's conversation with Adrian.

194

She opened the door with a strange mixture of disappointment and chagrin in her face.

'Well – ?'

'It was some old love affair,' she said, embarrassed. 'She's supposed to have had a liaison – you know, an actual relationship when she was at college – '

'We understand,' said Ester Henning with a smile.

'Well, thank goodness,' said Anna Gylling with a deep sigh of relief, 'then she's not as unhappy as I'd thought, after all.'

Kerstin looked uncertainly from one to the other.

'So now we had better consider how best we can support Cecilia,' said Ester Henning thoughtfully.

'Now I know some of you will despise me for all eternity,' began Jane, tears welling up in her eyes, 'but what I think is that we can do Cecilia and the movement no better service at the moment than by withdrawing her name for the time being. If we do that, Adrian will keep quiet – '

'So that's what you think?' Anna Gylling laughed.

'If we do the opposite, she'll spread the story far and wide, to make Cecilia unelectable.'

'I think it would be a crying shame,' said Anna Gylling with another laugh, 'to pass up this chance to gauge the moral standards of our association. That's my view.'

'But then,' said Jane Horneman in great agitation, 'she might very well get elected, and I will have to listen to my family saying that we are doing our best to elect loose women to the committee, and then the same will be said when the matter comes up in Parliament, if not in the Upper Chamber itself, then at least in the press coverage. That may sound narrow-minded, but I know that even the narrow-minded can be right sometimes.'

'You sound narrow-minded, certainly, but you are still not right,' said Ester Henning.

'Good God, as if I don't know it's an unbecoming attitude to adopt, but I'm thinking of the movement and its future,' said Jane Horneman, rather huffily.

Ester Henning's eyes began to blaze.

'We all love our cause,' she said, 'you too, I should know that. But are we to have so little faith in it, that we think it will collapse if Adrian and people like her withdraw their valuable support? Adrian, who really only wants the vote out of personal vanity, while all those who have truly crucified their souls for the suffrage would gladly forego it for themselves, if by doing so they could guarantee it to those among their sisters who need it more.'

'Very good,' said Anna Gylling under her breath. She looked as though she meant it.

'A movement,' said Ester Henning, her feelings running high, 'a movement that has awoken in the hearts of the strongest and most prominent women of their time, and then been carried forward by that time as if on the crest of a wave – dependent on arbitrary convention, on Adrian's caprices, it's simply grotesque.'

'But you said yourself, that it was borne aloft by the strongest and most prominent women,' put in Kerstin, who had yet to take sides in the argument, but could never stop herself noticing words, 'so presumably you think it matters what sort of women are now stepping into their shoes?'

'Yes,' said Ester Henning, 'that's precisely what I think. It's just that I don't necessarily consider as the strongest and most prominent those who dare not tread a straight path, but look to the left and right, mostly the right of course, to see what people will say. If we reach the point where people have nothing at all to say about us, then let's see how far we get! And don't forget that we are not discussing a crime or a case of disloyalty, merely something that is none of our business.'

'But just think – '

'I *am* thinking. I'm thinking that if the Adrian point of view prevails, then the future is not with us and I can no longer work with all of you.'

'You don't mean you'll walk away?' said Jane Horneman in alarm.

'If the future turns out as you envisage, then yes.'

'You can't,' said Anna Gylling, unruffled. 'You and the

movement can't go your separate ways even if you wanted to. As you well know, nobody tears the heart out of their own breast.'

'No, but if I go ahead and compromise myself in the company of Cecila Bech, can you imagine – Cecilia Bech! – then I shall no longer have a choice.'

'You just try that,' said Anna, and laughed. 'But you will never have time to do it really thoroughly.'

'Ester Henning's right,' announced Kerstin Vallmark suddenly, after thinking hard, 'a look at history shows us that. And I expect we could easily get Cecilia elected, if we put our minds to it. After all, we've achieved more difficult things than that between us. Jane Horneman – I shall speak to her later – can adopt some passive role for the sake of her conscience.'


The morning before the annual general meeting, Penwoman was lying in bed fresh from sleep, looking with eyes open wide at the streak of light from the window, heralding a new day of happiness, that happiness as precious to her as a child at whose sickbed one has watched.

Dick's doors were open once more, and their reunion had been as simple, as poor in words, as rich in joy as it can only ever be when you really do love each other. How they had joked about Cecilia, who had worried so unnecessarily; Penwoman had already completely forgotten all the strange thoughts that had been chased away by that first message in Dick's own hand.

What a world, she thought, there was Dick – and things were happening – Princess Charlotte had left her archduke, and tomorrow they were going to cut Miss Adrian down to size!

She gave a start as there was a loud ring on her doorbell, lay still, heard another ring and leapt up with the terror that is never far from those who have recently gone through some painful experience, and peered through the letterbox to find out whether she could safely open the door.

'What in the world, Klara? Is the domestic science college on fire?'

'Get back into bed quickly, and I'll tell you. Have you seen the paper?'

'No, I've only just woken up.'

'Read this then. Don't worry, it's not anything sad. Yes, just there.'

*'Princess Charlotte in Stockholm?'*

*Seen by an informant outside the general newspaper offices.*

*Denies her identity in confusion when asked and then disappears.*

'Well, well,' said Penwoman breathlessly. '"Wearing a dark-blue tailored suit and black felt hat with white feathers – ?" Good God Klara, it's you – '

'It's me, all right,' said Klara with grim emphasis on 'me'. 'You know I've been amusing myself by wearing my hair like the Princess, and now look where it's got me.'

'Are you quite sure?' asked Penwoman, her hand on the telephone receiver by her bed.

'Sure? A gentleman was standing there looking at me yesterday afternoon as I was buying the *Berliner Tageblatt* specially, to read about the Princess. Well the fact of a gentleman looking at me – you know – But then he comes straight over to me and says very firmly,'Vous êtes la Princesse Charlotte?' I was so taken aback, you know how stupid one can be, and then I blushed and answered him, 'Vous vous trompez monsieur,' and ran away. I thought he was going to follow me, but he didn't. He telephoned the telegraph office afterwards, of course, and now it's all round the world.'

Penwoman sat staring for a long time, as if turned to stone.

'Thank you for coming, Klara,' she said. 'You've done me a great favour, much greater than you can know. You can't imagine what a delightful article I shall make of this, but please will you stay indoors today? I shall send for food and anything you want, and I'll ring the domestic science college and say you're ill. Time for me to get up now.' She was already sitting on the edge of the bed, legs dangling, her hands clasped for the good journalist's prayer, when she surprised Klara by suddenly snuggling back down with a sigh and pulling the covers over her shoulders.

'No,' she said. 'The Devil can do it, for I shan't. I don't know much about her, and I would never run away from Dick, but then Dick is no duke, either. And I expect she's hiding somewhere at this moment, like a bird being tracked by the hounds. Let them come here and chase her, let them be thrown off the scent – I shall miss out on the glory, and God knows it's hard, but after all, *she's a woman, isn't she!*'

Klara remembered that this 'she's a woman, isn't she!' had been the only explanation Penwoman had considered necessary when she had helped her, and tears came into her eyes, over by the spirit stove, as she realised this was the simple perspective from which Penwoman saw both princesses and prostitutes.

When Penwoman entered the big hall of the YWCA, the auditorium was quite full despite the early hour. This was presumably partly to be accounted for by one of the daily papers publishing a piece that morning which, to the suffragists' astonishment, contained gratuitous claims that it was vital for the suffrage movement to be led by women without blemish. One could have imagined all manner of dreadful things, and only the initiated, of course, knew it was the work of Adrian, who had made use of the fat authoress at Bengtsson's boarding house.

Penwoman's entrance attracted a certain amount of attention; it was immediately obvious that she was in high spirits, that she knew something, that something was afoot. Kerstin Vallmark, her cheeks red, came in shortly afterwards, at the same moment as Miss Adrian and her anonymous letters, of whom there were more than usual, and who quickly spread out among the audience. From her place, Penwoman observed a certain disquiet becoming evident in the parts of the hall where they had found places, but other association members were arriving all the time, and the audience remained a mixture of initiates and puzzled faces. Kerstin Vallmark went round issuing instructions without entering into any explanation, and Penwoman could not help laughing to herself as she saw how many members, exhorted to do so by Miss Adrian, approached the Vice Chairman Ester Henning, who answered them with immutable calm in two short words. Miss Adrian saw it too, and grew steadily redder in the face, for she knew all too well from experience how hard it is to get anywhere, if the Vice Chairman sets her virtually unshakeable authority against something.

Suddenly every head turned as Cecilia entered, alone, a little stooped and not quite sure where to sit. She flushed under everyone's gaze, nodded to her friends, said good evening to Miss Adrian, who looked her calculatingly up and down with the incalculable contempt of a decent woman, and finally found herself next to Mrs Horneman, who was sitting on a bench to one side.

When they had asked her onto the committee, she had examined herself meticulously. She was more than happy to do the work that the position would involve; it was her only pleasure. But the possibility of rising to a position of leadership and shouldering responsibility made her feel miserably small and insignificant. The more she thought about the task, the more onerous a responsibility it seemed. This was where the fundamental design of society was quietly transformed and the weights in the scales were shifted. Those so entrusted surely could not be people like her, she who had been blind for so many years and could never become a whole human being like the rest? It was immensely hard to be a leader when you were conscious that every step taken on your authority was also a piece of the history of the women's movement. In the end, she brooded herself into such a despondent state that it took Ester Henning's resolute 'We have no one better' to make up her mind.

The election was first on the agenda. All the committee members except one were to serve a further term, so there was only one place to fill. When it came to the naming of the candidates, Kerstin Vallmark and Miss Adrian stood up simultaneously, but Kerstin had put her name down with the Chairman in advance, so she was allowed to speak first. She spoke for Cecilia's candidacy with a warmth and at a length that made Cecilia look up and wonder for the first time whether her election might be in doubt in some way.

As soon as Kerstin had finished, Miss Adrian rose, her voice quivering with vexation and zeal. She then named a rival candidate, commending her in such terms that no one could fail to grasp that she in Adrian's view had all the qualities Cecilia lacked: good reputation, firm character, unimpeachable integrity. Her anger, her fear of failing in spite of everything, caused her to go further than she had intended. She realised she had caused a scene, the like of which had never been seen at an annual meeting before, but she resumed her seat in the proud knowledge that she had done her duty.

Penwoman had her eyes riveted on Miss Adrian throughout, not caring that she finally noticed, and bridled.

'What can be the explanation for such behaviour, do you think?' whispered Penwoman, shaking with anger, to Anna Gylling who was sitting close by. 'Is it the men in her life, who have been so few and so stupid?'

'It's just like a spoilt little girl like you to leap to a conclusion like that,' Anna whispered back. 'That's not the solution to the riddle of what rules Adrian's psyche.'

'Well maybe I am a spoilt little girl, and I mistrust anyone who's so deliberate about their morality,' persisted Penwoman.

'It's tempting to think that,' replied Anna, 'but at the bottom of their muddled souls, under all the envy and self-importance, I'm sure there's some sense of it being one of the female psyche's achievements over the centuries that mustn't be lost. They want to be pure, at all costs.'

'Good God, who doesn't,' said Penwoman impatiently, 'it's just that most of us don't think about it all the time.'

'You're very clever, Penwoman,' replied Anna, 'But you are dreadfully young. Look, take Adrian, no, not her exactly, because she's malicious, but if you can imagine someone with her outlook, but a splendid, charming person, kind-hearted and whatever you will. She's learned to revere outward conventions

201

as the only things that can have a moral content. For her, they are a sign of the "elevated position a woman has always occupied at a man's side," and if we start disrupting those, then we're heading for perdition with our eyes wide open, that's what she believes. But that needn't stop us thinking it *our* duty to disrupt those conventions, even so.'

'Elevated position,' quoted Penwoman, contritely. 'How curious. But,' she said after a pause, 'even you with your immense objectivity can't very well deny that Adrian has behaved with unprecedented vileness? You see, as soon as you show any tolerance to morality, it ruins everything. What nonsense is this? Cecilia, why nobody could live a purer life than she does.'

'They know that, but she broke with convention that once, and it will never be forgiven her. You've got to let them draw some advantage from their own virtue.'

Poor, dear Cecilia, thought Penwoman, chancing a look at her for the first time. To the girl's astonishment and delight, the look was answered with a smile, a sad one admittedly, but a smile nonetheless. Cecilia, whom she had imagined to be going through the bitterest moment of her life. She did not realise that that moment lay far back in the past.

There was a rustling of ballot papers, a borrowing of pencils, an unusually lively conferring and advising. Cecilia felt a scarcely perceptible touch on her arm. It was Mrs Horneman.

'Doesn't all this make you feel uncomfortable,' she ventured, a little embarrassed.

'Oh yes.'

'It hadn't occurred to you – wouldn't it be best – to stand up and withdraw.'

Cecilia slowly turned towards her. Her eyes darkened to black, like a lake in a storm.

'*No*,' she said.

Penwoman, ever watchful, had been observing the pair of them, and when she saw from Mrs Horneman's expression that she had been rebuffed, her triumph was beyond words.

It still seemed to her like a fairytale; she did not know, of course, that on someone who has already condemned and hanged herself, in earnest, an attack like Adrian's does not make an overwhelming impression.

That last year had certainly changed Cecilia's perception of the standards by which one had the right to judge a person; her new sense of women's worth had brought with it a new way of seeing. But traces of shame, a bitter deposit left by all those sorrows that had run through her heart, had remained, and it was hard to say what stance she would have taken on the matter if influence had been exerted on her over a period of time. But it was spontaneous indignation that now saved her.

This judge had no dignity, and the view she was propounding seemed suddenly absurd and laughable. Here was a gathering assumed to contain the most broad-minded women in the land, and when someone dared to stand up in front of them and say that a person with *only* her irreproachable character to offer is more suitable to assume a leading role than one who has invested her whole life in the movement and done sterling work, but does not come up to convention's standards, then one's soul must stand up, too, and say: *enough is enough.*

As the meeting dragged on, and the chairman had her work cut out to get any decisions from the distracted audience, which was waiting to hear the result of the count, Cecilia sat there apparently unconcerned, repeating to herself those same words: '*Enough is enough*'. Her life was shattered forever, but that was enough, too. The dead would not come back to life, youth, hope, innocence and dreams of motherhood would all still lie in their big, common grave, but that was enough penance, shame and degradation, enough, enough, enough!

Cecilia was elected with an overwhelming majority, and when the meeting was over, her friends clustered around her, and the group was joined after some hesitation by Mrs Horneman.

She received their congratulations and smiled at them all; what she had felt, as her entire past life had been momentarily exposed to the whole gathering, nobody asked, and nobody was told.

203

She knew that her comrades were going to celebrate the victory at some restaurant, and that they would very much have liked her to join them, if she felt like it, but she went straight home with Kristin, who had been sitting in one corner of the hall.

'Well what do you say to that, Kristin?' asked Cecilia all at once. Kristin thought for a moment: 'Well, they have a go at each other in Simrishamn, too, but they don't call it morality,' she said.

# CHAPTER 22

Another winter had passed; you had high hopes, when it started, of getting through whole oceans of work, but now it was the vernal equinox and you found all that priceless time had gone by, without your managing to clear your desk: in fact, it was more overloaded than ever. New problems had cropped up where you least expected them, and the days had been crumbled to nothing by that indescribable labour which cannot be avoided or postponed, but which by mortal standards leaves so little trace and is so unglamorous to present as any kind of result. No one had performed miracles, not even the new parliament, which had turned out pretty much like the one before. But you had kept everything ticking over and demonstrated that you had no intention of tiring, if that was what your opponents were hoping for.

The Hard Labour Gang had to laugh when they convened, looking to a woman so worn down and exhausted by working for the cause and earning their keep as they did, and it was telling that they increasingly often discussed how they might find reinforcements to help with the workload, which was growing every day. During that winter's courses in civics* Kerstin Vallmark, the driving force behind them, had managed to rope in a few young girls that they hoped to use come the autumn, and their arrival was anticipated with eagerness, mixed with something like sadness, well hidden at the bottom of everyone's hearts.

One day, Cecilia gathered them all together for dinner, thrust Penwoman into the centre without warning, and obliged her to tell them that she was getting married. It ought not to have been a secret at all, since the banns had already been read for the first time, but it would not have occurred to any of them to pay heed to any ceremonies a certain Barbro Magnus was to undergo, unless they had been told explicitly that Penwoman was involved.

The girl herself was too embarrassed to pay attention to the impact of her news on each individual member of the Gang, but Cecilia, watching more closely, noted with a smile of pride and satisfaction the significant fact that while perhaps one among them was not surprised, not a single one was not glad.

Most astonished of all was Kerstin Vallmark, despite that autumn's events having taught her that not everything was as simple as she had previously believed.

'I shall have to swallow for a whole week to get this down,' she said. 'Oh Penwoman, are you really leaving us?'

'On the contrary,' said Penwoman, who was fighting back her impulse to tell Kerstin that 'your brother' and the much talked of architect were one and the same, 'on the contrary, I shall be much more use to you than before, now I'm leaving the daily and nightly drudgery of the paper to concentrate on writing about the suffrage and women's rights.' She seemed so delighted at the prospect that no one could have guessed it was the end result of a compromise with Dick.

'Those are noble intentions,' said Jane Horneman, 'but I think you are leaving your husband out of the equation. Believe me, most of them want you to work overtime on admiration, at least to start with. I know lots of women who had plans as proud as yours, but were obliged to relinquish them.'

'But I'm not marrying some old patriarch,' said Penwoman with unshakeable conviction.

It was a happy evening. Penwoman, who to her great gratification was as good as the only topic of conversation, had to put up with a succession of jokes and exhortations to educate her husband and children in the true faith and make sure she divided things fairly between her sons and daughters, as befitted a member of the Hard Labour Gang.

Penwoman generously promised to do all they were asking of her, and indignantly quoshed any conjecture that her fine intentions might encounter resistance from Dick, when it came to putting them into practice.

It was only when the party was breaking up that a more solemn mood suddenly descended on them.

'Goodbye,' said Penwoman, 'it's going to be a while until we meet again.'

'A while, eh?' said Kerstin, instantly suspicious.

'Yes,' replied Penwoman, not without a certain artless dignity.

'She is right,' determined Ester Henning. 'I certainly couldn't have got married in a lunch break, though that's clearly what Kerstin considers the proper way, if it is to happen at all.'

'But I shall be back, girls,' said Penwoman with tears in her eyes.

'We all look forward to that,' they said, and on the way downstairs Kerstin said hopefully, 'She'll come, everybody, you wait and see. She's got more gumption than to let herself be snuffed out like a candle.'

'Yes, we'll see,' Anna smiled her old smile, but if anyone had been able to see, they might have noticed that it was more melancholy than usual, not as bitter but infinitely sadder.

But Kerstin Vallmark had picked up the sceptical note in her voice; it annoyed her, and soon a full-blown dispute was in progress between the two friends.

Penwoman was the only one left at Cecilia's; she was spending the night there for the last time.

She had gone to prepare for bed, leaving Cecilia sitting alone in her study. Through the half-open door, Cecilia could hear Kristin and Penwoman exchanging views while the latter's hair was carefully brushed for the night. The two of them had had much to discuss since that wonderful day in the New Year when Dick had arrived looking entirely composed, but almost speechless with joy, to announce that he had been offered a partnership in an architectural firm with such good terms that it would be more than enough to set up house on.

'I've thought up,' said Penwoman, trying to be nice, and exerting all her willpower to initiate a conversation about something other than her own happiness, 'I've thought up a really good, simple way for you and Miss Cecilia to go down in History, Kristin, wouldn't that be splendid?'

'Well yes,' said Kristin, 'if there's somewhere Miss Cecilia has to go, I most definitely want to wriggle in there with her, because as you know, Miss, she really does need somebody to look after her.'

'Exactly,' said Penwoman, looking down so her smile would not be seen in the mirror. 'But I can tell you it's no easy matter to go down in History. I think there's only one way you could do it Kristin, and that's by setting up the Maidservants' Suffrage Club. Do you know the other suffrage maids?'

'Ye-es,' said Kristin, not greatly impressed with the idea, 'and they're nice enough, but we've so little to talk about, because none of us can complain about our mistresses. Augusta at Hornemans' says she'd always recommend a place with suffragists, but there are so seldom any vacancies. And there won't be one with you and Mr Block, either, because I'm going to see to that when I'm next back home in Simrishamn, and anyway, you don't need anyone until the autumn, do you?'

'No, that will be fine, but don't you think you could meet up all the same, and talk about the vote?' persisted Penwoman, reluctant to abandon her pet idea.

'Well that there vote, you keep telling me it'll be grand, but when everybody gets it, including maids, I don't see what point the gentry will see in having it.'

'No Kristin,' said Penwoman with a sigh. 'I've misjudged you, so let's not talk about it any more. I can't teach you anything, but the sorry truth is that I have a great deal to learn from you. Is it time for my wash? If so, I can start learning what all the different parts of the body are called in kitchen talk, so I know when I have to go to the market to buy food. Show me the sweetbreads, for example.' She was very proud of the word, which she had learned when Dick was still ill. Kristin brought the bath brush down with a rap on her soft neck.

'Ow, that's not where the sweetbreads are, is it? Well show me the hind loin, then. Isn't it down my back somewhere?'

'Yes indeed, Miss, God help you,' sighed Kristin, looking down pityingly at the naked little white frog in the tub.

'It doesn't really matter whether I learn any more,' the frog went on, 'because in my house' – Kristin laughed, and the frog for all its dignity found it hard to keep a straight face – 'in my house there won't be any plain, everyday cooking. "Away with homely fare!" will be my motto.'

'Oh Miss, you should be glad to serve homely fare every day,' said Kristin solemnly. 'Remember what happened to the girl who trod on the loaf.'*

And she gave the girl such a dousing with cold water that a roar from her patient roused Cecilia from her thoughts.

'Child, child, whatever are you doing in there?'

'I'm learning housekeeping,' whimpered Penwoman.

A few minutes later she was lying in bed, tightly and roughly tucked in right up to her nose by Kristin, who was now blowing her own very loudly, out in the kitchen.

Cecilia came in to say good night. Penwoman could see she had been crying, though she was smiling despite her smarting eyes. She came over and sat down on the edge of the bed.

'This is the last time you will be here with me in our old, easy way,' she began.

Penwoman protested vehemently: 'You make me feel awful when you say that, Cecilia.'

'But it is true, Penwoman's days are numbered. You cannot carry on running about with that nickname, once you are married.'

'But I won't ever be a proper wife deep down, Cecilia, so you see – '

'Just you wait, it will be different, even deep down, dear child. And it will be different between the two of us, too. But, no, come come, this is not a farewell; don't look so alarmed. Listen to me, Penwoman, you have become my dearest friend, and I am going to give you a wedding gift to thank you and to – ' she was speaking slowly, like someone keeping control of her voice only with extreme effort.

'But Kristin's already hemmed all my serviettes and towels, and you've equipped me as if I were your daughter,' said Penwoman, and threw her arms round Cecilia, not thinking that her words might be hurtful.

'As if you were my daughter,' repeated Cecilia, 'yes, which makes it very appropriate – I am giving you the finest thing I have to give,' she opened her hand, in which was concealed an old pendant, opals set in gold, that Penwoman had never seen before. Penwoman took it, enraptured; lying in her hand, the opals glowed like fire at the bottom of a lake.

'You see my name is engraved here,' said Cecilia.

'Cecilia Bech,' read Penwoman. 'But do you really mean to give me something so beautiful? This, you must love it so much yourself?'

'Let us try it,' said Cecilia, her tone one of forced cheerfulness. Against the lace of Penwoman's nightgown, the opals lay as white as tears and ice; the girl made an impatient movement: 'I can't see how it looks.'

'It really is beautiful,' said Cecilia, and smiled. 'I shall bring you a mirror.' But she made no move to fetch one.

'It is very old,' she said.

'Yes,' said Penwoman.

'In fact, it is practically immortal.'

Penwoman said nothing, not knowing what words would be appropriate.

'I shall die,' Cecilia went on in the same slow way as she had been speaking before. 'I assume it will not be for some time yet; creaking gates always hang longest, that is a fact. But I shall die, and before that happens I shall be very much alone.'

It was a very strange speech to make about a present, thought Penwoman. Everyone died eventually, after all.

'I shall die utterly, as every childless woman must. My thoughts will die, my heart will die, my sorrow will die, my whole essence, do you understand?'

Penwoman nodded.

'But the pendant will live. It is the only thing that I have held in my hand, owned, worn against my body and been beautiful with, that will endure, that will shine in the sun, that will gladden others when I am gone.'

'Yes,' said Penwoman. Now she understood.

'And that is why I want you to hold it in trust, you who bear immortality in your body. New generations will link in and carry on, as far as we can think and much further than we can see.'

'Maybe,' said Penwoman.

'I am a broken link, to which no new link can be fastened; I can still live out my time, anything else would simply be pretentious, but I want you to own the one part of me that will endure, you and those who come after you. The pendant and I have had our time together, and now I feel I am putting it in life's hand.'

The last words were scarcely audible. Slowly, she left the room, closing the door behind her. There sat Penwoman in bed with the pendant round her neck. She quietly took it off and sat looking at the stones, their tints shifting between joy and tears in her hand. Between joy and tears, as she was herself.

'My heart's beloved,' she said. And fell asleep with the pendant pressed to her heart.

— — —

211

# Afterword

## Sarah Death

A bestseller in its time, *Pennskaftet* (1910) was *the* novel of the Swedish women's suffrage movement, but its enduring popularity is also a testament to the quality of the writing. Possibly inspired by Elizabeth Robins' play *Votes for Women!* (1907), it served as an effective rallying cry, even though Swedish women did not finally get the vote until 1921. The novel's structure is masterly, contrasting kaleidoscopic crowd scenes and more focused ensemble episodes, and spotlighting the stories of a few, key individuals. If this sounds like a film, we should recall that a film version of the novel was indeed made in 1911. There is a tremendous sense of place; Stockholm is almost a character in its own right, seen in all weathers and all seasons, at all times of day and night. The characterisation of the central female figures is also strong: Penwoman's youthful optimism is the perfect foil for the melancholy of her somewhat older colleague Cecilia, as the two are swept up in the work of the suffrage movement.

Like much of Wägner's early fiction, the novel centres on a new phenomenon of the time: groups of middle-class, professionally active women not unlike her young self. The New Woman became the term for this intellectually and politically aware group. She is seen here starting to live her new life outside the home: riding the omnibus, reclaiming the streets, earning her keep, campaigning for women's rights, displaying a sisterly solidarity that made the more conservative factions in society deeply uneasy. The bafflement of one male character in *Pennskaftet* was probably a typical response: 'But what of women's mission in life, he thought, bewildered. When does a woman like that have time for loving, for us, for our joys and

213

sorrows, our food and our socks?'

But the novel also exposes the limitations imposed on the New Woman's freedom of action by critical, conventional society. Penwoman herself shows fierce honesty and rash confidence in entering into a loving, physical relationship with a man before marriage, and Cecilia too has 'a past'; her life fell apart after her engagement came to nothing. In their work as suffragists they find their personal lives subject to a public scrutiny neither had envisaged. Yet they refuse to be crushed, and the novel ends with a reaffirmation of their friendship and hope for the future.

Wägner had served her journalistic apprenticeship on *Helsingborgsposten* (1903-04) in her home town before moving to Stockholm to work on *Vårt land* (1904-05) and *Idun* (1907-17). Her fiction can be seen as a natural extension of the many columns and opinion pieces she was producing at the time. *Pennskaftet* was her first real novel, following the more episodic *Norrtullsligan*, which she saw merely as 'a commission like any other commission, dashed off on eighteen Friday evenings one winter, in the nick of time for the typesetters' deadline'.

The interplay between the journalist and the novelist is an important aspect of Wägner's writing life at this time, and one on which she later reflected in the revealing essay 'Indiskretioner' (Indiscretions. *Vintergatan. Sveriges författarförenings litteratur-kalender*, 1922). The piece strongly conveys her love of language and her skill in bending it to her purpose. The wittily iconoclastic style of *Pennskaftet* is typical of the young Wägner, the impressionistic, sketch-like feel adding pace and zest, enhanced by the author's wonderful ear for dialogue. It is worth mentioning that she later wrote a number of plays, for stage and radio.

Earning one's living by one's pen was not an easy business for a young beginner. Wägner looks back on the experience in 'Indiskretioner':

That was a time when one thought nothing of simply jumping aboard a royal train if one happened to have been sent to cover a meeting of monarchs; of venturing forth dressed as a fortune teller or baby farmer; or of writing a lively and detailed account in the morning of a function scheduled for the afternoon. But I never repeated that last trick, after they changed some vital parts of the programme at the last minute.[...] I remember the first lecture on women's suffrage I heard made not the slightest impression on me. I was interested in nothing but getting the speaker's words down; the only difference between me and a greying parliamentary correspondent was not indifference to the speaker's message but childish zeal and lack of training.

*

The translation of this novel into English threw up some interesting questions, beginning with the title. Its Swedish title *Pennskaftet*, meaning literally 'The Penholder', is not only the name by which the eponymous heroine is universally known, but also the generic nickname for the relatively few women journalists of the time. *Svenska Akademiens Ordbok* in fact cites this novel as the earliest example of this usage. The English 'penholder' obviously does not have these connotations. In addition, 'pennskaftet' is a neuter word in Swedish and our heroine is occasionally called 'det' (it) in the text. This will not strike Swedish readers as particularly odd because they are used to seeing, for example, a child, 'ett barn', referred to as 'det' in a text, even though its gender is known. Helena Forsås-Scott also argues in her *Re-Writing the Script: Gender and Community in Elin Wägner* (Norvik Press, 2009) that this use of a neuter word is a deliberate strategy on Wägner's part, calling society's standard gender assumptions into question.

It is not possible to do this in English without sounding totally outlandish, so in an attempt to make some sort of equivalent impact, one option was to choose a name outside the normal framework of male/female naming in society. This led to consideration of a name with superhero (or heroine) connotations: we have Superman, Batman and Wonder Woman, so why not Penwoman, a name which also echoes the New Woman

215

phenomenon discussed above? With her diminutive form, blonde hair, boundless energy, righteous indignation, long skirts and extravagantly large hat, Penwoman is an instantly recognisable figure about town, intervening to help in many situations involving women, be they prostitutes or princesses.

Elin Wägner's use of punctuation is at times idiosyncratic, particularly her use of commas, and although many of the oddities have been ironed out in the translation process, a few remain. Wägner also uses an elaborate system of sets of dots or dashes to signify a speaker tailing off, or a silence among a group, or even occasionally two lovers kissing. It has not always been practicable to replicate these in this edition.

Wägner makes liberal use in *Pennskaftet* of stream of consciousness and free indirect speech. She tends to introduce this with a dash, a Swedish *pratminus*. This is less obtrusive than English inverted commas, which do not seem appropriate for conveying thoughts that have not been uttered. *Pennskaftet* is a bold novel for its time, and does not shy away from experimenting with literary conventions, so it seems reasonable for the translation, too, to allow itself a more modern approach to stream of consciousness and dispense with speech marks in some cases where Wägner's *pratminus* introduces unspoken thoughts. The only slight caveat is that this may risk blurring the distinction between first-person musing and third-person narrative perspective.

Seen from the modern reader's viewpoint a century later, *Pennskaftet* is a historical novel, albeit written in a fresh and youthful idiom. There is an obvious need to avoid anachronistic, over-modern vocabulary, but one must nonetheless avoid sounding stuffy or archaic, as the young Wägner's style is anything but.

In keeping with the Swedish social conventions of the time, formal titles are very widely used in the original novel instead of names: *amanuens*, *arkitekt*, (clerk, architect) and so on. The challenge for the translator is to retain a feeling of formality whilst clearly needing to dispense with some of the Swedish trappings.

In the boarding house scene in Chapter 2, for example, those present routinely refer to each other, and are called by the narrator, by their titles and in the third person: *redaktören, assessorskan* (the editor, the deputy judge's wife) and so on. In the English of that period, it would be much more usual for them to call each other Mr Jessen, Mrs Bodin and so on, and for the narrator to follow suit.

Having lost her mother at an early age, Elin Wägner was partly brought up by her maternal grandparents in the vicarage at Tolg in the southern Swedish province of Småland and later spent much time in her uncle's home, the nearby vicarage at Berg. She grew up steeped in the language of the Bible, which accounts for the many Biblical quotations and allusions in *Pennskaftet*, some of which are identified in the Notes.

Elin Wägner has had a long wait to be translated into English. The efforts of British author and peace campaigner Vera Brittain, with whom Wägner had quite an extensive correspondence in the 1940s, led to discussions in the years following the Second World War with various publishing houses – Jonathan Cape, Hutchinson, Phoenix House and Allen & Unwin – about the potential of several Wägner novels for the English-language market. However, it was a time of shortages of almost everything, including paper, and sadly, nothing came of the initiative. The two short novels *Norrtullsligan* and *Kvarteret Oron* were published in English in the USA by Xlibris in 2002 as Stockholm Stories, translated by Betty Cain and Ulla Sweedler.

This is the first English translation of *Pennskaftet*. It was made from the 2003 edition published by Svenska Akademien in collaboration with Bokförlaget Atlantis, edited and annotated by Helena Forsås-Scott

Sarah Death
February 2009

# Notes

12    *the WSA, the Women's Suffrage Association*: the Swedish name is Föreningen för kvinnans politiska röstratt, FKPR. In 1903, six regional groups banded together to form a national association, Landsföreningen för Kvinnans Politiska Rösträtt, LKPR.

12    *the General*: there are two possible inspirations for the character of the General: Ann Margret Holmgren, secretary of the LKPR from 1903 and tireless speaker for the cause, nicknamed 'the suffrage general'; and the American Carrie Chapman Catt, Chair of the International Women's Suffrage Alliance.

13    *we had lost Norway*: the union between Sweden and Norway was dissolved in 1905.

18    *Forget-me-Not*: A popular weekly magazine, published 1895-1926, sold on trains and at other outlets.

19    *suffragists*: The Swedish suffrage campaigners ('rösträtts-kvinnor') are 'suffragists' rather than 'suffragettes', as they eschewed the acts of civil disobedience used by, for example, more militant branches of the British movement. Wägner herself had some sympathy with the latter, and during a visit to London in 1909, she was present when hunger-striking suffragettes who had been forcibly fed in Holloway were released. She also wrote some articles in the Swedish press to defend suffragette tactics.

26    *'They can vote for a man as Member of Parliament'*: Mrs Bodin and her daughter here reveal the depths of their ignorance: the women's suffrage campaign was demanding both the basic right to vote, and women's right to stand as

parliamentary candidates.

28    *'They deny their faith for fear of the Jews'*: cf. John 7:13 'Howbeit no man spake openly of him for fear of the Jews.'

30    *Kristina Gyllenstierna*: (1494-1559) widow of Sten Sture, helped to defend Stockholm in 1520 against King Kristian II of Denmark and was taken prisoner when the city fell.

36    *Liberal Morning News*: the Swedish, *Frisinnade Morgontidningen*, is an invented, generic-type name, presumably meant to represent the score or more Swedish newspapers of the time with liberal views.

39    *the Athanasian Creed*: one of the three creeds accepted by the Roman and Anglican churches, so called because it embodies the opinions of Athanasius (c.298-373) respecting the Trinity.

41    *Stockholm Daily News*: *Stockholms Dagblad*, a conservative daily paper, founded in 1867.

42    *Women and Dress Reform*: the campaign for dress reform began in the USA in the 1850s as a reaction against the fashion of tight corsets for women, which doctors came to view as a threat to the wearers' health.

42    *Fredrika Bremer Society*: *Fredrika Bremer-förbundet*, a society founded in Sweden in 1884 to campaign for 'the elevation of women'. Named after the nineteenth-century authoress and champion of women's rights, Fredrika Bremer, 1801-65, it is still campaigning 125 years later.

45    *Rosenbad*: a building at the eastern end of Riddarfjärden, opposite what is now the parliament building, and today synonymous with government offices. It then housed a bank, shops and apartments, and a restaurant.

50    *Victoria Hall*: *Viktoriasalen*, a large meeting hall at 19 Tunnelgata, now renamed Olof Palmes gata. The hall was demolished in 1967.

62    *as excellent an advertisement for women's suffrage as the sewing machine*: the advent of the sewing machine in the later nineteenth century had forced down seamstresses, wages and increased their awareness of the need to organise

themselves to demand better conditions.

65 *an endeavour to gird women's loins and carry them whither they would not*: the words of Jesus to Peter, cf. John 21:18: 'Verily, verily, I say unto thee, When thou wast young, thou girdedst thyself, and walkedst whither thou wouldest: but when thou shalt be old, thou shalt stretch forth thy hands, and another shall gird thee, and carry thee whither thou wouldest not.'

73 *surveyed the works of their hands*: cf. Hebrews 1:10: 'And Thou, Lord, in the beginning hast laid the foundation of the earth; and the heavens are the works of thy hands.'

77 *give a superstitious curtsey to the new moon*: curtseying to the new moon: a superstition supposed to bring good luck.

77 *farm for the poor*: a 'fattiggård' was a sort of farm offering employment to more able bodied recipients of poor relief. Men worked in the fields and gardens; women did housework and weaving, and cared for the sick and the young.

83 *cigar shop assistants and all that sort of thing*: because their clientele was exclusively male, the female assistants in Stockholm tobacconists' shops were often viewed as prostitutes, and some cigar shops did function as covert brothels.

90 *shaving token*: a token entitling customers to a shave at the barber's at a discounted rate.

90 *Self-Supporting Educated Woman*: *Självförsörjande Bildad Kvinna*, often abbreviated as S.B.K., was a fairly widely used expression at the time. There was even a holiday home expressly for this group of women, its linen monogrammed 'S.B.K.'.

90 *Susan B. Anthony*: American campaigner for women's rights (1820-1906), known for the saying 'Failure is impossible'.

94 *Mrs Skogh*: Wilhelmina Skogh, managing director of the Grand Hotel in Stockholm, 1902-1910.

98 *she could stand in local government elections*: new legislation in Sweden had extended the right to stand in local

government elections to single women taxpayers in 1910. Married women had been eligible since 1908.

99   *Gärdet*: an area of Stockholm, north east of the centre, where there had been little development at this time.

106  *Upper House*: the Swedish parliament at this time comprised two chambers. The 150 members of the Upper Chamber were elected indirectly by county and town councillors. From 1909, they were elected for a period of six years.

114  *student caps*: in Scandinavia, these distinctive white caps with black peaks were traditionally worn by students, and are still worn by upper secondary school students as they graduate in May. Wägner uses them here to evoke a sense of impending summertime freedom.

114  *'Do you think that's the done thing?'*: An allusion to a famous novella by Carl Jonas Love Almqvist (1793-1866), *Det går an*, (literally 'That is allowed' or 'That is proper'), later translated into English as *Sara Videbeck*. Written in 1838, it features an unmarried liaison between Sara and Sergeant Albert, and sparked huge public debate in Sweden.

115  *Marcus Larsson*: Swedish artist (1825-64) whose favoured subject matter was Swedish nature at its grandest and wildest.

123  *Fredrika Bremer*: see note to page 42. *Mrs Olivecrona, Mrs Adlersparre*: Rosalie Olivecrona (1823-98) and Sophie Adlersparre (penname Esselde) founded the influential women's periodical *Tidskrift för hemmet* (Journal for the Home) in 1859. Adlersparre was also among the founders of *Fredrika Bremer-förbundet* in 1884 and a patron of women writers.

126  *Lady Patricia*: probably a reference to Victoria Patricia Helena Elizabeth of Connaught (1886-1974), granddaughter of Queen Victoria.

130  *'Those that come after us will be greater than we'*: cf. Mark 1:7: 'And preached, saying, There cometh one mightier than I after me'.

132 *Villa Borgis*: the name of the rented cottage is a play on words, linking to Penwoman's familiarity with print journalism. Borgis/bourgeois is a type size, the French name possibly derived from the name of the type-founder. The fact that it is mid-sized type, larger than brevier and smaller than longprimer, could also refer to their enjoyment of acting out the roles of an average, middle-class couple.

136 *isinglass*: called '*klarskinn*' in the Swedish text, this is one of several preparations traditionally used for clearing coffee and other liquids, derived from the swim bladders of certain fish.

137 *how well our page layout works*: again, it comes naturally to Penwoman to borrow terminology from the print room to describe how well she and Dick are suited.

140 *Rembrandt hat*: a style of ladies' hat modelled on those of Rembrandt's time: broad-brimmed, plumed and made of velvet.

141 *Central League for Social Work*: *Centralförbundet för socialt arbete*, a group of organisations working together to disseminate public information about social issues. It had its offices at 6, Lästmakargatan at this period.

144 *Berns*: a famous restaurant and music hall.

145 *Votes for Women*: *Rösträtt för kvinnor* was a 4-page broadsheet published by the Swedish national suffrage association LKPR for its first public rally in Stockholm in June 1909. Elin Wägner herself sold this paper on the streets of Stockholm, and is said to have dressed in the British suffragette colours of white, green and purple to do so – a somewhat provocative act.

145 *'I couldn't possibly not have time'*: *'Jag har omöjligt inte tid'*: the double negative, which means the opposite of what Ester Henning's cousin really means, can be interpreted as an expression of her discomfort.

150 *historici*: historians (Latin, plural of *historicus*)

152 *Miss Morgonvind*: the name Morgonvind is a reference to *Morgonbris* (Morning Breeze), the journal of the Social

Democrat women, published since 1904. The character may be modelled on Ruth Gustafson, who was its editor at the time in which *Penwoman* is set.

153 *Axel Danielsson* (1863-99) was a newspaperman and politician.

153 *barred from working and earning money until they are four weeks old*: legislation of 1900 stipulated that women could not do industrial labour for four weeks after childbirth, though there was no maternity pay.

154 *suffrage on the same terms as men*: working-class single mothers and widows with children could rarely avoid resorting to social welfare. The Swedish law of the time was that men dependent on such welfare forfeited their vote.

155 *Carl Larsson's words: 'Now is the time to set great, clear bells ringing'*: the opening line of the poem 'Dalarnes ungdomsmarsch' (March of the Youth of Dalarne) in the collection *By och bonde* by Carl Larsson of By (1877-1948).

157 *Frigga Carlberg*: an activist, one of the founder members of the Gothenburg women's suffrage association.

165 *Goshen*: a happy place of light and plenty, from the abode of the Israelites during the plague of darkness in Egypt; cf. Genesis 45:10.

166 *entailed estate*: Swedish *fideikomiss* (from the Latin *fidei commissum*) is an estate settled on a series of exclusively male heirs so that the immediate possessor of it may not dispose of it. An entailed estate and its impact on a family of daughters is famously used as a plot device in Jane Austen's novel *Pride and Prejudice* (1813).

172 *Gustaf Adolfs torg*: at this period Stockholm's main square, opposite the Royal Palace. It was the home of the general newspaper offices (*Allmänna tidningskontoret*), where all the latest dispatches were displayed in the window.

174 *ward five*: for this election, Stockholm was divided into five wards. Number five comprised the parishes of Katarina and Maria Magdalena on Södermalm.

175 *great was their fall*: cf. Matthew 7:27, about the foolish

223

man who built his house upon the sand, 'and great was the fall of it'.

177 *Scriver's Spiritual Treasury:* German theologian Christian Scriver's classic *Seelenschatz*, a work of edifying Lutheran reflections published in 1675-92. The Swedish translation *Scrivers själaskatt* was published in six volumes in 1723-27.

179 *ballot papers*: in Swedish elections, by contrast with their British equivalents, ballot papers are sometimes also handed out by representatives of the political parties outside polling stations.

188 *à la Strindberg*: August Strindberg, Swedish author and playwright (1849-1912), whose three marriages were frowned upon in more conservative circles.

188 *'You could thank your God, if you were as they are'*: cf. Luke 18:11: 'The Pharisee stood and prayed thus with himself, God, I thank thee, that I am not as other men are, extortioners, unjust, adulterers, or even as this publican.'

205 *courses in civics*: courses educating women for full citizenship were an important part of the Swedish suffrage movement from about 1907. Topics included workers' rights, housing, poor relief, world peace, local and national politics, the cooperative movement, temperance, morality, and smallholding.

209 *the girl who trod on the loaf*: a folk legend tells of a girl who threw a loaf of bread into a bog and stepped on it to avoid dirtying her shoes. She was sucked down into the underworld as a punishment. Hans Christian Andersen wrote a version of the tale entitled *Pigen, der traadte paa Brødet*.